THE MAIDEN

CELIA AARON

The Maiden
Celia Aaron
Copyright © 2018 Celia Aaron

This book is a work of fiction. While reference may be made to actual historical events or existing locations, the names, characters, places and incidents are products of the author's imagination, and any resemblance to actual persons, living or dead, business establishments, events, or locales is entirely coincidental.

Content Editing by Evident Ink

Copy Editing by Spell Bound

CONTENTS

CHAPTER 1

*S*heer white fabric covers me from neck to toe. I keep my eyes on the dirt path ahead of me as I move through the dark, my thin shift a beacon in the night calling every sort of predator to me. I try not to shiver. Keeping my steps even becomes my world, my only focus. One step, then the next.

I can't think about the crackling branches, the footfalls through the crisp leaves, the low chant floating through the chilly air, or the women ahead or behind me. No. Only my own steps. Right, then left. The frozen earth beneath my bare feet. The momentum that carries me deeper and deeper into the woods.

Firelight casts a faint glow as we continue moving forward, each of us rushing toward the cage, desire in our hearts, and fervor in our souls. We want to be shackled, owned, moved only by the spirit of our God. And our

God has anointed one on earth to embody His good will. The Prophet Leon Monroe.

The deep chant thrums through my veins as I approach the firelight, the orange glimmer flickering over my dirty feet and up to play against the soft fabric of my night-gown. Though clothed, I am bare. I enter the circle of men, each one of them dressed in white pants and shirts —holy men, handpicked by the Prophet himself.

I follow the girl ahead of me until all of us form an inner circle, pressed between the fire and the men along the outside. It's a new circle of hell, promising an agonizing burn no matter which way I move.

A woman in all black walks along the line of women, handing each of us a small pitcher of water. My head bowed, I don't look her in the eye as she approaches. But I already know who she is—Rachel—first wife of the Prophet. Her limp gives her away. I take my pitcher, the weight of the cold water steadying the shake in my hands.

A strong voice silences the chanting. "We thank God for this bounty."

"Amen," the men chorus.

"We remember His commandment to 'Be fruitful and increase in number.' As a sign of our obedience to His will, we take these girls under our care, our protection. We also take them into our hearts, to cherish as if they were of our own blood."

"Amen."

His voice grows louder as he walks around the circle. "Just as Rebekah was called by the Lord to marry a son of Abraham, so have these girls been called to serve the godly men gathered here tonight."

A pair of heavy boots stops in front of me. A light touch under my chin pulls my gaze upward until I'm met by a pair of dark eyes. The Prophet peers into my soul.

"Do you remember the tale of Rebekah, Sister?"

"Yes, Prophet."

"I'm sure a child of God like you knows all the stories in the Bible." He smiles, his white teeth bleached like a skeleton's.

"Yes, Prophet."

"'The woman was very beautiful, a virgin; no man had ever slept with her. She went down to the spring, filled her jar and came up again.' And then what happened to Rebekah?"

"She was taken by Abraham's servant."

"That's correct." He leans closer, his gaze boring into mine.

A shiver courses through me. He glances down at my chest, a smirk twisting the side of his lips as he sees my hard nipples through the gauzy fabric.

He releases my chin and steps back, continuing his circuit as he speaks of Rebekah's destiny. I steal a look at the man standing opposite me. Blond hair, blue eyes, a placid expression—the Prophet's youngest son. Something akin to relief washes over me. Being Cloister Maiden to Noah Monroe wouldn't be so bad. He was rumored to be kind, gentle even. I let my gaze slide to the man standing at his left. Dark hair, even darker eyes, and a smirk like his father's on his lips as he stares at me— Adam Monroe. I drop my gaze and silently pity the Maiden to my right.

"We will keep you safe. Away from the monsters of this world who would seek to use you, to destroy the innocent perfection that each one of you possess. Remember the story of Dinah: 'When Shechem, son of Hamor the Hivite, the ruler of that area, saw her, he took her and raped her.' And so it is with any man who is not within this circle. They would take you, hurt you, and cast you aside once they've spoiled your body and heart. Only in the Cloister can you lead peaceful lives without fear."

I wonder if Georgia heard the same speech. She must have. How long did they let her live after this ritual? The thought churns inside me, surprisingly strong, and hate begins to override my meek persona. Breaking character for a split second, I glance back up at Adam Monroe. Had he been the one to slit her throat? Had his large hands done untold violence to Georgia while she was still alive?

He scowls at the shivering Maiden standing in front of him, then snaps his gaze to meet mine. His eyes round the slightest bit, and I drop my focus back to the dirt, then close my eyes. I shouldn't have done that. I silently berate myself as Leon—*no, he's the Prophet*—as *the Prophet* continues his lesson on the safety of the Cloister. I let my disguise fall back into place. I am a devout follower of the Prophet and eager Cloister Maiden. The hum of my thoughts grows louder, and I realize the Prophet has stopped talking.

I open my eyes and peek at the Maiden to my left. She's lifted her pitcher, her eyes still downcast. I do the same.

"The water signifies an offering from Maiden to her Protector. A righteous man—one who will teach her and lead her in the light of the Lord our God. The Protector is sanctified by God, and his decisions will always be made in the best interest of the Maiden under his protection. Just as God instructed in Genesis, the man is leader, the woman his helpmate. And so it will be here. The Protector—with God in his heart—shall lead his Maiden and show her the ways of true believers."

"Amen." The men's voices seem to have grown louder, hungrier.

"Now, Maidens, offer yourselves as vessels made to carry the knowledge and light of our Lord, to your Protector."

With shaking arms, I hold out my pitcher. A brief brush of fingers against mine, and the weight lifts. After a few moments, the drained pitchers fly over our heads and crash into the fire at our backs. A primal roar rips from the men—wolves with appetites whetted for blood.

"Protectors, lead your gentle lambs back to the Cloister where we will welcome them into the fold."

A hand appears, the wide palm up. I take a deep breath and remind myself that Noah is a good draw. Slipping my hand into his, I lift my eyes to find the entirely wrong man attached. Noah leads a different woman away from the bonfire.

Adam's smirk darkens as he grips my hand too tight. "Shall we, little lamb?"

CHAPTER 2

ADAM

The Cloister—a vast log cabin complex—appears through the trees. I pull the Maiden along with me, her bare feet skittering over dry leaves and pine needles. She doesn't complain. They never do. My father's little army of Maidens always behaves perfectly at first. The problems wouldn't begin until later tonight.

We exit the woods, and she picks up her pace on the grass expanse. The other Protectors and Maidens follow us, none of the women making a sound as the men grunt and laugh.

I yank my Maiden closer. "Hurry up."

She starts to pull against my grip, then seems to recon-sider and allows me to continue half-dragging her to the Cloister. A little hint of spark flares in her eyes, then quickly dies. I saw it at the fire ritual—the great theater my father just loves to put on every year when we have a new Maiden crop. I'd switched with Noah because of that hint of something hidden inside this one, but it was likely a stupid choice on my part. After all, she'd signed up to be a Cloister Maiden. There was no backbone inside her, no keen intellect. Just another lamb to the slaughter. The thought makes me grit my teeth as I pull her inside the doorway leading to the banquet hall.

A few Spinners kneel to the side, bowls of warm water next to them.

"Wash." I shove my Maiden toward them and point at her filthy feet.

She follows my command like an obedient little supplicant, pulling up her shift and allowing one of the Spinners to sponge the dirt away. When I first spotted her walking through the trees, I did a double take. A fairy—her hair white, her skin pale—she seemed to float along the path. Watching her now, I realize she has gray eyes, ones that hardened to flint as she peered at me during the ritual. I thought I'd sensed something more in her ... A trace of defiance. But it can't be. If she was dumb enough to fall for my father's line of "chosen one" bullshit and leave her life for the Cloister, there was no way she had any real wheels turning in her skull. Just blind devotion, ignorant worship, and foolish faith.

A Spinner dries the girl's feet. My Maiden looks young, early twenties at most. Features too delicate to be real, easy to break. Medium height, small build, light pink nipples at attention beneath her shift and a waist that narrows before flaring out to full hips. Light penetrates between her thighs, giving me the outline of her sex. That one little hint isn't enough. I want more.

"Come." I hold out my hand.

She glances down at the Spinner, hesitation in her eyes.

"I said *come.*"

There it is again, a flare of defiance, but she buries it and slips her small hand into mine. Something flaps in my chest, its wings dry and brittle, the feathers rotted and the bones showing through. Interesting.

The others begin filing in, the Spinners washing the girls' feet as the men wait, their claws desperate for the soft touch of new flesh.

I pull my Maiden through to the Banquet Hall. The Spinners decorated it for the ceremony, white fabric covering the tables, hanging from the wooden rafters, and draped all along the platform at the front of the room. The familiar throne sits at one end of the stage, the gaudy velvet cushions better suited to a seedy champagne room. Candles burn in the black wrought-iron chandeliers overhead, the faux antiques mixed with modern equivalents and electric lights. After all, this is a show.

My father's booming voice echoes into the room, the dark corners greedily devouring his words. "Welcome, Maidens. Welcome to your new home." He strides in, all eyes on him, just the way he likes it. "Every need you have will be met. Only you, the Spinners, and the Protectors are allowed into the sacred space of the Cloister. Each of you will be assigned a room and given tasks to further your service to God. But more about that later. First, we celebrate your arrival!"

He struts down the center aisle, the Maidens following him, their eyes downcast. My Maiden seems to forget herself and lifts her chin, watching the scene as if she isn't part of it. I disavow her of any such notion by thrusting her into the line of Maidens. She stumbles, then rights herself, falling into line and walking toward the front of the room.

My father takes the first girl's hand and leads her up the three steps to the white platform. He waits as all the Maidens rise and take their places. Lambs patiently waiting for their throats to be cut. I stand in the shadows as the other men line up, practically salivating.

"Why'd you swap?" Noah sidles up to me.

"Not sure." I focus on my Maiden, her hands folded in front of her.

My father sermonizes on the tale of Esther, his voice having long ago fallen to nothing more than background noise for me.

"She's got a strange look." Noah stuffs his hands into his pockets, resigned to our father's yearly song and dance. "I was almost looking forward to her."

"She's just another idiot. Like all these. Eating up Dad's lies and asking for another serving."

He sighs, but doesn't comment on my blasphemy. "I don't know if I'm up for another year of this. I'm spending so much time on the money side. The Maiden duty is going to cut into that."

"No way out of it." I scowl at my father as he weaves his tale about old kings needing young virgins. "He says this is a perk, you know? Giving us women like this. But it's just a chore. Another fucking job to be done."

"One that doesn't pay off. At least not for us." He shakes his head.

"No shit." I cross my arms over my chest, my gaze wandering back to my Maiden. Her hair covers her face in delicate curtains, her hands clutching each other as if she knows something bad is coming.

She has no idea.

"And so, to honor the Lord our God, I shall give each of you your new names. In the light of love, and of rebirth, you must come to me as a child." My father strides to the throne and sits, an indulgent smile on his face. "Come to me." He motions the first girl to him.

She walks over, eager to please him.

"Remove your garment, my dear, and I shall receive you as a child and give you the name that God intended for you." He licks his lips. The wolves circle closer to the stage.

The girl blinks. "Naked?"

"Yes. You are being reborn. All children come into this world innocent and naked." My father states it as if it's perfectly normal to ask a young woman to strip in front of him and a bunch of strangers.

But the girl is under his spell. She truly *believes* that what he's saying is right. Slowly, she lifts her shift, revealing a patch of dark hair between her thighs and full breasts with brown nipples.

That's my father's gift—he can tell a crowd of ten thousand to stop drinking milk, start taking vitamins, stop vaccinating their kids, start wearing more pink, and *they will do it*. He can make the absurd seem reasonable. People believe he has a direct line to God. And why do they believe that? Because he told them. His gift manifests in many ways, the yearly crop of virgins at Heavenly Ministries being one of them.

"My child, you are truly blessed." He runs his lascivious gaze all over her body. "And because of this, your name shall be—"

"Mary." Noah rolls his eyes. The first one is always Mary.

"Mary." My father proclaims.

"Thank you, Prophet." She reaches for her shift.

"No, my dear. Stand proud with your sisters." He points to the next girl as a Spinner pulls the girl's shift from her grasp.

Over the space of the next ten minutes, each girl is required to strip, their bodies laid bare as the men watch. The recruiters picked well this year, brainwashing mostly attractive women into the Cloister program with promises of safety, peace, and sisterhood. The sales pitch leaves out a few key elements, but they'll learn it all soon enough.

When it's my Maiden's turn, I find myself becoming a little too interested.

She approaches my father, and, unlike the other girls, removes her shift before he even asks, and tosses it to the floor. Now, for a man like my father, he'd take that as a sign of faith in him, of devotion to the Cloister. But me, I take it for what it is—an open "fuck you" to my father. She's meeting the ugliness of the charade head on. The bird flaps its bony wings inside me again, waking after a long slumber.

"You, my dear, are sacred. Just look at you." He twirls his finger, and she turns in a circle at his command. Her long white hair flows down her back, light pink nipples pebbled in the cool air, and a hint of blonde curls between her thighs. Her gray eyes remain hidden from me. I want to see them, to see *her*. Not her body, but whatever simmers inside.

"Come closer." My father takes her hand and pulls her until their knees are touching. He darts his tongue to his lips.

My hands close into fists. It's not his time. It's *mine*.

"What's the matter with you?" Noah must have been watching. "You're all tense."

"I'm fine."

I loosen my fingers as my father asks, "And who is your Protector, sweet girl?"

She turns toward me, her gaze finding mine with ease. He follows her look.

"Noah? Adam?"

I nod.

"Well." He turns his focus back to her and grips her waist, his hands profaning her smooth skin.

She doesn't flinch.

"I think I'll need to deviate a bit here. Give you a name that suits anyone who has to deal with Adam on a daily basis." He fakes a consoling look. "Not that he'll hurt you, of course. He's a Protector, after all. Hmmm."

I itch to punch him in his smug face even more than usual, which is saying something.

"How about we call you Delilah?" His hands slide lower, easing across her hips.

"Thank you, Prophet." If you weren't paying attention, you could miss the faint tremor in her voice. I hear it just fine.

"Go on now." He lets his hands drop, and she steps back into line, all the girls bare for the leering assholes below them.

"God is good." Dad stands and motions to the Spinners. They rush forward, golden dresses in their hands, and help the girls put them on.

Once the show is over, the men disperse and sit down at the tables, their rough voices overcoming the quiet chatter on the stage.

"When is he going to stop doing this?" Noah yawns and motions his Maiden over to him. She comes like an obedient little dog, her gold dress skirting her ankles.

"I suppose whenever these girls stop falling for this shit."

Noah's Maiden gives me a shocked look before inspecting the floor again.

Noah leans close. "Don't let Dad hear you saying any of that."

"I'm careful."

"I know. But we can't risk it."

"I know." I walk away from him, ignoring whatever warnings he wants to add. My Maiden, Delilah, stands at the edge of the stage, the gold dress giving her an even more unearthly look.

"Come." I take her hand and pull her to the nearest table. She sits opposite me, not a word from her light pink lips.

Who was she before she came here? I'd have to investigate her file. Plenty of the girls who expressed an interest in the Cloister came from broken homes and, above all, had intense daddy issues. Ones my father took full advantage of. Is that who Delilah is? Another broken cog in a wheel that was never made for her?

It doesn't matter, I remind myself. Who she was doesn't matter. Because now she's in the Cloister. She likely didn't notice it when we walked in, but each door with outside access has a keypad, cameras set up everywhere, and the windows similarly monitored. Once the faithful supplicants enter my father's clutches, they don't leave. Not on their terms, anyway.

"What's your name?" The question pops from my lips though it should have stayed tucked away with all the forgotten things that resided in my mind.

"Delilah." The sound barely reaches my ears.

"Your real name."

"Delilah."

"Fuck." I lean back in my chair, staring her down.

She doesn't meet my gaze, her mask of obedience firmly in place.

"We have one more small ceremony before you girls can retire for the night." My father strides to me with Abigail at his side, a small green device in her hand.

"I'm sure you're ready to get on with it." He grins down at me.

I hold my hand out to Delilah.

She looks at it as if it's a venomous snake.

"Take my hand."

She glances at my father.

"Don't look at him. Look at *me*." I keep my tone even, but no less lethal. Showing weakness in front of my father isn't an option.

She puts out one delicate hand. I engulf it with mine, keenly aware that every Maiden in the room is watching.

Abigail, her graying hair wrapped up in a tight bun, loads the plastic gun. "Hold her."

I yank Delilah across the table.

She cries out in surprise, but I don't let go. Instead, I rise and pin her arm down with both hands. After only a second of struggle, she returns to placid, as if someone flipped a switch inside her. She's learning quickly, adapting to the violence that is this place. That is me.

"It'll only hurt for a second, little one." My father runs a hand through her hair, touching what's mine.

In that moment, I hate him more than I ever have.

"Here we go." Abigail places the end of the gun against Delilah's upper arm. "It'll sting, but you'll be fine." She squeezes the wide trigger, and the microchip slides under the pale skin. Then Abigail grabs a syringe from a tray held by another Spinner. "This is to stop your monthly curse. We value clean women here."

Delilah doesn't make a sound, her tenseness the only way I can sense that both injections hurt. The tracker insertion point bleeds a little, so Abigail applies a bandage.

"Well done." Dad gives Delilah a pat, as if she's a faithful dog who fetched him a prize duck.

They move on to the next girl as Delilah sits up and presses her palm to her arm.

One of the nearby Maidens leans over to whisper to another. A Spinner hurries from her spot along the wall and steps between them, a deep furrow in her brow. "No speaking when the Prophet is present unless it's to say please or thank you." She doesn't draw her small baton and hit the talker.

Not yet.

CHAPTER 3

DELILAH

I follow Adam down a long hallway. Doors break off to the left and right at intervals, and Spinners stand at a few of them, their hands folded in front of them, eyes down. I don't need to see their faces to know I'm headed for a dark fate. My instincts scream at me to run. I don't. I'm here for a reason, and I won't leave until I get what I came for. I force my fear to take a backseat to my determination.

After what feels like one hundred yards of walking, he turns to the right and pushes through a set of double doors. A Spinner stands inside the new area. She's young, maybe not even twenty-five, and a scar cuts across her forehead and disappears beneath her blonde hair.

"Which is hers?" Adam asks, impatience slicing the spaces between his words.

She turns and leads us down the hall. I count a dozen doors, each named after a book of the Bible. She motions to the Psalms door, and Adam pushes past her and into the room.

Something cold slithers around my spine, squeezing and cutting off my ability to move. If I go into that room, what will happen? Nothing good. But this is what I signed up for. I have no illusions like some of the other girls. The Cloister isn't a haven, it's a prison, and I walked right into it. This is just the iron bars clanging shut behind me.

"You'd best follow," the Spinner whispers.

I glance at her, but she gives nothing away.

"Delilah." Adam's low voice carries more than a hint of menace. "Get in here."

I steel my nerves and step into the room. Adam sits on the bed, his eyes on me. The room is bigger than what I'm used to. A small bathroom connects on the right, a closet on the left. The furniture is simple and matches the log cabin décor. A white bedspread covers the bed.

"Close the door." He hasn't taken his gaze off me.

I do as instructed, pushing it shut. The click of the handle carries a finality that chills me.

"Come." He points to the floor in front of him.

Swallowing hard, I move to stand in front of him. He looks up at me, his eyes dark and fathomless. So much like his father's that bile rages in my stomach.

"Down." He taps his foot on the pale blue rug.

Heat seeps up my neck and into my cheeks.

He must see it, because he smirks. "I've never had one who won't do what she's told."

Shit. I can't stand out. Fitting in with the other Maidens is the only way this can work.

Slowly, I sink to the floor and keep my gaze on the rug.

"Closer." He reaches out and plucks a lock of my hair, rubbing it between his thumb and forefinger.

I scoot nearer. He spreads his knees wider and yanks on my hair. "Closer."

I clench my teeth, but I obey, moving until I'm between his legs, my face level with his stomach. I don't look down.

"What's your name?"

"Delilah." I flinch as he yanks my hair again.

"What's your real name?"

I look up at him. "*Delilah.*"

His nostrils flare, and his eyes widen. I quickly drop my gaze.

"You're different." He uses both hands to stroke down my hair. "I mean, obviously you look different. Albino or something?"

I'd been called that by mean children since the first grade. His use of the term rolls off like water on a duck's back. My skin and hair are the result of a genetic defect, a close cousin to albinism, but he doesn't need to know that. I've dealt with rude comments on my odd looks my whole life. I could deal with his, too.

"So white." He studies my hair. "Like a fairy."

I remain still and silently hope that he will lose interest, that his perusal of my hair will be the end of the evening, and he'll leave me in peace.

A few more moments pass, then he leans back. "Take your dress off."

God, it had been so hard to do it the first time in a room full of gawking men. Now, in a quiet room with just one man, it seems infinitely more difficult.

He taps the small buckle at the front of his belt. "You'll learn that you need to obey me. Every time. Immediately. I'll give you a pass tonight since it's our first time together, but from now on, when I tell you to do something, you do it. No hesitation. Now, take your dress off."

My lip trembles as I reach down and pull the gold fabric from beneath my knees, then ease it over my head.

Goosebumps race all over my body as the cool air hits me in secret places, but I won't cry. I drop the fabric next to me, then resume staring at his stomach, though now my eyes are drawn down to the shiny silver buckle.

"Good lamb." He presses his index finger under my chin and draws my gaze up to his face. Square jaw, sharp nose, full lips, dark hair, and those unreadable eyes—he is handsome. I assume Satan is, too.

"Whenever I come to visit, I expect you to strip and kneel before me immediately. You don't ask questions. You don't hesitate. Do you understand?" His gaze flickers to my lips.

"Yes."

"Good." He releases my chin, and I return my gaze to the floor.

He clucks his tongue. "Don't hide from me. Always look me in the eye when I speak to you."

"But the Spinners told us never to—"

"When we are in this room, we do it my way." He shoots a glance to a vent in the ceiling, then refocuses on me. "I'm your Protector. I would never lead you astray."

I meet his gaze again, feeling its weight settling all over me, pulling me down to an abyss full of dark shapes and moving shadows.

"Good lamb." A smirk toys with the edge of his lips. "Now open your mouth."

I will not cry. I will not cry. I open.

He frowns. "Faster next time. And wider."

I spread my jaws, pulling my lips back from my teeth.

"Better." He slides two fingers into my mouth, pressing down on my tongue. "Have you ever taken a man in your mouth before?"

I shake my head slightly.

His smirk blooms. "Liar."

Panic threatens to constrict my throat. Getting into the Cloister required virginity. I had that in the technical sense, which was supposedly "confirmed" during the exam required for all applicants. A virgin? Yes. A saint? No.

"How many dicks have you sucked, little lamb?" He presses down harder, his fingers sliding closer to the back of my throat.

I gag, but he doesn't remove his fingers. My gorge rises, more from a memory than anything he's doing to me.

"How many?"

"One," I say around his fingers.

"One?" Seemingly satisfied, he pulls back. "Leave your mouth open."

Spit pools on my tongue, but I can't swallow.

He gives me a hard look, one devoid of pity. "Do you have any idea what you're in for? What a year in this place will do to you? What *I* will do to you?"

I can't respond. But I want to tell him I'm not afraid. That I will do whatever is necessary.

"You're a fool for coming here." He sighed. "Close your mouth."

"Spinner!" His sudden yell makes me jump.

The door opens, and the scarred blonde enters. "Yes, sir?"

"Begin throat training tomorrow for this one. Her gag reflex needs work."

She nods. "Yes, sir."

"Get out."

"Yes, sir."

She disappears, and the door clicks shut again.

"Get on the bed, and spread your legs."

My knees go weak, but I try to stand. He doesn't help, just watches with cold eyes that seem to miss nothing. Humiliation courses through me as he treats my nudity like a banality, as if nothing is off about this, *all* of this.

"Delilah, you're testing me." His hand strays to his belt buckle again.

I walk to the far side of the bed and sit down, then force myself to lie back. Telling my legs to open is one thing—them actually following the command is another.

Adam rises and stands at the foot of the bed, his face cast in shadow. "Spread them."

My chin trembles, and for a second, I don't think I can do this anymore.

He unfastens his belt and slowly pulls it from the loops with a *schick* noise as a girl starts crying next door. "Last chance."

I clamp my eyes shut and open my legs.

"More." His voice seems to drop an octave, taking on a rougher edge.

My heels scoot across the white quilt until cool air caresses the most intimate parts of me.

"More," he grates.

I open all the way, and a tear slips from my eye and rolls into my ear. He doesn't say anything else.

The girl next door wails, and another girl screams from down the hall.

The bed dips, his knees between my ankles. I clutch the quilt, fisting the material as he looms over me. I can't open my eyes.

A scream sounds from down the hall. I jump.

"Shh." His warm breath fans out along my inner thigh.

"What are you doing?"

"Look and see."

I open my eyes. He's between my legs, his mouth hovering along my bare skin, moving up, up, up my thighs. His gaze locks with mine, pupils wide, as he stops only an inch from the part of me that no man has ever seen.

"Do you taste as good as you look, *Delilah*?" His warm breath tickles along my sensitive skin.

Every rational thought in my mind grinds to a halt.

He breathes in deeply, and I clutch the quilt so hard my fingers ache.

"I think you do." His tongue darts to his lips. "I think you'll beg me to taste you. Soon."

My heart pounds and stumbles as he inhales me, his gaze holding me prisoner. He doesn't touch me, but he's staking a claim all the same. I can't relax, can't think, can't look at anything but him. His light breaths ignite little sparks along my skin, and I'm horrified at how I'm reacting to him. Something warm unfurls low in my stomach, a faint longing that shouldn't be there. Not in this place. Not with this man.

27

He licks his lips, and I gasp in a breath. With a smirk, he leans back and stands, then grabs his belt from the bed. He strides to the door, then pauses. "Don't open the door for anyone but a Spinner or me. Understand?"

I can't even nod.

"Goodnight." He leaves, and I finally take a breath.

CHAPTER 4

ADAM

I lean back in my chair and take a long draw from my glass.

"That bad?" Noah walks in and tosses his jacket onto the pool table.

"How was yours?" I don't want to think about Delilah. From the first moment I saw her, my thoughts have been circling her like a vulture around carrion, and it has to stop.

"Fine." He shrugs. "She had no problem obeying. Then again, I'm never hard on them, even if they're not quick on the obedience thing."

"Which leads to trouble."

"Maybe." He fixes himself a drink and plops down next to me in his favorite leather chair. "But I don't want to hurt them."

"You're the only one."

"I know." He frowns. "I wish Dad wouldn't let Craig or Newell near them. They shouldn't be Protectors."

"Perks of being in the Prophet's inner circle." I snort and drain my glass, then rise to make another.

Noah's phone pings.

"Fuck." I slam two ice cubes into my glass. "It's him, isn't it?"

He checks his phone. "Yeah. He wants to see us. Upstairs."

I down my drink and follow Noah up the curved staircase that leads to the main floor of the Prophet's house. Everything up here gleams—the floors, the chandeliers, the priceless art. How many heads of state have walked into the Monroe Mansion on the Heavenly Ministries property and taken a deep breath, the taste of money on their tongues?

"Office." Castro leans against the wall beside the French doors to my father's lair. He's been with us for a few years, but hasn't proven himself enough to be a Protector and get his very own Maiden to play with. Maybe next year. The bitterness in his eyes tells me he's well aware of what Noah and I have been doing in our stupid white outfits.

He opens the door for us, and we walk into the office, the familiar smell of cigars tainting the air as my father scrutinizes us through the smoke.

"Are you two happy with your picks this year?"

"Sure." Noah sinks onto the tufted leather couch as I stand next to the fireplace.

"And you, Adam? What do you have to say about that bright white gal you got?" He opens a cross-shaped box—handmade by one of his congregants—and scoops a bump of coke onto his pinky nail, then snorts it.

"She's adequate."

My father laughs, though no lines appear in his forehead, no crow's feet at the corners of his eyes. Botox is a hell of a drug. "Adequate?" He chuckles. "Is this the year when you take one for yourself?"

"Is that what you want?" I keep my tone level.

His eyes narrow. "If you want to challenge me, boy, best come at me with all you got. If you don't, I'll end you."

"Dad." Noah's gentle tone floats through the acrimony, falling like a gentle snow on my father's anger. "He's just not ready yet."

"He's thirty years old. Plenty ready!" He takes another sniff of powdery courage.

"Sure, but he's in charge of our operation. His focus is—"

"I can defend myself just fine, Noah." I level my father with a glare. "I'm not taking one of these fools as a wife. If they're stupid enough to fall for your song and dance, then I want nothing to do with them."

Dad stabs his finger through the air. "I am the Lord's Prophet, Adam. God has chosen me for this. And He has chosen them to serve me."

Out of my father's many delusions, this is his favorite. I could argue, could spell it out that he is a whoremonger of epic proportions. I don't. All I want is to go to bed and forget this day happened. That isn't really an option. I'll be met with my fucked-up reality the second I wake up in the morning. But the bliss of sleep—hours of nothing but utter darkness—is my only remaining pleasure.

His anger turns suddenly serene, which is never a good sign. "I was going to let you say goodnight to your mother, but since you both insist on being obstinate, I think I'll pass."

Noah holds a hand out. "Dad, please." He doesn't realize that pleading will only feed my father's refusal.

Besides, it's a trick. Dad hasn't let us get near our mother in years. She's watched even more closely than the Maidens.

"That's fine." I stand and stretch, easily hiding my hatred in nonchalance. "I'm ready to hit the hay anyway."

When my father realizes he can't make me squeal, his ire returns triple-fold. "Get out of here! Both of you. Service in the morning. This one will be beamed in at our new ministry in India. Surely some of those dot-head idiots can gather up rupees to send over here. Godless heathens." He stubs out his cigar in a crystal ashtray, his dark eyes cutting into my back as I walk away.

I lie in bed, my thoughts drawn back to the ritual, to Delilah. Her thin file rests on the pillow next to me, a snapshot of her oval face pinned to the front. Twenty-one, went to college, from northern Louisiana where her parents still live. She started attending services at Heavenly about a year ago, right after the murder scandal broke.

She came to church every time the doors were open. Always alone, despite a handful of attempts from some of the male members of the congregation. Perfect for the Cloister—a spotless record and distant parents. She'd come to Alabama for school, but like so many others, she'd fallen for the siren song of the Prophet.

I drum my fingers on my bare chest, her image on the backs of my eyelids. The way she'd looked on that bed. *Jesus.*

I've trained a Maiden every year for the past five years, and I've never reacted to one the way I did to her. I pushed her too far, forcing her to look me in the eye and give me more of her than I'm allowed to have. And I was hard on her, but not as hard as I will be. Going easy on her like Noah does with his Maidens would only end in trouble. My hand strays beneath the sheet to my bare cock. It's already hard—the simple thought of her, legs spread, small hands fisting the quilt—that's all it takes. I begin to stroke myself, imagining devouring her sweet cunt as she writhes, fighting the pleasure and then giving in. When she comes on my face, I shoot a thick load all over my stomach.

When I come back down from the euphoria, I realize I can't let this happen again. Fantasizing about her will only cloud my mind, will make me rethink all the shit I have to do to prepare her. I wipe myself clean and toss the sheet to the floor.

She'll be ready.

I won't fail.

Not this time.

CHAPTER 5

DELILAH

The congregation buzzes, each voice added to the others until the 20,000 seat auditorium crackles with energy. I kneel, my head down, my hands folded, a white veil over my face. My fellow Cloister Maidens do the same on either side of me. Twelve innocents on a pedestal for the crowd to watch, to covet.

The Prophet is nothing if not a showoff. The gilded floor of his stage says as much, and when he walks out in his shiny black shoes, the crowd turns into a living monster, the roar of approval drowning out the constant hum of sin.

He grins, the smile of a kindly father figure, and waves at the congregation. His image is magnified on the huge monitors on either side of the stage. The girl next to me shivers, though I doubt it's from fear. Religious rapture, hero worship that endures despite whatever terrors may have befallen her the night before.

"Now, now. The glory goes to God, not me." The Prophet speaks through a small microphone that curves around his cheek and hovers at his lips.

I can't turn around. The Maidens are required to kneel, the perfect image of devout femininity during the service. Our veils cover everything in a whitewash and hide some of the bruises. I realized this morning that I was one of the lucky ones—many of the girls had suffered during the night as I rocked in a corner, my arms wrapped around my calves.

Even if I can't see behind me, I know the sanctuary is full of devout believers. At our backs, the children have been brought in from the nursery, all of them in white jumpers. There's no talking allowed during service, and I've seen the women assigned to childcare yank a child out of the sanctuary on plenty of occasions. I cringed, but no one else batted an eyelash.

A row of Heavenly Police Officers line the sides of the aisles. The State granted the Heavenly campus municipality status a few years back, allowing the Prophet to form his own police force and government. His influence spreads more each day, like an all-consuming rot.

"We have a new crop of Cloister Maidens, praise be to God." He motions to us, twelve pawns in his game of power. Stage lights make him shine. The crowd applauds. Their hunger is a harsh wind at our backs.

"These coveted spots have been filled with young women who will become the future for our church. Twelve months of intensive training in the ways of the Father, Son, and Holy Spirit will yield a set of females that walk in the light and love of our Savior." He sweeps a hand at us. The applause grows.

He holds a hand up, and all sound stops. "As a treat for our new Cloister Maidens and for all of you, we have a very special guest with us this morning. A woman who embodies everything a young woman should be. She is the shining example, the future that we want for all our Cloister Maidens, especially since she was one herself. Please welcome our First Lady of Alabama, Mrs. Miriam Williams."

The crowd roars as she walks onto the stage, her blush pink heels, long legs, and impeccable cream dress accenting her flowing blonde hair. She waves, a huge beauty-queen smile on her face as she embraces the Prophet and kisses him on each cheek.

When they finish beaming at each other, she lifts a microphone and steps forward, her gaze roving over the Cloister Maidens at her feet.

"Blessed are you among women." Her voice, the perfect blend of high and low, rolls over the arena. "For you are the hope for a better future."

Another burst of applause, and then the crowd quiets.

Her clear blue eyes are almost as sharp as her smile as she surveys us. "The Lord has brought you to the Prophet, just as He did for me. I praise God every day for that blessing, and I have no doubt that all of you do the same. The Prophet knows your hearts, your minds, your wants, and your dreams. And only through him will you reach your full potential as a Godly woman in a fallen world."

A chorus of "amen" rises from the spectators.

"Trust him. Listen to him. Only the Prophet knows God's plan for your life." She lifts her eyes and sweeps her dramatic gaze over the crowd. "The Cloister Maidens are blessed to be in the care of the Prophet. As are we all. May God continue to shine his light on and through his one true representative here on earth." She turns and drops a deep curtsey before the Prophet. He nods, then strides to her, takes her hand, and pulls her upright.

"A true woman of God, is she not?"

The churchgoers erupt, a volcano of approval for both the Prophet and Miriam. She struts off the stage with a wave, her white teeth glinting like the stage lights in her eyes.

I chance a glance at the Prophet as he begins his sermon, but my gaze is drawn to the right. Adam stands to the side of the stage, obscured from the crowd but visible to some of the Maidens. It's difficult to see through the veil, but his attention seems to be locked on me. His dark eyes pinning me with something akin to curiosity—or perhaps disgust. I shouldn't care which it is, even though I do.

Adam isn't a man for me to be interested in; he's just another obstacle I'll have to defeat on my way to the truth.

Dropping my gaze, I focus on the edge of the stage. I don't listen to the Prophet. I never have. That's not what I'm here for.

I take my plate of vegetables and a tiny portion of meat and sit at one of the tables in the dining hall. Smaller than the banquet hall, this room is strictly utilitarian—metal tables and chairs, tile floors, and a full kitchen staffed by Spinners. We eat lunch and dinner here. The Head Spinner told us that the Prophet believes breakfast is for the weak; therefore, we skip it at the Cloister. I suspect the lack of breakfast and the low quality of food has more to do with keeping us tiredly compliant, or perhaps attractively thin. Maybe both.

Another Maiden sits next to me and opens her milk carton. "Hi."

"Hi." I spear a piece of droopy broccoli and put it in my mouth.

"I'm Melin—I mean, I'm Sarah." She smiles, her dark hair curling around her forehead. She looks barely old enough to drive.

"Delilah."

"Where are you from?" She cuts off a corner of her meat chunk and gingerly puts it in her mouth.

"Louisiana. You?"

"Birmingham." She wrinkles her nose but swallows.

"How old are you?"

She smiles and spears a green bean. "Old enough."

I glance up and see another Maiden watching us. "Hello."

She drops her eyes—one of them with a black half-moon beneath it—and picks at her food.

"That's Eve. She was—"

I jump as Sarah yelps.

A Spinner stands next to her, a short baton in her hand. "No speaking during mealtimes."

Sarah clutches her bare neck where she'd been struck and cringes against me. I wrap my arm around her. The Spinner rears back again. I flinch as the baton lands against the side of my neck.

"No contact between Maidens!" She scowls as I release Sarah.

"I'm okay." Sarah sniffs, a tear running down her light brown cheek.

My neck stings, but I refuse to touch the sore spot. I won't give the Spinner the satisfaction.

She threads her baton through a loop on the belt of her skirt and walks toward the kitchen, her long black skirt almost touching the ground.

I reach under the table and squeeze Sarah's knee. She gives me a brief nod, then begins eating again.

I wonder about the women who signed up for this under the delusion that the Cloister would be some sort of sisterhood-paradise. Have they come to terms with what it really is? After last night, I can't imagine any of them still believe in the Prophet, in the safety they were promised. But as I glance up at one of the Maidens, the smug satisfaction in her eyes as she gazes at the welt forming on my neck tells me that some of these women are exactly where they want to be.

"Training begins in five minutes." A different Spinner stands at the hall door, her voice a harsh bark. She doesn't look a day over thirty, but, given her air of authority, she appears to be in charge. Her hair is hidden beneath a black habit, and her eyes seem to bore through anyone she looks at too directly. I drop my gaze, lest she see the true me.

I down what I can of my lackluster food. By the time I'm done, the rest of the Maidens are filing out the door. I join the line as we wind our way along the corridors, the

Cloister like a honeycomb. When we emerge into a large room, some of the women gasp.

Three high tables—the type you see at doctor's offices—sit to the right, a Spinner at each. Then another set of three tables with some sort of odd IV bags hanging on their corners, a large sink at their back. Beyond the tables is a wall covered in a dark lattice. Whips, clamps, crops, chains, and a large selection of dildos dangle at intervals. In the corner is a large wooden structure in the shape of an X, and the straps along the top and bottom of it tell me it's not just for decor.

"God smiles on women who please their masters. You must be precious in His sight." The Head Spinner spreads her arms wide. "This is your training room. You will spend quite a bit of your time here every morning. The afternoons will be spent in prayer or performing chores. And your nights belong to your Protector."

One girl makes a slight sound, as if her throat swallows a fearful groan.

The Head Spinner smacks her baton into the palm of her hand. "Remove your clothes. All of you."

I've already become accustomed to forced disrobing, so I drop my dress to the floor without complaint. They don't give us underwear here.

The Head Spinner walks to the first girl in line and uses her baton to tilt the girl's chin up. "All body hair is unseemly in the sight of the Lord."

And what Bible verse says that, exactly? Porn 1:69? I keep my thought to myself.

She slides her baton down the naked girl's torso and stops at the patch of hair between her thighs. "Shameful. All of you. Your bodies are shameful. We have twelve months to try and mold you into females that God and the Prophet can be proud of." She lets out a labored sigh and moves to the next girl. "But I have never had such a bottom-of-the-barrel class of Maidens in the past five years." She uses her baton to poke at Eve's curvy waistline. "That one's a sasquatch, this one needs to lose weight." She continued down the line until she came to me. "Now here's one that shows promise. Trim body, good hair—of course we'll need to remove that mess between your legs." She presses the baton under my chin, lifting my face to hers. "Oh, dear." She frowns. "These eyes simply won't do." She clucks her tongue. "There's something in them I don't care for. Something that is displeasing to the Lord." She hesitates for another moment before moving down the row, criticizing hair, weight, dimples, cellulite, skin tone, and even the location of moles. "Is this a tattoo?" Her disgust coats the air like oil on water. "How on earth did you make it into the Cloister with this evil mark of the fallen world on your body?"

By the time she returns to the front of the line, we've all shrunk about six inches, and I hear some sniffles in the back.

She smacks the baton in her palm. "The Cloister was created by the Prophet to train young women, such as yourselves, to follow the Lord's teachings and obey His will. Some things that happen here may confuse you." A hint of a smile creeps across her thin lips. "They may even scare you, but be assured that everything is done in accordance with the Prophet's plan for your life. You will understand in time."

She speaks with a sureness I've only seen in salesmen and politicians. It makes my skin crawl.

"You three Maidens, here." She points to the first set of tables.

"The next three, here." She motions with her baton to the second area.

I'm the last woman to take one of the tables with the odd IV bag.

"Up." The nearest Spinner pats my table.

I climb and sit, my arms wrapped around my knees. Dread pulses through me with each beat of my heart.

"The rest of you, come with me." The Head Spinner leads the remaining women to the lattice wall.

"I need the three of you on all fours." One of the Spinners behind the tables grabs an IV bag and turns on the water, testing its warmth with her fingertips.

That's when I realize they aren't IV bags. Too big. Too not-entirely-medical.

I saw one of these hanging behind the door in my grandparents' bathroom and thought it was some sort of special balloon. Fun, right? No. They're enema bags.

Sick fucks.

I exchange a glance with Sarah on the table next to me. Her brows are drawn together as she stares at the bag hanging from the hook above her table. I silently mouth the word "enema" to her.

She doesn't understand.

I mouth it again.

When her brown eyes widen, I know she caught the word.

"All fours, I said!" the Spinner at the sink barks.

We all turn over and get on our knees. Humiliation washes over me in a dreadful torrent. I dig my nails into the top of the padded table. Another thought adds to my cocktail of shame: is there a camera in here like the one in the vent of my ceiling? Has to be. Maybe Adam's watching right now, getting off on my torment.

A yelp draws my attention to the other three tables. One of the Spinners is waxing Eve, yanking her dark pubic hair out and tossing the strips aside. Another girl is on hands and knees as a Spinner applies something between her cheeks. She doesn't rip it away. Must not be wax. A memory of Georgia and me watching "Bridesmaids" and giggling together floats through my mind. Are they bleaching her asshole?

I bet mine will be glowing white before the day is—this thought is interrupted when I feel cold hands on my backside and then the unmistakable insertion of a hose into my ass. My reaction is to push it out.

A sharp whack on my side tells me that isn't the correct response. "Don't push!"

The head Spinner appears in front of me, a gag in her hand. Instead of a ball like I'd seen in the movies, this one has a dildo. "She needs throat training sooner than usual, according to Protector Adam."

"Yes, ma'am." The enema Spinner reaches for the contraption.

"I'd like to administer this myself." The head Spinner holds the black dildo in front of my face. "Open."

I don't want to. But I don't have an option. I open.

The Head Spinner shoves it into my mouth.

I gag, but she straps it around my head and buckles it at the back. Using my teeth, I try to bite down and push it with my tongue, but it only makes me gag more. An odd sense of claustrophobia sets in. I could die like this. Choke on my spit. Asphyxiate. All while the Head Spinner stares at me with a coldness that terrifies me.

I close my eyes and focus on breathing through my nose. In, out. In, out. The tube snakes farther up my ass, warmth filling the space and forcing me to clench my cheeks to keep it all in.

"I want to leave." A small voice from one of the tables to my right.

I don't look up. I have to focus on my breathing or I'll die. I know it. The pressure keeps building in my ass as spit drips down my chin.

"Please, let me leave."

I want to warn her. To tell her it's too late for that. There is no way out of here. It's a trap, and once it closes around its victims, the bars are permanent. When I hear a thud and she starts screaming, I keep my breaths steady. *In, out.* Another scream and someone else is crying. *In, out.*

"You are here to serve the Lord. You made an oath, and I and my sister Spinners are here to make sure you keep it." The Head Spinner's voice is oddly serene. "We will save you from the fires of hell despite yourselves. Now stop your sniveling and get back on the table."

"Why? I thought we were here to—"

Another *thunk* and a squeal of pain. "You are here to do as we say, as is commanded by the Prophet!"

Several of the girls cry, their eyes awash in shock. They truly believed they'd be safe in the Cloister, that they'd remain untouched, unmarred. Fools.

I walked into this trap, fully aware of the bars and the rusted metal bits that promised pain and despair. I did it for Georgia.

I will find her killer. And then I will repay what happened to her with blood.

CHAPTER 6

ADAM

*S*he sits on the bed, her gaze downcast, as I enter the room. Red lines run along each of her cheeks. The Spinners did the throat training as I'd instructed.

I close the door behind me and flip the lock.

She doesn't move, doesn't strip and drop to her knees as I instructed.

I sigh and slip my belt from its loops. That catches her attention. She looks up, the same fire in her eyes I saw yesterday.

"Take it off."

She knows I mean her white dress. I'm wearing black pants and a dark blue button-down shirt—my business attire. The all-white charade has ended for me. Not for her, though.

"Why?" The word is barely a breath from her pink lips.

"Didn't the Spinners tell you not to ask questions?" I slide the belt through my palm, it's top grain, soft like butter when it moves slowly. Fast is another story.

"What are you going to do?" Her eyes lock with mine.

"Tonight, I'm going to have to give you an obedience lesson. After that, we'll see."

"I'm not a dog."

The challenge in her voice sends a current through me that ends in my cock. It stiffens, nudging against the front of my pants.

"You've already put three strokes onto the agenda." I let the belt hang at my side. "Would you like another?"

She swallows hard.

"Take off your dress and get on your hands and knees like a good dog." My heart careens against my ribs, drunk on the thought of her naked flesh reddened with my belt.

With one more look that telegraphs a pure, undiluted hatred, she stands and pulls her dress off. Inch by inch, I take in every delicious bit of skin.

"I see the Spinners jumped right into the waxing routine." I stare at the bareness between her legs, the skin still pink and irritated. I want to run my lips, my tongue, my cock all over it.

She says nothing and climbs onto the bed, keeping her thighs together and crossing her ankles she lets out a breath. Her hair cascades on either side of her face, hiding her from me.

I move to stand behind her. When I get the full view of her bare pussy, my mouth waters. It's a perfect pink tulip, the untouched center likely the sweetest thing I've ever tasted. Gripping the belt tighter, I focus on her discipline. She's a thing, not a person. I began telling myself that little mantra when I became a Protector for the very first time. It was the only way I could do what was necessary. Now, I realize how empty it is, how diseased I've become. I *want* to strike her. I salivate for it.

I used to lie to myself—*I'm only doing this for her own good. She'll have it much, much worse later if I don't break her now.* Those words are just as hollow as my diseased heart. I hurt her because I want to, because I fucking crave it, because I've become the monster my father always wanted. The same monster he is.

Drawing back, I savor the moment before the strike. The appetizer. With a vicious swing, I paint a red stripe across her ass.

She yelps and bucks, her ankles coming apart as her head hangs. I don't give her a moment to rest. My beast needs to be fed. I strike again, her agony reaching my ears on an exquisite cry. Rearing back, I put even more strength into the last hit, letting the leather travel a little lower, striping across her most delicate flesh. Her howl lights up every pleasure receptor in my brain, and my cock pushes against my zipper.

Collapsing, she rolls over into the fetal position.

"We're not done with this lesson." I point to the rug.

She peers at me from beneath her curtain of angelic hair, then edges off the bed, her knees hitting the floor with an ugly *thunk*.

I refasten my belt and sit in front of her as she stares at the floor. "Like this, every night, understand?"

She nods.

"You can do better than that." I want to touch her hair, soothe her. I shouldn't. The desire doesn't fit. It's a soft curve in a sea of broken glass. I shake it off. "Delilah."

She looks up, tears gleaming in her light gray eyes. "I understand."

"That's better." I draw my finger across the red marks on her cheek.

I wonder how much self-control it takes for her not to flinch away from my touch. Her eyes remain locked with mine, though they give me no insight. They aren't windows at all, but a steely wall she hides behind. Not that I can blame her.

"How did your gag reflex training go today, little lamb?"

She shrugs, her narrow shoulders barely rising. "I still gag."

I grip her chin. "Open."

She does, and I push my fingers against her soft tongue and to the back of her throat. When she gags, I draw back, then do it again, and again, and again. Spit pools and drips down her chin.

I withdraw my fingers and simply admire the slightly ruined look of her—watery eyes and a succulent red mouth. "You're better than yesterday. It'll take time. But it's necessary."

"Why?"

"There you go with the questions again." I drag my fingers across my belt buckle. She doesn't look down, but I know she can see the threat. "Besides, you know why."

"The Prophet said we'd be safe here, that we—"

I smirk. "And you believed it?"

I don't know why, but I get the sensation she's toying with me. It's unprecedented, and I can't tell if I like it or not. I suspect I do.

Leaning forward, I grab a handful of her hair and yank her head back, bending her spine so she looks straight up at me. "I think you knew the Prophet's promises were lies." A hint of paranoia whispers in my mind. "Are you a cop?"

"No."

I know she isn't. We've had the county sheriff on our payroll and his family in the reserved front row every Sunday. But there *was* something different about her. Off.

"Some sort of reporter?" I shake her, enjoying her wince of pain.

"No."

The church has enough fingers in the national and local media pie to figure out if anyone has sent in a mole. So, it wasn't that. But what?

"Why would anyone who knew what the Cloister truly is volunteer to be a Maiden?" I voice the question that's been bothering me since the previous night. My other Maidens—they actually believed in my father's circus sideshow. But Delilah isn't like them. The fact that I can't quite delineate what sets her apart is a thorn that is slowly working its way into my gray matter.

"God led me here."

I release her and sit back. "Bullshit."

She barely keeps her balance, but settles back onto her knees, those ethereal eyes locked on mine. "The Prophet will keep his promises. I am where God wants me to be."

If she had any idea of what the Prophet truly intended to do with her, she wouldn't be bothering with this charade.

"What other training did you get today?"

"They performed an..." Her gaze almost wavers, but she holds it. "Enema."

"Do you know why they do that?"

She shakes her head, genuine curiosity in her eyes. The darkest part of me hungers for what she will reveal next. Shock, disgust, maybe even interest?

"For when I take your ass."

Her eyebrows lower. "What?"

"They're preparing you for when I decide it's time for you to feel me deep in your ass." I take a little too much pleasure in the explanation.

"But, I thought... I'm a virgin, and I thought that's why the Prophet—"

"Oh, you'll still be pure afterwards." I want to devour every last drop of despair she lets slip through. "Still a virgin."

A shiver cuts through her, and she crosses her arms over her stomach. "I'll never agree."

"No?" I smile, perhaps because I can sense it infuriates her.

"You can't force me." Her fire lashes out, burning me in the most indulgent way.

"I can't?" I grab another handful of her hair and yank her up.

She yelps as I throw her on the bed and cover her body with mine. On all fours, she tries to buck me but can't. She thrashes as I slide my hand down her back and ass.

"See?" I spread her cheeks apart and push my knees between hers.

Still struggling, she yells, "Stop!"

I don't.

I run my finger down her ass and press it against the hole. "I can do whatever I want with you, Delilah. I could face fuck you right now. Plunge into your ass. Bite your pussy and tongue this tight little hole." I push just a little, almost breaching her.

"Stop!" Her yell is muffled in the comforter.

I push back and stand as she flips over and scuttles until she hits the headboard.

"Stay away from me!" She breathes hard, her breasts rising and falling, pink creeping up her neck and into her cheeks. Beautiful.

"I can't." I give her another smirk. "But that's all for tonight."

When I close and lock her door, I feel her sob before I hear it.

"Where are the rest of the receipts?" I sift through the pile of information on my desk, dropped there by the dumbest bagman we've ever hired.

"Oh, I guess they must be in the car still." He turns, his redneck "Duck Dynasty" t-shirt even more offensive from the back.

Once he's left my office, I hit a button and turn on the flatscreen on the wall. There she is, Delilah, sitting on her bed and chewing her thumbnail. She does that a lot. Sometimes she hugs her knees and rocks. I watch it all. Before, I would check on my Maiden once a month at most. With Delilah, I can't stop looking.

I scared her tonight. I had to. No, I *wanted* to. The fear in her was like the scent of fresh blood to a hound. I crave it.

A knock sounds at my door and Franklin walks in.

I scowl and flip off the TV screen. "What do you want?"

"Me and the boys are heading to the Chapel."

"So?"

He shifts from one foot to the other, his bald pate shiny with oil. "The Prophet said we had to check in with you before we could—"

"Go." I wave him away. "But don't do any permanent damage like last time. That costs us money."

His smile somehow makes him even uglier. "I won't."

"Fuck off." I flip the screen back on as he hustles down the hall, ready to spend his evening snorting blow and getting his filthy dick wet.

Returning my attention to Delilah, I stare at the curve of her neck where it disappears into her white gown. Would she end up at the Chapel? The thought rots in my gut as I consider her delicate features.

"I got 'em." The Duck Dynasty dipshit returns with a tattered notebook in his hand. "Wrote it all down just like you told me."

"Leave it." I point to an empty spot on the scarred wooden surface.

He drops it there, then glances at the TV. "She's a looker."

"Get the fuck out!" I reach for the pistol in the holster under my desk, my control hanging by a thread. Offing this lowlife would go a long way toward stress relief.

"Sorry, boss." He holds up his hands and backs away. Each step farther from me he gets, the easier I feel. I release the pistol and settle into my chair.

Grabbing the notebook, I flip through to check what amounts he received from our smattering of all-cash business. We didn't need many to cover our money laundering side of the business. By far the easiest place to launder money was the church. No taxes, all cash, no IRS problems. We built an empire on it, along with quite a few other unscrupulous avenues.

I tally up the numbers and make the additions to a handful of spreadsheets. The drudgery eats away at me. But I can't escape it. My die was cast a long time ago. I'm almost as trapped as my Maiden. At the thought, I look up at the screen.

Rage blots out whatever thoughts I have as I grab the pistol and rush out the door.

CHAPTER 7

DELILAH

a soft knock at my door tears my attention away from the thumbnail I've been chewing on for half an hour.

"It's me." A low voice—the Spinner with the scar along her forehead. Spinner Chastity, I think they call her.

I walk over and flip the lock. The door shoves forward, knocking me back. Chastity gives me a wide-eyed look before the Protector who grabbed her thrusts her aside, enters my room, and slams and locks the door behind him.

"Get on the bed." He isn't familiar—his brown eyes, brown hair, and pockmarked skin nothing to remember.

I scoot back across the floor until my back hits the wall next to the bathroom. "You can't be in here." My stomach churns, acid splashing up my throat.

"I'm a Protector, bitch. I can do whatever the fuck I want." He glowers. "Except the one fucking thing I want the most. But I'll make do with everything else."

"Please—"

He rushes forward and grabs a handful of my hair, then wrenches me off the floor. I scream and slap at his forearm as he yanks me to the bed.

"Bitch." He draws back one hand and slaps me.

My ears ring, but I keep fighting, clawing at his arms.

He slaps me again, and this time I taste blood. He's yanking at my clothes, trying to rip the dress off me. I keep screaming, hoping Chastity or even the Head Spinner will burst through the door. But they don't. The dress tears along the seams, the material cutting into my skin as it shreds.

"Fucking bitch!" he yells as I scratch his face, then wraps his hands around my throat.

I try to pry his fingers away as my throat burns, my eyes water, and I can't draw a breath. He settles on top of me, his crushing weight only added to the pressure at my throat.

I'm going to die like this. The hate in his eyes tells me that's the truth. I will end because of his violence. He squeezes tighter, and I can't feel anything except the burning in my lungs, the pain at my neck.

A crack shatters my agony, and he collapses on top of me. Warmth rushes over my face as I gasp in a breath, then another.

His weight lifts as Adam throws him to the floor, then Adam fires another shot into his prone body. Without casting me so much as a glance, he strides out of the room.

"Clean this mess up." He spits the words at the Head Spinner who comes into view just outside the door.

She frowns at the body, then at me as she rushes in. "This is your fault. You tempted him in here with your whoring ways, and now he's dead because of you."

I can't summon the energy I need to be incredulous. All I can do is relish the oxygen returning to my lungs despite the burn that accompanies it. Is that what happened to Georgia? Did she die of idiotic rage? No. That can't have been it. The memory of the crime scene photos resurfaces—the marks carved into her body, the elaborate way she was staged. Her death was no thoughtless act. It was a well-planned sacrifice.

The Head Spinner snaps her fingers. "Are you listening, Delilah?" Her voice has dropped to a lethal tone.

"I am."

"Good. I expect you to have Protector Newell's body cleaned and laid out neatly on your bed when I return in a few hours."

"What?" I croak.

"Get to work." She swings the door shut behind her, and I'm left alone with the dead man.

I just lie there for a few long minutes, breathing. Being alive. My throat swells, the skin hot to the touch as I gingerly feel the damage. My hands shake, and a tremor rockets through me every so often. My brain tries to piece together what happened, because my recollection is jumbled. When did Adam come in? Concentrating, I go through the attack step by step. Adam appeared at the end. He killed the man who'd hurt me. The scene came together like a movie where I was only a spectator—a piece of dust floating lazily in the corner. Adam killed a man without a second thought. But did he kill for *me*?

Sitting up seems to help my breathing, though I have to inhale and exhale to clear the black dots swirling in my vision. I touch my fingertips to my cheek. They come away red. My haze begins to clear. The bed is splattered with blood, and crimson streaks up the wall along with chunks of gray matter.

My stomach heaves. I bite the back of my hand, trying to keep from throwing up. It would be just another thing the Head Spinner would make me clean.

Another soft knock at my door makes me jump. I stand on wobbly legs and skirt the dead man's boots, then open the door.

Tears fall down Chastity's face. "I'm so sorry."

"It's not your fault." My voice is a rasp, and it hurts.

"Can I come in?" She has towels piled on one arm and a container of Clorox in the other. "Please?"

I nod and back up as she scurries in and closes the door. "I'm not supposed to help, but Spinner Grace won't notice." She swallows hard. "I hope."

"The Head Spinner's name is Grace?"

She shrugs. "The Prophet assigns our names." Kneeling, she leans over the body. "Let's get him into the tub. We can strip him there and wash him off."

I want to mention that a quarter of his head is gone, that gore is everywhere, that there was no way we could ever clean the blood off him. Or me. Instead I join her on the floor, my hands still shaking, my body going cold, and help her drag his still-warm corpse to the bathroom. His blood oozes onto the white tiles, leaving a slippery trail of human carnage.

"You seem used to dealing with bodies." I can barely understand myself, and my throat makes an ugly clicking noise as I speak.

She freezes for only a second, then continues working without reply. How many deaths had she seen at this place? Had she seen Georgia's? The burning need to know almost overcomes my caution, but I keep my lips firmly shut. She won't tell me anything. Not until I have more time to work on her.

"On three." She grips one of his arms and motions for me to take the other. "One, two, three."

I lift as hard as I can. The body flumps into the tub, marring the surface and the wall with more garish crimson. My stomach churns again, and even Chastity seems to pale.

She wipes her hands on one of the towels, then gives me a steady look. "Now we need to remove his clothes."

I cringe.

"We can do this." She reaches over and squeezes my wrist. "We have to."

"Okay." I lean over the tub and grab the hem of his t-shirt. The Confederate flag across the front has become more of a modern art piece, red seeping through the white parts. With a yank, I get it up to his chest, his pale skin the sickly shade of a fish's belly.

"I've got his arms." She nods, encouraging me to keep working.

After an hour of labor, we sit back and stare at the man in the tub. He's naked, turning blue, but clean except for the wounds in his head and back. They aren't bleeding anymore, but if we move him, little runnels of red still ooze out.

"This is as good as we can get him." She stands and puts her hands on her hips, stretching her back and popping her neck. "Let's get him onto the towels. Then you can shower off while I clean the room."

Before I know it's happening, I feel tears on my cheeks. Some dam suddenly breaks inside me. I'm already coming apart, and I've only been in this hell for two days.

Her eyes soften, and she pulls me into her arms. "You survived. Shhh, now. Shh. You survived. That's what's important. You're alive. He's dead. He'll never hurt you or anyone else again." She strokes down my back, slow and steady, as I sob on her shoulder.

"Am I in bad trouble?" I whisper.

"You?" She shakes her head. "No. Protector Adam, though, I'm pretty sure there'll be consequences."

I can't think about him right now. About what he did or his reasons for doing it. He threatened me not four hours ago. Then he protected me. I thought I knew what I was getting into when I volunteered for the Cloister.

I don't understand. My gorge rises again, and I throw myself away from Chastity and heave the entire contents of my stomach into the toilet.

I was already afraid when I *knew* what was coming next.

Now that I'm in the dark? I'm terrified.

CHAPTER 8

DELILAH

Five years ago

"This makes me look fat, doesn't it?" Georgia twirls in a blue dress, the fabric flowing out around her knees in an arc of sky.

"No." I lay on her bed, my hands propping up my chin and my feet in the air. "You look like some glam queen."

"Oh, stop." She waves a hand at me, then reconsiders. "No, go on. Tell me how cute I am."

"You're the worst." I lay my head down and stare out the second-floor window of her bedroom. Everything is so soft here—the bedspread, the carpet, the voices of her parents as they go about their weekend in the house below. Nothing like my home.

"I would kill for your platinum hair, you know?" She sits next to me and runs her fingers through my long strands.

A lot of people compliment my hair. But Georgia hits on the exact problem with what she doesn't say. She wants my hair, sure. But she doesn't want the pale skin and grey eyes that come with it. Whereas Georgia is all blonde curls, tan skin, and bright blue eyes, I'm the ghost of the girl I'm supposed to be. That's how I think of myself, as if I'm a black and white spirit while my real self is someone technicolor, like Dorothy over the rainbow.

"At least I got your nose." She points to the slightly upturned tip. "The boys don't know that it's the nose that gets their attention when it comes to babes like us."

"You're delusional." I still smile. Georgia always has a way of tapping into the deeply-hidden vein of happiness inside me. Maybe because we share a father. Or maybe because of who she is—an effervescent beauty queen who rules her high school with a benevolent, but firm, hand.

Georgia Evans is a teen dream, and I fantasize about going to her school and living in her inner circle. But I'm a Barnes, and I don't belong here in this clean, bright world. That doesn't mean I can't imagine how different things would be if I had a stepfather who cared enough to give me his name, or a mother who didn't have to work three jobs just to keep it together.

"Girls, time for church," her mother calls from the bottom of the stairs.

I push up from the bed and eye the dress Georgia has chosen for me—a pink A-line that I already know will hang loose in the bust.

"I can't wear that."

"You can." She floats to her closet and bends over to drag out some white mary janes.

"I'll look like a little girl in those." I frown and strip off her long night-shirt emblazoned with Taylor Swift's face.

Georgia knows I'm shy, so she looks away as I adjust my barely-needed bra, then pull the dress over my head.

"Do we really have to go to church?" I roll my eyes as I catch a glimpse of myself in her dresser mirror. Just as I figured, the bust is made for Georgia, not for me. It hangs, and the dress is wearing me instead of the other way around. So pale, I'm a white rabbit caught in a puff of cotton candy.

She frowns, then her expression brightens, just as it always does. "I've got it." She turns and rummages through the stack of plastic storage drawers in the side of her closet, then yanks a white cardigan from a hanger. "Here." She whips me around, then futzes with the back of my dress. The front tightens up.

Suddenly, a real teenager appears in the mirror, not the ghostly girl I am used to seeing. The dress molds to what little curves I have and—while not perfectly fitted—is easily the best thing I've ever worn.

"Now—" she helps me with the cardigan"—Perfect!"

I turn and whatever she used to gather the dress fabric is hidden beneath the soft cardigan. I want to say "wow," but my throat feels too tight.

She grins and pushes me so I fall onto the bed, then kneels and puts the too-big shoes on my feet. "You are so pretty when you let me force you into it."

The tightness fades as I stare down at her halo of golden curls, the familiarity of her soothing the too-raw emotions of the past few moments. "I don't know why I have to dress up this time. Your parents never cared what I wore before—well, except the time they made me change The Kinks t-shirt."

She pops up and smiles at her handiwork. "Oh, this time is a special occasion."

"Why?" I follow her into the hall, my ankles wobbly as we head down the stairs.

She turns, her big blue eyes looking up at me. "Because the Prophet is coming today."

CHAPTER 9

ADAM

*T*toss my shirt to the floor as I enter the sacred circle. Crosses—some upside down, some right side up—pentagrams, and various other symbols greet me from all angles.

Noah walks along the circular wall and lights candles. Dad and his fucking love of spectacle.

"Why?" Noah crossed to me, his bare feet disturbing the salt circle.

"She's mine."

"So?" He frowns. "That's not a good enough reason."

"Newell was a cunt. What does it matter?" His filthy blood all over my hands barely scratches the surface of what I'm capable of. Killing Newell is the lightest of my transgressions, perhaps even a mark in my favor.

"Because of *this*." He points to my bare back and the criss-cross of scars that live there. "I fucking hate it."

"He would have killed her." I shrug and stretch up, looping my wrists through the wooden cross in the center of the room.

"No, he knew better. He would have..." He shakes his head. "But she'd be alive. And so would Newell."

"Goddammit, Noah!" I yank on the self-tightening restraints. "Sometimes we have to make a choice. I fucking made it. I'll take the punishment for it. End of story. Now light the candles and enjoy the show."

I love my brother. So much that I want to shake the fuck out of him. He's been steeped in the culture of Heavenly Ministries since he was too young to know any better, and it fucking shows. Evil isn't a bad thing when it's all you've ever known. It's a comfortable blanket, a warm sun, a lover's kiss. For him, all this makes sense.

But I remember a time when my father was just another preacher at one of the larger Baptist churches in Birmingham. I went to the religious school, had a nearly normal life, and pretended to believe in all the crap my father spouted. Over time, he became the head pastor. And that's when everything changed. Power allowed my father to preach a new message. One of fear, of a coming apocalypse, of the need for the congregation to tithe more and more to support the church. To support *him*.

I shake off the memories as the Protectors file into the room and stand in a circle around me. None of them look too happy about me killing Newell. I smirk and hope they know I'd just as soon do the same to them.

"Son." My father's voice slithers into the room. "Why have you disappointed me yet again?"

"I guess old habits die hard." I see Noah flinch at the sarcasm in my tone.

"You think this is a joke?" My father moves closer.

"I think I killed someone who had it coming."

"Had it coming?" He seems genuinely confused.

"I thought you'd be all in favor of what I did, considering Newell was about to break your number one commandment."

"You have no proof of that."

I realize there's no point arguing. Gripping the wooden cross, I steel myself for what's next.

"Oh, son." The faux dismay in my father's voice is laughable. "I don't enjoy this. You know that, don't you? But what else can I do? You killed one of my godly Protectors. There can be no other outcome."

A rumble of agreement pulses through the circle.

"Just get on with it."

He lets out a heavy sigh, as if he isn't looking forward to the blood and pain. But I know the monster too well to believe it. This is what he thrives on.

"Just as in the story of Abraham, I must take my own son and lay him on the altar of the Lord. A sacrifice to show my adherence to God. And just as Abraham, my heart aches as I lash my son to the altar." He moves around and checks my wrists, making sure they're held fast, then takes the whip from a frowning Noah. "And I must be steadfast in my sacrifice, for if I am, the Lord says 'I will surely bless you and make your descendants as numerous as the stars in the sky and as the sand on the seashore. Your descendants will take possession of the cities of their enemies, and through your offspring all nations on earth will be blessed, because you have obeyed me.'"

The Protectors answer with a steady "amen" as my father backs away.

I want to say that in the story of Abraham, he never sacrifices his son at all. The son is reprieved by God, not harmed by his father. But that thought is seared away with the first strike of the whip. More follow in rapid succession.

I don't cry out, not even when I feel the blood trickling down my back. My teeth grind together, possibly on the verge of breaking as my father puts everything he has into the final blow. Black flickers across my vision, but I refuse to pass out, refuse to give in.

When he's done, he's winded, his voice breathy. "Atonement has been paid for the loss of Protector Newell."

Another "amen" and the men file out, some of them giving me satisfied smirks as they pass. Despite the overwhelming fire roaring across my back, I want to lunge at them. To take these monsters down the same way I did Newell. But that thought ignores the obvious.

After all, I'm a monster, too.

I lie on my side, lazy smoke from my joint twisting in front of my face as I stare at the wide TV screen on my wall.

Delilah sits in a corner of her now-clean room. She rocks back and forth, her wide eyes focused on the door. She's the picture of terror, the sort that, once it touches a person, leaves a mark.

"These aren't the worst you've ever had." Noah tends to the tears in my skin, the wounds that will heal and add to the scar tissue inside and out.

I take another drag on the joint, holding the smoke in my lungs as he pulls me into a sitting position and begins wrapping gauze around my torso.

Exhaling, I watch as her head slowly drops to her knees, then bobs up again, her gaze on the door. Is she afraid that I might come through the door? Another Protector, maybe?

Fear is the best thing for her. The sooner she breaks, the easier it will be for me. In the past, I had quite a few Maidens who—despite the stark reality of the Cloister—still believed my father was the Prophet. The rituals helped with that notion. And they didn't require me to break them. Instead, they were eager to please, to learn, to become the Prophet's favorite.

In the end, all of them—the true believers and the broken ones—all believe that the Prophet favors them, that they are chosen, that God has put his mark of favor upon them. I try to imagine how it must feel when they wind up at the Chapel or the Cathedral instead of on the arm of a politician or one of the South's millionaires. Betrayal. I'm intimately familiar with that sensation.

Her head nods forward again, resting on the tops of her knees. This time, she's out. As out as she can be.

"You've never watched one before." Noah tucks the end of the gauze into the tight ribbons around my chest.

I let out another puff of smoke, the weed finally giving me that perfect sensation of soft disconnection. "She's different."

"Why?" He checks his handiwork.

"I don't know."

"Is she going to be a problem?" He takes the joint from my fingers and pulls in a long drag. "I mean, more than she already is?"

"She'll fall in line. Mine always do." The few times I've had to break my Maidens, I always managed it before the trials that begin at the 6-month mark. Maybe because I'm methodical. Maybe because of the consequences if I fail. Or, more likely, because I enjoy it.

"She looks so weird. With the hair and the white skin." He shakes his head.

I reach for the remote. He shouldn't be looking at her. At what's mine. And his criticism cuts through the smoky haze of my high. I click the screen off.

"Touchy."

"Fuck off." I lie back down, the lines of fire across my back pulling a groan from me.

"After Newell, how many is it now?" he asks quietly.

"How many what?" I know what he's asking, but the sadist in me wants to hear him say it.

"How many ... you know ... people have you..."

"Killed?" I stick the knife in.

He winces.

I should feel something. Maybe remorse. But there's nothing there. Not even the emptiness bothers me

79

anymore. "At current count, seven." I grin. "But there's always tomorrow."

"God will forgive you." He stubs out the joint. "You did it all for His glory." He swallows hard. "Even Newell, since he may have had intentions of defiling one of the chosen Maidens."

I open the top drawer of my nightstand and pull out a flask of whiskey. My brother's blind belief is doing more to tank my high than even the pain in my back.

"Which god?" I take a draw, the heat pouring down my throat. "The one up top or the one below?"

"They are both one." He pulls the blanket up to my waist. "You know this. There can be no light without dark. Our Heavenly Father and our Father of Fire have already forgiven you. Even Mom believes—"

"How do you know what she believes?"

He pinches his lips together, then relents. "I'm just guessing." He sighs. "I don't know. Anyway, I'm sure you're forgiven. Doing things that seem wrong, if they're done for the Heavenly Father or the Father of Fire—that makes them righteous."

I take another long pull from the flask. I don't berate myself for the way Noah is. Not anymore. He's too steeped in my father's bullshit, too much of a true believer, for me to ever pull him free. Maybe I've failed him, or maybe this was the way it was always meant to be.

"Get some sleep." He stows the flask. "We've got the Ritual tomorrow night."

"I know." I settle into my pillow as he turns out the light. "Now the real mindfuck will begin."

He shakes his head. "It's for—"

"His glory. Yeah, I got it." I don't even want to shake him anymore. He's too far gone to understand.

He closes the door, and I grab the remote. The screen glows to life, and there she is. Her fairy hair falling around her shoulders as she sleeps in a huddle. I hope she dreams of me, even if it's a nightmare. How could it be anything else?

"It can't be," I answer myself. Like a lunatic.

She stirs and lifts her head as if she can hear me. She can't. But she turns and looks straight at the camera, at me, her eyes luminous in the low light.

"Why?" I ask her. Why did I kill for her? Why is she different? *Or,* my mind answers, *she's not different at all. You're just desperate for something new. For someone else besides the usual brainwashed acolytes*

"Why?" I ask her again, more demanding this time.

Do I detect a faint quirk to her lips, a touch of fire in her gaze? I blink hard, and when I open my eyes, she's hidden from me again, her head resting on her knees, her breaths slow and even.

CHAPTER 10

DELILAH

"*D*elilah." The Head Spinner approaches as I stand in line for "training."

I turn toward her, my eyes down, my hands clasped in front of me. The picture of demure purity, despite the fact I'm utterly naked.

With a deceptively light voice, she says, "You will train with me today." She continues walking, and I step out of line and follow. Sarah shoots me a worried look, but doesn't say anything as I file past.

Goosebumps race down my body as the Head Spinner makes a beeline for the large wooden X suspended from the ceiling. The one with the straps.

She stops abruptly, her black skirt swishing forward at her ankles. "Step up."

I want to turn and run, but there is no way out. I force my body to cooperate, to move forward despite the paralysis of fear. I walk past her and stand in front of the X, then lift my arms.

"Turn around."

I spin and face the room, the Maidens in various states of training—some with dildos in their mouths, others on all fours with plugs in their asses, still others on top of benches, their legs held in place as Spinners wearing strap-ons fuck them in the mouth. One Spinner demonstrates the differently-sized dildos with a metal ruler, which she also uses to discipline any Maiden who she feels isn't paying perfect attention.

The Head Spinner reaches up and fastens first my right wrist and then my left, pulling the leather bindings tight. She pauses for a moment to inspect the bruising on my neck, then steps back.

I wiggle my fingers, the circulation already slowing in them. They'll be numb in a few minutes, and maybe that will be a good thing.

There are leather cuffs for my ankles on the bottom of the X, but she doesn't fasten them. I breathe a small sigh of relief. If she'd spread my legs and left me completely open, the terror might have overtaken me.

She edges past the X, then reaches for a green industrial-looking button in the nearby wall. Foreboding coats my tongue like a sour taste. A loud mechanical click sounds from above. I look up and see the chain receding through a small hole in the ceiling. The X rises, pulling my arms taut, and cinching the leather even tighter on my wrists.

I struggle, trying to loosen the bindings and ease the ache, but the leather only grips tighter. My back is pressed against the X, a crucifixion before an audience of Maidens and Spinners.

She slows my ascent, just as I go up on my tiptoes, the very last chance I have to keep at least some of my weight on the ground. The machine quiets, and I'm left mostly hanging, my body protesting the strain, my mind yelling at me to focus on something other than the fear, the torture, the smug Head Spinner.

"This is an important lesson, and I'm glad to be the one to teach it." She eases around me until I can see her again.

The room is silent, all the other training halted.

She raises her hand and presses it to my chest. I can't get away from her touch. She lets her fingers trail between the valley of my breasts, down my stomach and then lower.

Her eyes glint as she cups my sex. "This is what happens to sluts who disobey the Lord's commands," she whispers so low that only I can hear.

I tremble and press my legs together even though it puts more strain on my wrists. She releases her grip and backs away.

"The Prophet demands your obedience." Her voice rises, the sound piercing every woman in the room. "God demands sacrifice from all his chosen. And if you fail to comport yourselves as the godly women you are meant to be, there are consequences."

"Amen." The Spinners in the room form one voice.

"Cloister Maiden Delilah caused the death of a Protector. His blood is on her hands. Because of her whorish Jezebel ways, she has broken the Prophet's law. Does she deserve punishment?"

"Yes!" the Spinners cry.

"I asked you all, does she deserve punishment!" Her voice is a whip.

The Maidens react, even Sarah crying yes under the harsh gaze of the Head Spinner. Some of the girls look on with expectant, hungry eyes. But others seem locked into their own horror, though I can't tell if their trepidation is for me or themselves.

"Better." The Head Spinner walks to the wall of implements and chooses a crop, the handle long and thin, and the end a piece of flattened black leather.

"The book of Isaiah tells us what happens to the wicked among us. 'I will punish the world for its evil, the wicked for their sins. I will put an end to the arrogance of the haughty.'" She stands in front of me and runs the crop along her palm. "Your arrogance is an affront to the

Prophet. You must learn your place. It is at His feet. At the feet of your Protector. At the feet of our mighty Prophet. And at the feet of our Lord." The fervor rises in her voice. "Here, with your sisters, you will learn to be a model female, one that carries the blessings of God wherever she goes. But first, you must be punished."

I can't look away from her, the mad sparkle in her eyes, the sheer weight of belief in her voice, and the violence in her arm as she swings the crop right at my vulnerable sex.

My scream rips through the room as the most intense pain I've ever felt rushes through me. I cross my legs, but my wrists feel like they're shredding as the leather digs in. I have to put my feet back down, leaving myself vulnerable. Tears well, though I try to fight them back.

"You see, Maidens? Disobedience, wickedness, or a return to your fallen ways will not be tolerated." She swings again.

I can't get enough air, and I pull my knees up to try and defend myself, even though I can feel blood trickling down my forearms.

"Soon, you will speak the truth of the prophets! 'Let me die the death of the righteous, and may my final end be like theirs!'"

"Amen!" shout the Spinners.

My legs give out, everything in me vibrating to the frequency of agony, and the Head Spinner draws back.

When her arm flies forward, my wail comes from a deep reserve of suffering somewhere inside me. One I didn't know was there. A primordial well of terror and hurt.

""The Lord rewards everyone for their righteousness and faithfulness.'" The Head Spinner's voice is full of rapture. "I will make each one of you righteous and faithful." She pulls up my chin, forcing me to meet her stony gaze. "Even you, sinful Delilah."

She releases me, and tears leak freely down my face as my body goes limp. I lean forward, my shoulders twisting as I let the leather tear into my wrists. Deep sobs wrack me. I don't know how long I hang there, my tears dripping onto the floor, but I feel when someone lifts me, their shoulder under my stomach. Then hands gently release the leather at my wrists.

Someone carries me over to one of the waxing tables. I blink away my tears to find an older, stout woman hovering over me. I recognize her from the microchipping. She's Abigail, the oldest Spinner I've seen.

"I'm going to tend to your wrists and your maidenhood."

I glance around wildly, looking for the Head Spinner through the haze of tears.

"She's gone." Abigail scowls. "Likely to do some sort of high and mighty business. Who knows. Now just lie still, and I'll fix you right up."

Sarah stands next to me, her face pale. Chastity assists Abigail with bandages as the other Spinners bark at the women to return to their "studies."

"I'll stay." Sarah pushes my hair from my forehead.

"I didn't do anything." The words bubble up, as if my guilt or innocence matters in the least.

"I know. I know you didn't." She wipes my cheeks with her palms. "It's not your fault."

"Sarah!" A Spinner barks. "Do you need another demonstration of what happens to those who disobey?"

"Go. Please go." I close my eyes.

"I'm sorry," she whispers.

"It's okay." I don't want her to suffer. My pain is plenty.

Her warmth fades as she leaves, and then Abigail's shadow falls over me. She mumbles under her breath, none of her words particularly Spinner-appropriate. I want to ask her how she got here. She clearly wasn't a passed over Cloister Maiden like so many of the others seem to be. She is too old, too smart, too clear-eyed.

"This is going to sting." She presses something cold against my wrist. Then the burn sets in. I clench my eyes shut.

"You aren't too bad off. The leather only tore your skin in a couple of places. With a little salve, you won't even scar. Thank the Lord. Scarring would send you right to the

89

Chapel when your year is up." She resumes grumbling. "Could've used ... and there are padded cuffs...damn sadist."

She cleans first one wrist and then the other as I wonder what the Chapel is and try to keep from crying out. I stare up at the rustic logs, each one forming an elaborate lattice above me. Planned, perfect, and built with human hands. Just like the Cloister. But instead of holding up a structure, the Cloister is designed to rip a person down to the barest foundation.

"Your maidenhood will recover just fine." She bends over my crotch.

Only a week ago, I would've felt uncomfortable with someone hovering so close to my private area. Now, I sigh with relief as she applies some sort of cooling gel to the skin, easing the burn of the crop.

"Are you all right?" Chastity stares down at me, her voice barely a whisper.

"I think so. And ... thank you for ..." For helping me with the dead man. The words are there, but I can't seem to utter them.

"You're welcome." She moves down the table and begins wrapping my wrists.

The rest of the room continues with training as Abigail and Chastity tend to me.

My thoughts veer past the punishment, rewind on the spool of my mind, and stop on Adam bursting into my room. He killed without a thought. The sureness in his shot, the coldness in his voice all telling me that he was no stranger to murder.

Was it him? Had he taken Georgia's life with the same lethal calm? And would he one day take mine?

The Cloister dormitory is eerily silent as night falls. No heavy footsteps from the Protectors, no whispering Spinners outside the door.

I wait for Adam, dreading him but also wondering if he'll talk about the murder. It's funny how quickly I accepted it. A man tried to kill me only hours ago, and now he's dead. Simple as flipping a switch. It certainly was that easy for Adam.

I shiver. He took a life as if it were commonplace, something he did as easily as closing a door or flushing a toilet.

He'll want me on my knees, my nudity on display. But I don't strip yet. Not until I have to. My last little bit of rebellion, I suppose. Though it's stupid. I knew it would be like this, what I'd have to do if I wanted to be a part of the Cloister. The Prophet's chats with the hopefuls— ones centered on being a pure child of God, an example for a fallen world—hadn't fooled me.

I pick at the bandage on my right wrist. Would Adam ask what happened? Would he even care? What if he saw the red marks on my—

My door opens without a knock. I look up, but it isn't Adam. Chastity motions for me to come, and I see several Maidens lined up in the hall, their white dresses ghostly.

"What's going on?" I whisper as I pass her.

She doesn't respond. I take my spot at the end of the line. Sarah and Eve come out of their rooms just as the Head Spinner appears through the double doors to the rest of the Cloister complex.

"God will bless those who are obedient, those who receive him with fear and trembling." The Head Spinner walks down the line, her sharp eyes taking in every Maiden with close attention to detail. "Only those who bow down before the Lord and his Prophet will have a place in the heavenly realm beyond this one." She hesitates as she reaches my side.

A ripple of fear courses through my blood, but she continues on, her voice loud and steady. "Once a week, the Prophet sees fit to allow you filthy Jezebels into his presence. I expect all of you to be on your best behavior. You will not speak unless the Prophet bids you to do so. You will not look the Prophet in the eye. Keep your eyes down with deference to his holiness. Try to rid your selfish, worldly hearts of anything other than pleasing him." She walks back down the line, her black baton in her palm. "If any of you fail to comport yourselves appropriately, rest assured that the punishment will be quite memorable." With a wave of her hand, the front Spinner begins marching out of the dormitories and into the hallway.

We follow, our eyes down, our hands clasped in front of us. Down the long corridors and then into a hallway we've never visited. We keep going until a Spinner enters a code on a keypad and opens a set of outer doors, sending a blast of cool air and dried leaves skittering onto the tile floor.

A white bus waits just outside, the engine idling and sending up puffs of white exhaust into the starless night. We must be at the back of the Cloister—the only area where a road connects it to the rest of the Heavenly Ministries compound. Though satellite images of it are obscured thanks to some deal the Prophet made with the tech companies, a well-flown drone had no problem giving me the exact layout of the "compound" as they call it. The Cloister, though large, is not the biggest building on the grounds. The main church sits at the front of the property, facing the main road. It's larger than several of the football stadiums in the state. Behind it, the rest of the compound is encircled by acres of wrought-iron fence with spikes at the top and, in the wooded areas, ten-foot-high chain-link fences with looping barbed wire.

The only way in and out is through a guarded gate house just off the main road. The Prophet's house sits just inside the fence near the church. It's three stories of grandeur that would have made a Pharisee blush. On either side, smaller homes in the same Georgian architecture dot the grounds—the biggest ones belonging to the Prophet's sons and the others to favored Protectors and their families. Beyond that, a line of trees and a slight ridge obscures the rest of the buildings from the public eye.

What the buildings are for? It's anyone's guess. But there are several of them, each large and often surrounded by vehicles. The entire campus is a humming hive, though in an affront to nature, each worker bee seeks to please the king instead of the queen. The Prophet rules over it all, taking far more than he's ever given.

"Move!" A Spinner gives me a light shove, and I climb onto the bus. It's a short school bus that's had every single surface painted white. The stiff seat is cool beneath me as I sit, and Sarah slides in next to me.

"Are you okay?" she whispers. Her eyes dart to the Protector in the driver's seat, his gaze focused on the Maidens via a wide mirror above the windshield.

"I'll live."

In a gesture of pure rebellion, she grabs my hand and squeezes, then lets it drop as the Head Spinner boards the bus. She grabs the handles on either side of the aisle, and then we take off, easing over the smooth paved road that serves as the artery between the different parts of the compound.

The white windows give no clue about what lies on either side of the road. The only glimpse I get is through the windshield, but I can only glance every now and again.

We travel for a few minutes, moving up a steep slope, then cresting it and rolling down the other side. I consult my mental map, and try to place myself. It doesn't help. We could be at one of three ridges on the sprawling compound. The ground levels out again, and the driver turns to the right. Another minute and he slows to a stop.

"Remember what I said, Maidens." The Head Spinner opens the bus doors. "Best behavior."

She steps out, and we follow, two other Spinners herding us into a line as we step out into the night and then through another set of double doors, not unlike the ones at the Cloister. But this building is different. The hallway we walk down is lined with various paintings and photos of The Prophet. He watches from every angle, sometimes smiling, sometimes stone-faced, always looking down. Unlike the log cabin look of the Cloister, this building has golden wallpaper in an intricate pattern and fancy chandeliers hung at intervals.

A low hum charges the air, and it grows louder as we take the twists and turns that lead us deeper into the structure.

The Head Spinner stops in front of a set of golden doors and holds up a hand. "You are entering one of the holiest places on the campus. This is the Temple. Here, you are like children before your Lord. Remove your clothing." She snaps her fingers, and we dutifully obey, used to the dehumanizing constant nudity at this point. "When you are in this place, in His presence, you are more than yourselves. You are made holy, but only by the grace of the Prophet." She adds an unnecessary note of menace. "Act accordingly."

We stare at the floor like good little Maidens as the other Spinners gather our garments. The hum increases, low voices reverberating through my chest as they chant in unison. I can't tell what they're saying. I don't want to know.

The doors open, and we file into a huge, circular room. The ceiling swirls away above us, veins of gold converging on a center golden emblem, an upside down cross gilded and glinting in the light of the candelabras. A dozen men kneel at the edge of the circle, their backs to the golden walls. Shirtless, they chant. I search for Adam. He sits at the back of the room, his eyes on me while the rest of the men bow their heads. White gauze wraps around his chiseled torso, though I can't see any injury. I have to drop my gaze before the Head Spinner sees.

"Welcome." The Prophet sits on a huge, crimson dais—made for a giant, not a man—at the center of the room. He wears a robe of white and a crown of golden laurel on his head. The circular floor has lines running through it, forming a pentagram. The Prophet sits at the center on his blood red throne.

"'Suffer little children to come unto me, and forbid them not: for such is the kingdom of God.'" He smiles, his angular face still handsome despite the corruption that dwells within.

The Spinners lead us forward until we form two lines in front of the Prophet. He motions for us to kneel on the pillows strewn about at his feet.

I sink onto a plush emerald pillow, the velvet soft on my knees but doing nothing to stop the chills that rake my skin. Another Maiden kneels directly before me, the one with the tattoo on her hip. Hannah, I think her name is.

The men's chanting flows to a slow halt, a stream blowing away from a windy waterfall.

Silence.

Everything in the room focuses on the self-appointed God on the throne, his Christian and heathen regalia reeking of a special cocktail of blasphemy.

"Sit, my doves. Sit and relax." He snaps his fingers.

The Head Spinner walks swiftly out the door and returns with a brigade of Spinners, each one carrying trays laden with fruit, cheese, wine, chocolates, and everything that has been forbidden to us over the past few days in the Cloister.

Is it a trick? I shoot a look toward the Maidens to my right. Like me, they peek at the bounty as it's set around them. A fat purple grape taunts me from the corner of my eye, but I don't dare reach for it. Not with the Head Spinner within baton range.

"Very well." The Prophet plucks a strawberry from the plate to his right. "My darling Spinners, for this special evening, I'd like all of you to take your leave and spend the time in quiet reflection."

The Head Spinner takes a step forward. "But the Spinners always—"

"Grace!" The Prophet's roar makes every one of us jump. Then his voice quiets, "Do you see these precious children gathered at my feet, Grace?"

"Yes, Prophet." Her voice trembles, and I take what satisfaction I can from that little fact.

"Do you see how obedient they are?"

She hangs her head. "Yes, Prophet."

"Go and spend the rest of the evening praying to the Lord that you will be more like them. More humble. More *gracious*." Venom drips from the word. "And certainly more willing to be in harmony with your Prophet."

"Yes, Prophet." She shuffles backwards, then turns and walks out, the rest of the Spinners following her.

When the doors close, the Prophet's low snarl dissipates until he is once again smiling. "Eat and drink, my fair Maidens."

I glance at the Maiden next to me. She reaches for a cube of cheese, takes it with shaking fingers, and pops it into her mouth. As she chews, I wait for the axe to fall. When she swallows and takes another piece, I chance the grape. When I pop it into my mouth, it bursts on my tongue with a sweetness that promises a verdant spring.

When nothing horrible befalls us, we begin to eat more freely. The Prophet smiles from his throne as the men remain on their knees along the periphery. I take a sip of wine and glance at Adam. His gaze pierces me, and I doubt he's looked anywhere else since this strange ritual began.

It's unnerving, but also... somehow gratifying? I don't sense menace in him right this second, but I know it's there.

"Why can't we eat like this at the Cloister?" Sarah hisses and snags a thick chunk of cantaloupe from my tray.

A few of the other Maidens are whispering, but no one reprimands them. The Prophet motions to the Maiden nearest him to come sit with him.

We quiet at that and watch.

He pulls her to his side and pops a green grape in her mouth, then whispers in her ear. Her cheeks flame and she smiles. His hand stays at her side, never wavering from the smooth flesh of her waist as they talk in low tones for a few minutes.

I have no clue what's going on, but I'm not going to waste the chance at eating well for once since I've been here. I devour the rest of the red grapes on the silver tray to my right as the Prophet sends the first Maiden back into the crowd and takes the next to his lap. More whispering and smiling as he feeds her a sugary blackberry.

Sarah leans over. "I-I think it's real. Like it's actually okay." She's mid-chew on a brie-covered cracker.

"We'll see." I can't seem to stop looking at Adam. Every time our gazes lock, a warning sounds deep inside me. But is it telling me to worry about him, or the Prophet, or the Spinners? There are too many dangers for me to sort out. Instead, I drink my wine and lounge on the pillows. The other Maidens have already lain themselves out, feasting and whispering. If someone painted us right now, we'd look like sinners at the feast of Dionysus, or some similar pagan rite replete with nudity and excess.

I finish my glass and set it aside as Eve twirls a lock of my hair between her fingers. The bruising on her eye has turned a deep purple, but it doesn't seem to bother her.

In a dreamy voice, she says, "Your hair is the color of light. Pure white light."

I giggle. Then I stop and realize what I've done. I stare at the wine glass. I've been drunk before, but that's not what this is. This is something deeper that verges on euphoria, a dangerous abandon that threatens to pull me down.

"The wine." I tap Sarah on the shoulder. She looks up at me with big brown eyes that swirl and sparkle.

When she smiles, her effervescent soul shimmers between her lips. "I want more."

"I think it's been laced with—"

"Delilah, my child. Come." The Prophet crooks his finger at me, the wide smile back in place and dazzling like a toothpaste commercial.

I stand on wobbly feet and walk to him, then plop down at his side. He pulls me close.

"You are chosen. Better than every other female in the world. Truly special and blessed. When the world ends, and I ascend to the heavenly throne, you will be at my side, for you are the most precious of all my Maidens, holy in the light of your Prophet."

I close my eyes as his words sink into me like his fingertips into the flesh of my waist. Or does he have claws? Tilting my head back, I open my eyes and stare at the golden cross above me, upside down and pointing toward me. Damnation hangs over my head. Isn't that what this is?

"Your whole life, people have scorned you for this." He strokes down my cheek, then runs my long hair between his fingers. "Isn't that true, Delilah?"

I refocus on him, his dark eyes swallowing me like a bottomless void. "Yes. They used to call me Casper, or Powder, or ask me if I was late for the Queen of Heart's party."

He strokes my cheek gently with a warmth that coats my senses. "They were jealous of you. They could see the heavenly spark that lives here." He strokes my left breast only once then returns his fingertips to my face, his voice hypnotic. "And they wanted it for themselves. But you saved yourself for the Prophet. Isn't that right?"

"For the Prophet." I nod, my brain sloshing through my skull.

"Here, you are cherished, loved, and protected. The filthy men out there who want to hurt you, to take your spark, to abuse your purity, they can't touch you here. I will keep all your enemies at bay and force them to grovel at your feet. For you are my beloved." He kisses my fore-head. "Now go forth in the knowledge that you have been chosen by your Prophet, and you are holy in his sight."

I rise and manage to return to my cushion as Sarah takes my spot on the crimson throne. But the crimson dais is no longer static. It pulses. Like a beating heart. And tendrils of light flow from it to each Maiden, touching her chest. One tickles against my left breast, reaching into my body and wrapping around my heart in a gentle embrace.

I am chosen. I am loved. I am made whole through the will of the Prophet.

Georgia flits in and out of my vision, her golden hair flowing out behind her like a river of heaven. She's dancing, floating, spinning. I want to follow her, to tell her how much I miss her. She moves farther away, her light fading but her connection to me still shining brightly. We will always be connected, always be there for each other. My eyelids grow heavy, but something pulls my gaze to the gloom that rings the circle of light created by the Prophet.

A man watches me. I know him. Adam. He waits in the outer darkness, his teeth bared, his soul corrupted, and his heart crying out for my blood.

CHAPTER 11

ADAM

*T*he look on her face chills me to the fucking bone, which is saying something.

She's in the grips of the LSD, her pupils huge as she watches me. I wonder what she sees, what picture my father painted for her as she sat by his side, his lecherous hands caressing her fair skin.

I know the litany, the lies, the promises of being the chosen one. But why does she look at me as if I'm a threat when it's obviously the snake who was only moments ago whispering in her ear?

Noah snickers. "Do you see mine?"

His Maiden seems to be chasing invisible butterflies, her body swaying as she swirls and dives for whatever she sees. But I can't take my eyes off Delilah for long. She's beyond stunning, like a princess from some fairytale that normal children heard at bedtime. Every movement, every glance from her, sets me on alert. My palms sweat from the need to touch her, to drag her away from the drugged indulgence. But this is just the first of many visits to the Temple, and I'm rooted to the spot, frozen like always.

She relaxes on her pillows, her wide eyes taking everything in, but whenever she looks in my direction, her delicate brows draw together.

My father finishes with the last Maiden, sending her off to collapse onto her sister Maidens in a peal of giggles.

"Blessed are my Maidens, the chosen of God." He raises his glass. Though his back is to me, I'm certain a smug grin rests on his lips. *Asshole.*

He nods toward the door, and Gray rises and opens it, allowing the Spinners back inside. Grace keeps her gaze on the floor, her earlier chastisement likely still ringing in her ears.

"Refill the plates of my chosen ones." My father stands, surveying the feast of flesh on the floor before him. Some Maidens sleep, others laugh, still others trail their fingers through their hair and along the skin of their sisters. The drugs make everything new, sending a coursing current of electricity through their collective consciousness.

My gaze returns to Delilah. One of the girls is braiding her long white hair. Now she's a wood nymph, completely at ease. Open, even.

The Spinners bustle back out and return with fresh platters of food. But by this time, the Maidens are too deep in the high to notice.

"Are we done?" Noah stage whispers. "I've got a couple of girls from the Chapel coming over."

I sigh. "Not until he says we're done. You know that." Besides, I won't leave until I know Delilah is safely away from my father.

"We don't even get to do anything." He points to his Maiden, still chasing butterflies, her nude body on full display. "I can't touch that, so why am I here?"

"To serve God." My father's voice cuts through the hum of giggles, and his gaze settles on Noah. "And to please me. Do you have a problem with that?"

Noah straightens and clasps his hands behind his back. "No, sir."

"Good." My father shoots me a scornful look, as if I were the one who'd questioned him, then rises. "My good and faithful Maidens, our evening is at an end. You may return to the Cloister. Go with love and the knowledge that you are the very jewels upon the Lord's heavenly crown."

More giggles, and then the Spinners march in with the girls' dresses.

I stand, my knees groaning from all the time spent on the wood floor. The Protectors stand at attention as the

Maidens are dressed and herded from the room. The Spinners treat them gently under my father's watchful eye, though I suspect the gloves will come off as soon as they arrive back at the Cloister.

Once the doors close, my father whirls on Noah. "If you have a problem with our rituals—"

"I don't." Noah flinches. Interrupting is one of the worst sins you can commit against the Prophet.

My father strides over, his jaw tight—and not just from his last procedure. "Return to your home. Pray to the Lord to grant you forgiveness for your errant ways."

Noah nods, relief pushing from him like a wave over dry sand. "Yes, sir."

My father smirks, cruelty in every line of his face. "Do you still have that lizard Adam gave you what, ten years ago on your birthday—the birthday I told you we no longer celebrate but Adam disobeyed me?"

My hands clench into fists behind me. I remember the lashing for that. In fact, I remember every one I've ever gotten. It was nine years ago, on Noah's sixteenth birthday. Dad had outlawed birthdays for his faithful, demanding that we spend that day in contemplation of the Prophet's ultimate divinity.

But Noah was only going to turn sixteen once. I took a chance, and I paid for it. Noah was allowed to keep the lizard, Gregory, but only after my back had been lashed so badly I had to be sent to the hospital.

"Yes, I still have him." Noah's words drip with apprehension.

"And didn't you have a kitten or a puppy or something, too?"

"No." Noah is smart enough to lie about his cat Felix.

"The lizard will have to do. Sacrifice it to the Father of Fire. Show him your repentance."

Noah wilts at my side, though he keeps his face stoic. "Yes, sir."

"You know the rules, Noah. Make sure you burn him *alive*. Then bring the ash and bone to the house. I'll inspect them before bed."

"Yes, sir."

He cuts his gaze to me. "Eyes on the floor, Adam. Or do you need to relearn the lesson of deference?"

"No, sir." I train my gaze on the curve of the pentagram beneath my feet while lava bubbles in my veins. Noah may be twisted and ruined, but somehow, a part of him survived. From the moment I gifted him that bearded dragon, he took care of it. Fed it, nurtured it, even took it out and carried it around on his shoulder. When he found Felix wandering around the compound, he took him in and did the same.

Noah falls in line with my father, and he's done plenty of things that would make normal people shiver, but he still has a stripe of humanity emblazoned across his heart. My father is determined to stamp it out. Maybe it's best if he does.

"Protectors." He motions everyone to form a circle around him. "We are set upon our work with full hearts. Continue to do my will in all things, and you will be rewarded. Disobey me—" he shoots me a glare "—and face the consequences."

"Yes, sir." All in unison.

"We have the issue of Protector Newell to discuss." He clasps his hands in front of him and adopts a thoughtful look, even though I know he's already decided who he wants to fill the position. "God and the Father of Fire have both informed me that Trey Reynolds—one of our longtime associate pastors and a devoted servant to the ministry—is the correct choice. He will take over Newell's Maiden. Parker?"

"Yes, sir." Zion Parker steps forward, his bald pate shiny under the candlelight. Many of the Protectors are almost twice my age—their shirtless bodies pudgy and pale. Juxtaposed with the young, nubile Maidens, it makes my stomach turn.

"Have him and his family settled on the campus, and make sure his daughters are enrolled in the school. We don't need any more worldly influences dirtying their minds."

My father—though a charlatan through and through—is also a clever visionary of sorts. Instead of pulling Maidens from society, he's decided to engineer the future of Heavenly Ministries through his separate schools for boys and girls. The schools, though new, are growing rapidly and solidifying the Prophet's stranglehold on the community. Not to mention all the new additions that show up from the Cathedral.

"I'll get to work on it first thing."

"Good man." My father pats him on the arm, then turns to me. "As you know, Newell was in charge of the celebrations for the winter solstice in a month. The Father of Fire will be displeased if we fail to honor him through our rite. Since you are the reason Newell is no longer with us, the preparations now fall to you."

God-fucking-dammit.

"I expect this year's celebration to be the best we've ever seen. You are required to work closely with Grace to get this done. I take it that won't be a problem?"

"No, sir." Not a problem, no. Likely a huge fucking calamity. But a problem? Not at all.

He regards me with a knowing smirk. "Good. And with that, our business is concluded. I expect you all to continue educating the Maidens as is your duty. Report any problems to me. We already have plenty of interest in this year's crop, and the trials will be here before we know it. Otherwise, enjoy your spoils." He grins, the wolf finally showing through.

"Yes, sir." Another chorus of assent circles the room as we're dismissed.

Noah hurries toward the door, and I follow.

Once we're out in the night, a chill breeze cutting through our clothes with ease, he turns and faces me. "Not Gregory. He's like a friend."

"He's a lizard."

"He's mine." The word ends on a choked sound from his throat.

God, his face reminds me of when we were still kids. Or, perhaps, it was just when he was still a kid. I grew up fast once my father anointed himself the Prophet and began Heavenly Ministries. Five years separated Noah and me, but it may as well have been a lifetime. The anguish in his eyes turns into anger as he whirls and stomps toward our houses.

"Noah, come on." I pointed toward one of the many golf carts on the property. "Let's ride over. It's freezing."

"And make it go quicker? Kill Gregory faster?" Each of his steps thumps hard on the pavement.

"No." I catch up and stuff my hands in my pockets. "I'll walk with you."

The movement brings the pain in my back to life, and I wonder if I'm bleeding through the bandages. Doesn't matter.

"I can't do it." He runs a hand through his light brown hair. "I can't."

"You have to."

"No." He crosses his arms over his chest as we climb the first ridge toward the front of the campus. "I'll take the lashing instead."

"It won't *be* just a lashing. Not for this. He'll take it further, and you know it."

He stops, his eyes wild as he turns to me. "He wouldn't."

"He would." I hold his gaze. "To save face in front of his goons that heard his pronouncement. He definitely would. You know how this works, what he'll do."

"Fuck!" He walks a few more steps. "Maybe, maybe we could burn something else and then—"

"He said bones, Noah. Bones. He isn't going to take anything else." I want to save Gregory. I really do. But the price is too steep.

We trudge in silence, our breaths steaming out into the moonless night. I know Noah. I know he's wracking his brain for any possible way to snow our father, to grant Gregory a reprieve.

When we make it to his house, next door to mine, we push through the back door and into the den area. Two girls from the Chapel are laid out on his couch, their faces painted in bright hues and one with a distinct white ring around one nostril.

"Out." I hold the door open.

"But we were supposed to—"

"Out." I keep my tone even as they rise and pull on their flimsy coats. I don't recognize them, but I've probably met them before. The plastic surgery, fillers, and never-ending parties and coke have turned them into different people. Ruined and twisted, just as my father intended.

They hustle past me, their stripper heels clacking on the walkway outside. Noah has already disappeared upstairs. I follow and find him in his guest room, Felix purring in his lap and Gregory perched on his shoulder.

"I can't." Noah's voice is thick, but he doesn't shed a tear. Crying had been beaten out of us long ago. "I can't burn him."

"I know." I sit next to him and give Gregory a look. His colors have faded, but he still appears mostly the same. He blinks at me, first one eye and then the next, as if to say "hello, youngster."

Noah runs his finger down Gregory's back, the pebbled skin reacting to the touch.

I sigh. "I'll do it."

Felix meows, his orange eyes large as he watches me.

Noah shakes his head. "I can't burn him. I won't. Not alive."

"No." I watch as he continues stroking Gregory. "The Prophet may think he's all-powerful, but he won't be able to CSI the cause of death on a lizard."

Noah chokes on a laugh. Felix meows mournfully. Everything in the room grows a little sadder.

I hold out my palm. Gregory climbs onto it slowly as Noah turns away.

This won't be the first time I've shed innocent blood in the name of the Prophet.

And I know it won't be the last.

CHAPTER 12

DELILAH

a knock at my door has me hurriedly throwing on my white dress. Chastity walks in as I wrap my wet hair up into a towel.

"How do you feel this morning?" She peers into my eyes, one at a time.

"I'm okay." I'm better, actually. The food last night seemed to give me new strength, and the drugs have left my system entirely. No more weird light and shadows.

"Your wrists?" She pulls them up and inspects my bandaging.

"Still ache. Neck does too."

"Your ..." She glances at my lap.

"It only hurts if I touch it."

"You mustn't touch it." She looks at the camera, then back at me. "Not like *that*," she whispers. "If Grace found out..."

The thought of touching myself intimately in this place makes my gorge rise. "I just meant in the shower when I was washing."

"Oh." She smiles, the scar along her forehead pulling a bit, and seeming somehow redder. "That's okay."

"How did you get that—"

"Head Spinner!" Sarah hisses through the crack in my door.

I rise and toss my towel into the hamper next to the bathroom and dart into the hallway, falling in line as expected.

The Head Spinner raises an eyebrow at me and rolls her baton in her palm as she approaches. When she glances at my wrists, she seems to reconsider smacking me, and continues walking down the row of girls in white.

"This morning, your education will be in the viewing room." She spins on her heel, her habit swirling, and walks back to the front of the line. "I expect each of you to give these films your full attention. The Prophet has handpicked them for your edification."

We follow her to a new room, one with three risers, like a movie theater, and a motley assortment of chairs on each.

"Sit," she instructs and presses a button on the wall that lowers a white screen at the front of the room.

Abigail stands at a small table to the side, her gnarled fingers hunting and pecking at an ancient laptop. I settle into a striped green chair that smells faintly of weed. It reminds me of college, fun, and Georgia. I swallow the memories and get as comfortable as I can.

After a brief argument between the Head Spinner and Abigail on how to properly use the media player, the screen flickers to life, the projector overhead sending a beam of light through the dimness.

A clearly homemade video begins, narrated by a man with the creepy Old South accent that only truly exists in small wealthy enclaves or timeworn movies.

"The world is a dangerous place," he tells us. Images of war, riots, and violence clog the screen as the narrator continues, "Man has fallen from the place God intended for him. From Eden, thanks to the original female sin, to now—we have never been able to show God the love and the reverence he deserves." The image changes to one of the Prophet, his arms wide open, standing in front of the huge entrance to the Heavenly Ministries Church. "Until now. Finally, God has anointed one person to be his emissary to the fallen. The Prophet. By following him, we are reborn. By following him, we will live our lives as God intended. And only through perfect obedience to him will we receive our eternal salvation."

"But sisters, I tell you now, be wary! Guard your hearts against sin." More images—this time unflattering photos of Hillary Clinton, Ruth Bader Ginsburg, Michelle Obama, Ellen DeGeneres, Oprah Winfrey, and several others I don't recognize—flash on the screen. "Sin has put these women above their station." The voice turns harsher, colder. "Sin has led them to believe their place is lording over men, dominating men, and forcing their evil ideas and desires upon men. The Bible tells us this is not the way. The Apostle, Paul, states clearly in Timothy, 'I do not permit a woman to teach or to assume authority over a man; she must be quiet.' And the Prophet tells us that God despises a woman who would seek to make herself a leader of men." The images flicker to women hanging from trees, women burning at the stake, and others on their knees as men with pistols walk behind them, pulling the triggers.

My empty stomach churns as more and more violence against women is praised as the righteous end to sinful females.

"But you." The voice lightens again. "You are the chosen of God. The blessed among women. Others will seek to harm you because of your purity, because of your perfect obedience." Footage of men catcalling at a woman on the street, then a man watching a woman through her windows, and finally several clips of women screaming and crying as they are raped fills the screen. "This is what the world would do to you without the protection of the Prophet. This is the evil that thrives outside the gates of

Heavenly Ministries. But the Prophet will smite the wicked and lift you up. He is good and true, and will reward you for turning away from sin and falling at his feet."

I glance to my right. A Maiden chews on her fingernail, her eyes wide. She nods along with the narrator's words.

The Head Spinner hisses at me and points to the screen. I turn back to it and settle in for my morning of "edification."

After a lunch of greens, the thinnest pork chop I've ever seen, and a tiny side of white rice, we enter the training room. All the usual areas are set up, but there is a new one in the corner. A table with a large white apparatus next to it, along with an older man in a white coat.

"Hannah, come here." The Head Spinner strides over to the man. "Remove your dress."

He peers over his glasses as Hannah approaches, her dark hair swept up in a tight bun. She slips the dress from her shoulders and steps out of it. The rest of us do the same as we stand in line near the wall of implements.

"There, the mark of the world is along her skin." The Head Spinner turns Hannah around so the doctor can examine the ink twirling along her hip.

"Shouldn't be too difficult to remove." He pats the table. "Lie down on your stomach. I've got some spray to help ease the pain."

"No." The Head Spinner crosses her arms over her trim waist. "No pain relief. She should feel the sting of the fallen world leaving her."

He hesitates.

"The Prophet wills it," she adds.

"Oh." He nods. "Well, in that case." He grabs a wand attachment from the machine and flicks a switch. It whirs to life, the digital screen glowing. "Give it a minute to warm up, and we'll get started."

"Delilah," Chastity whispers and points to the floor. "Come on now."

I drop to my knees. She gives me an apologetic pat before placing the dildo in my mouth. It tickles the back of my throat, but I breathe slowly through my nose and fight the gag reflex. A sharp electric *snap* cuts through the room, and Hannah makes a small noise.

The Head Spinner lifts her baton.

Another zap, and Hannah gasps.

Thwack! The Head Spinner slams the wooden rod against Hannah's thigh. She shrieks, which earns her another hit.

The Head Spinner raises the baton and waits.

Zap. Silence, but I can see Hannah shaking from the corner of my eye.

"You must be pliant for the Lord. For your Prophet." Another Spinner walks among the Maidens. "You must use your bodies only to please the Lord. To please the Prophet. You must remain chaste, pure, and clean. Your purpose is to serve the Prophet, to do what he asks, no matter what that might be. In return, he will keep you safe from the wicked world outside these doors."

The Spinner scoffs as she makes a circuit of the room. "So many women claiming they were harassed and molested at their workplaces. *Me too*, they say. What a load of lies. Those whores asked for it, deserved it. They thrive on attention from men, and want to be used up and thrown away. They begged to be defiled, then blamed the men for their own sin. But you don't have to worry about that. For you are chosen. Protected. Loved. Cherished. No filthy worldly man will ever touch you. Their grime can't stain you. As long as you follow the Prophet and do as he commands."

Chastity leads me to the nearest bench, they call it the 'horse', and helps me up. I sit astride it, my ass in the air. I'm exposed. I don't fuss. The Maidens who balked on the first day still wear those bruises.

She smears lube all around my asshole. "Relax. Deep breath."

I inhale as she presses the plug into place. It hurts at first, then my body accepts it, molds around it. I want to push it out, but I can't. Instead, I keep breathing through my nose and trying to keep my focus, even when the scent of singed flesh permeates the air.

Georgia. She's the only reason I'm here. But I've made zero progress toward finding out what happened to her. I underestimated how closely monitored I'd be, how the Cloister would structure my time so that I couldn't speak to anyone for any length. The locked doors and microchips aren't enough; the Prophet wants to control every second of every day. He'd begun to haunt my dreams.

"You can get down." Chastity takes my hand and helps me to my feet.

I wince as the plug presses against the inside of my cheeks. But I can't protest. Not with the gag. Maybe obedience will get me what I want. Playing along, allowing the Cloister to seep in just a little bit—perhaps that's the way for me to break this place wide open. But that would also mean allowing Adam to bend me to his will. An unwelcome tingle shoots through me at the thought.

"Delilah." Another Spinner motions me over to the X where I'd taken my beating. A Maiden is cuffed to it, though her feet remain on the floor. She looks at me over her shoulder, concern arching her brows.

I give Chastity a glance, but she's already working with the next Maiden on the horse.

I walk over to the Spinner who called me.

She hands me a flogger, the handle braided leather. "Girls, gather 'round for this lesson."

The other Maidens form a semi-circle at my back.

I hold the flogger by the end, as if it's dirty and vicious all at once. She glowers and wraps my hand around it. "Cooperate, Maiden. Learning to wield these tools—she gestures toward the wall—is just as important as allowing them to be used on you. Who is your Protector? Adam, right?"

I nod, my hands shaking.

"He's dominant." She seems a little too impressed. "*Very* dominant. So these techniques will be of no use to you with him. But—" She pulls me back a step and helps me line up to the Maiden on the X. "There are plenty of men, even some Protectors, who prefer to be on the receiving end. You'll often find that powerful men have secret desires to be punished." She steps to the bound Maiden and runs her fingers down her skin. "These areas, here and here, are the most sensitive spots on the back." She speaks as if she's going over different cuts of meat on a pig and glances at the Maidens behind me to make sure they're paying attention. "If he is a true lover of pain, those are the spots to focus on." Her hands lower to the Maiden's ass. "Here, you can have a bit broader use of the flogger. Light touches can be playful. Repeated medium or hard touches can verge into pain, or stay there and ramp up." She steps back. "But the most important thing is for you to read him. Pay attention to his sounds. Listen for when he's enjoying it. Listen for when he's perhaps being pushed too far. And make sure that once you get him into the space he wants, you keep him there until it's over. That is your duty as one of the Prophet's chosen."

One of the Prophet's whores, you mean. Maybe it's a good thing I'm gagged.

"Hit her." The Spinner clasps her hands in front of her dark skirt and watches.

I manage a faint slap of the leather against her bottom.

The Spinner frowns. "Again. Harder. And keep going with it. You can do a figure eight with your wrist or simply twirl it over and over."

I give the same effort, barely brushing her.

"Perhaps Delilah would like for me to give the demonstration." The Head Spinner's voice sends chills up my spine. She's standing right behind me.

The Maiden on the X, Ada, throws a wide-eyed look over her shoulder. I can't let the Head Spinner do to her what she did to me.

I shake my head again, and step closer, rolling the flogger in my wrist.

"We'll see." The Head Spinner's low voice urges me onward.

I swing harder and keep going, the buttery soft leather turning into strips of pain as they hit flesh. The Maiden cries out. I don't let up, slapping her bare skin again and again with the fronds of the flogger, her skin turning a light rose.

"Listen to her," the Spinner instructs.

Soon, the Maiden is panting, her head lolling back. I go a little easier, then give her a series of full-force strikes. Her cry isn't the wail of pain. It's something deeper and just as raw. Desire.

"You have her." The Spinner takes the flogger from me. "This is where you want your secretly submissive males to dwell." She pops her once more, and the girl moans. "Hear that? Ecstasy. There's a plateau in pain where the most profound pleasure lives. Here, when your subject is pliant, you can get information, plant ideas, and reinforce the love and bounty that flows only from the Prophet. Do you understand?" She reaches around the Maiden, her hand disappearing as the Maiden begins to shake, her breathing growing harder. The Spinner's arm moves in rhythmic strokes until the Maiden cries out, her pleasure rising and bursting in a crescendo of sparks.

The Spinner removes her hand and wipes her fingers on her skirt. "And that concludes the lesson for today."

CHAPTER 13

ADAM

"*T*his isn't what we agreed on." I stare at the man sitting across from me, a pile of cash in a black garbage bag on the dingy desk between us. We're in the basement of a decrepit warehouse near the railroad tracks in downtown Birmingham. No man's land.

"That's all we got. That's it." Ratty G shrugs.

I have no idea what his real name is. I don't care. All I care about is that he's short on the money for the heroin we've been providing to him and his dealers. It won't stand. Two of his associates guard the door at his back, their eyes cold, the gunmetal glinting from their hips even colder.

"I have to say I'm disappointed." I lean back in my creaky metal chair.

His men twitch.

Ratty G twirls one of his dreads and shrugs. "Way I see it, this is the start of a new deal. New terms. Go on back and tell your cult daddy that we want a ten percent cut in prices. We deal everything you send, always. You don't got no one else who can guarantee movement like that."

In fact, I have two other dealers who move twice as much product as he does. Ratty G is expendable. I toy with telling him that fact to see if he reconsiders. I opt for choice number two.

I address the beefiest guard by the door. "Currently, Ratty G gets a three and a half percent cut of everything he sells for us. He has a problem with paying what he owes on time. I am willing to pay one of you four percent to do Ratty G's job, and you can keep that job as long as you pay what is owed on ti—"

Ratty G's eyes widen. "Whoa, man. That's not—"

His brains are splattered all over the garbage bag and the desk before he can finish his protest.

"I'll take that job." The beefy killer looks at his partner who hasn't moved. "Be my right hand man?"

He nods.

I pull a handkerchief from my pocket and wipe a splatter of blood from my forehead, then rise to leave. "Pleasure doing business with you, gentlemen." Hefting the gory money bag over my shoulder, I climb the stairs, get in my car, and head to my next collection stop.

When I enter Delilah's room, I'm surprised to find her naked and on her knees beside her bed. I'm even more surprised at the disappointment that wells within me. Broken so soon?

I sit on her bed, my body groaning with relief. The ache in my back subsides as I settle before her. It had been a long day of dirt, and I'd been looking forward to the reward of my squeaky clean lamb. She doesn't disappoint.

"Look at me."

She lifts her chin, those otherworldly gray eyes meeting mine.

"Why so obedient today?"

Her face stays impassive. "I want to please you."

"Oh?" I smile. Playing with my food always lifts my spirits. "How best do you think you can please me?"

"By being obedient to the Prophet."

I narrow my eyes. "You mean to me."

She drops her gaze for a split second, then meets mine again. "To you, as a representative of the Prophet."

She's not broken at all. Just toying with me again. My cock begins to express its interest, coming to life as I stare down at her. Plump lips, rosy cheeks, pert breasts. Fuck, how can a man be expected to concentrate? It has never been a problem before.

"Foolish little lamb." I stroke her cheek with my thumb. "You are still lost, wandering around in the pasture, ignoring the wolves all around you."

She pinches her lips together, likely to stifle a sassy comeback. I want her to let it out.

"Stand up."

She rises, her pale skin almost shimmering. Her neck is still bruised from that idiot Newell.

I pull her hand toward me and move aside a bandage on her wrist. "What's this?"

"Just a few scratches."

They aren't scratches, more like tears, and there are bruises forming a ring around each wrist.

Gripping her forearms tightly, I ask, "Who did this?"

She blinks a few times. "The Head Spinner."

"Why?" I skim my gaze down her body and find more bruising between her thighs. Red coats my vision for a moment, and I taste blood.

"The man you killed." She swallows hard. "It was my fault for tempting him. So the Head Spinner—"

I reach up and grip behind her neck, yanking her face down to mine. "*I* killed him, not you."

"She said that it was my fault."

"She's a moron in a costume who hasn't the faintest clue." Her lips are close to mine. Her breath whispers across my lips, her long hair tickling along my cheeks.

"I'll have a talk with her." I'd have to do it for the Winter Solstice preparations anyway. *Fuck.*

She tries to shake her head, but can't while she's in my grasp. "Please don't. She already has it in for me."

"You don't tell the wolf what to do, little lamb." I push her back down to her knees. "Let's get back to the matter at hand. You said you wanted to please me."

"Yes." Her voice quavers.

"What do you suggest?"

Her fingers tangle in a knot, and her cheeks redden. "I could... I could—"

"Suck my cock?" I love the flare of her nostrils, the fear that darts across her features.

"I-if that's what you want me to do."

"Of course I do." I grip her hair and pull her close, then nestle her face against my erection.

She stiffens, letting me hold her still but doing nothing else.

I laugh. "If this is how you sucked your last cock, I can't imagine a happy ending to that relationship."

She pulls against my grip. "It wasn't a relationship."

"No?" I release her, and she sits back, her breasts heaving as she tries to calm herself.

Looking away, she says softly, "It wasn't my idea."

I pinch her chin and pull her to face me. "Who was the not-so-lucky fellow?"

"My stepfather."

CHAPTER 14

DELILAH

I'd never told anyone, not even my mother, and here I was spilling my guts to a cult leader who intended to rape me, at the very least.

"How old were you?" He leans back on the bed, but still seems to loom over me.

"Twelve." I don't let the memory creep into my mind, not his smell, not the way he told me I was his 'good girl.' My eyes water. "I-it happened only once." I trip over the words as I fling them out. As if it happening just once means that I'm not dirty. I know it wasn't my fault, but deep down, I'll always carry the stain of what happened to me. "When my mother was away. And then they broke up not long after, but it was over something else."

"Twelve." His face pinches, but then smooths out, his dark eyes trying to pry me apart and see inside. He lies back and stays silent for several minutes.

Fear seeps through my pores and wets my underarms. But I don't know if I'm more afraid of the memories or of Adam's judgment.

I begin to think he's fallen asleep, but then he sits up. "Get on the bed. Spread your legs."

Fighting back my tears, I obey. Part of playing this game is doing what he says. Trying to get close to him to learn what I can. I have to repeat this litany just to get on the bed. He stands as I lie down.

"Legs open." He stares as I ease my heels apart.

Dropping to his knees, he prowls over me, his eyes burning through me with an intensity that verges on terrifying. His shirt brushes against my taut nipples, and I suck in a breath.

"This is how you show obedience to me. To your *Prophet.*" He practically spits the last word. "You do what I say when I say it. You don't ask questions. I expect your complete trust."

I want to ask what I get in return, but I don't dare. Not when he's on top of me like this. Not when the only thing separating us is inconsequential fabric.

His eyes, pools of darkness that I can't begin to fathom, focus on me with unmistakable predatory intent. "Trust." He lets the word slide along his tongue until it ends with a flick. "Can you do that? Trust me?"

Trust isn't something I can give anyone. Not in this place. Not after what happened to Georgia. "I can try," I answer honestly.

He dips his head, his lips at my ear. "Trying isn't good enough. I need your word, little lamb."

Goosebumps race down my flesh, and I grip the blanket. A weight settles in my mind, as if my choice will sway the balance of my life irrevocably. Why is he asking me for anything? He could take it, just like he said a few days ago. Why would he care if I trusted him? I chew my lip and think back to when he killed Newell. Though I'd tried to block out the blood, I couldn't forget the look in Adam's eyes, the pure rage. He wasn't a man I wanted to anger. Not ever.

With a deep breath, I gave him my answer: "I will trust you. Yes."

The world stills, his breath catching. Does he sense the lie or fear I'm telling the truth?

"Good." He finds my eyes again. "If you trust me, I will never force you. But if you cross me—" his gaze slides to my hard nipples "—you are mine. I will use this body however and whenever I see fit. By the time I'm done with you, you'll think Newell was a gentle angel by comparison."

My voice sticks in my throat, and all I can do is nod.

"Then we have an agreement." He pushes off me and stands.

I sit up, my mind grasping at the frayed strands of this 'agreement.' "So, as long as I trust you … you won't touch me unless I say it's okay?"

He arches a brow. "Oh, silly little lamb. Didn't you listen? I won't *force* you. Touching is an entirely different matter, don't you think?" He sits on the bed next to me and runs his fingers down my cheek, past my collar bone and between my breasts.

My breath snags as he circles one nipple, but he never touches it. The peak hardens, tingling and hyper-sensitive. He does the same to my other breast, his eyes on mine as his warm caress begins to cross the wires inside me. Fear melds with heat, which both twirl around a central circuit of desire. Mortification washes over me as wetness builds between my thighs, and I close my eyes.

"Eyes on me, lamb."

I force my gaze back to his. Dark eyes consume me as he keeps up his sensual tease. My breathing speeds up, and I press my thighs together to try and stem the pressure.

He smirks and pulls his hand away as he stands. "You'll be begging me to touch you in no time. And to do plenty more than that."

"Never." I shake my head. Whatever game he's playing isn't what I'm here for. I hug my knees.

"We'll see." He strides to the door. "Until tomorrow night, then."

"Your back. There's blood." A stripe of red has seeped through his light blue shirt.

"Don't worry about it." He doesn't turn around, just leaves my room and pulls the door closed behind him.

I roll over and snatch my dress from my nightstand and yank it over my head. What was that? I stare at the door long after he's gone, replaying his voice in my head. His warm breath at my ear, the way his hard body barely brushed against mine, the length of him on my cheek. I press my thighs together, because something wrong is happening inside me. I can feel myself getting wet, can feel the heat flowing through me as I think about his eyes, his lips, his body.

It's wrong. So wrong that I bound off the bed, hurry into my bathroom, and flip on the shower. I get in and turn the hot water down until it's chilly, my body aching from the cold.

"Better." My teeth chatter as I step out and towel off, my unexpected heat extinguished by the shock of the cold water. This is better. I can handle cold and pain, but desire for my captor? No. Unacceptable.

I slip into bed and turn out my light. His face appears when I close my eyes, but I push that thought away and, instead, get lost in a memory of a fun weekend with Georgia when we were both fourteen. Her golden hair flowing in the wind as she runs soothes me to sleep, though the phantom feeling of Adam's breath at my neck crashes through the memory right as I drift off.

A soft knock at my door has me sitting straight up. In the faint bathroom light, I see the handle turning back and forth, squeaking lightly. Flashbacks of Newell have my heart beating so loud I can feel it vibrating through my chest. I yank my blanket to my chin, as if that can ward off whatever devil is at my door.

"Delilah!" A whisper hiss cuts through the silence. Sarah's voice.

I tamp the dread down and creep over to the door.

"Hurry! The Spinner will get us." Another voice.

What is going on?

I flip the lock and open the door. Three girls rush inside and plaster themselves against the wall under the camera.

"Delilah?" A Spinner enters the dormitory from a powder room near the main door. She can't see the terrified Maidens to my right.

"Sorry... I, um, thought I heard something."

Her expression sours. "You shouldn't be up. Go back to bed immediately. Do this again and I'll notify the Head Spinner."

"Yes, ma'am. Very sorry." I lower my chin in deference and close the door.

The Maidens have disappeared into my bathroom.

I don't look at the camera, even though it takes every ounce of self-control I have, and shuffle to the bathroom.

"Close the door!" Sarah points.

I push it shut and lean against it. The small bathroom is crowded with four bodies in it.

"What are you doing?" I try to keep my voice low, but an edge of hysteria creeps into my whisper. The punishment if we get caught—I can't even think about it without my stomach flipping.

"We need to talk." Sarah perches on the side of my tub, and the others sit. Hannah and another Maiden I think is named Susannah.

I shake my head. "Talk? The Spinner is going to catch us!"

"That one goes to take a piss every half hour. Like Old Faithful. That's why we picked tonight."

"Picked it for what?"

Sarah rolled her eyes. "To come see you."

I freeze when I hear the floor creak. We all hold our breaths, but the sound doesn't come again.

"Okay, we don't have much time, so here it is." Sarah leans forward, her gaze intent. "We're getting out of this dystopian nightmare."

I shake my head. "There is no 'out'."

"There is."

I pull the sleeve up on my night dress. "Did you forget about these?" I point to where the tracker is embedded under my skin. "Or the cameras? Or the locked doors? Or the barb wire fence? Or the fact that every policeman within miles of this place works for the Prophet? No one will help you. Everyone you meet will turn you in to the Prophet."

"We just have to get to Birmingham."

"You think he doesn't have people there, too?"

She shrugs. "Maybe, but not everyone is on his payroll. Birmingham's a big place, not like here. If we could just make it to the city, we could disappear."

"How do you expect to get fifty miles from here before they realize you're gone?" I clutch my elbows. "And when they catch you..." I shudder.

"We won't get caught." Sarah puts a bite into her tone. "We can sneak out when that Spinner—" she cocks her head toward the hallway "—is on duty. We'll get out of the dorms. Susannah knows how to pick locks and—"

"It's Piper." She speaks up. "Not Susannah. That's not my name."

"Piper, yes." Sarah continues, "So she can get us onto the grounds. Maybe we can roll up our blankets and carry them with us so that when we get to the fence, we can lay them over the top to get past the barbed wire."

"How do you expect to get past the guards? You do realize they patrol the place?" My drone had shown me a few men keeping watch over the main areas of campus during the days and nights. There was no way to know when or where they'd be.

"I know, but we'll have to take our chances. Maybe that night will be cloudy or raining or something." Sarah shrugs. "I don't know, but we have to try. I can't do this anymore! I thought it would be different. I thought—"

"That the Prophet was a man of God?" Cynicism, ugly and prickling, creeps into my voice. "That you'd be safe here? That joining a cult was a great life choice?"

Sarah brushes her dark hair back from her face and glares at me. "You're here, too. You know that, right? You're trapped right along with the rest of us. You fell for it, too."

I can't tell her I'm different, that I have my reasons. So I simply say nothing.

"Are you in or out?" She stands.

"Who else is involved?"

"Just us. We can't trust anyone else. Some of them are—I don't know—it's like they still believe. Even after everything that's happened since that first night. They still think the Prophet is preparing them for something special." She steps in front of me, her gaze hard. "And you can't say a word. I told the girls we could trust you."

"You can."

"If you rat us out and we're stuck here…" Hannah moves to stand behind Sarah.

The bathroom feels even smaller. I clutch the door handle. "I won't tell anyone."

"Are you in then?" Sarah asks.

Do I want to escape this hell? Yes. Can I? No. I shake my head.

Sarah's face falls. "Why?"

"I have to see this through." *For Georgia.*

"What?" Susannah hisses.

"Shh." Sarah holds up a hand. "Are you scared of getting caught? Is that why?"

"No."

"Then what? Don't tell me you believe this shit? That you're chosen? That the Prophet wants to use you for anything other than a whore or a pawn?"

"No." I can't give her what she wants. An explanation. My truth. "I just can't."

"She's going to rat us out." Hannah glowers.

"I won't." I meet Sarah's gaze, putting every bit of conviction I still have into my words.

A tense few seconds pass, all three of them peering at me.

"She won't." Sarah's shoulders relax. "I trust her. But we should go."

"Come on." I turn the handle, then walk to the hallway door.

I press my ear to it and hear a faint shuffle. Holding up my hand, I bid the Maidens to wait. After what feels like an eternity, a faint, rusty squeak breaks the monotony.

"She's in the bathroom." I ease my door open and they hurry into the hallway.

Sarah hesitates and grabs my hand. "Tell me if you change your mind."

"I will." I glance at the bathroom door. "Hurry."

She darts away, and I close my door, then lean against it. My heart is pounding, and I stand there for a while, listening for trouble. None comes, and before long, I hear the Spinner walking along the dormitory corridor, the wooden boards groaning quietly at intervals.

I return to my bed and pull the covers over my face. Like a burial shroud, it gives me a measure of peace, the sense of finally being alone, of blissful isolation.

The three of them will try to escape. I couldn't miss the determination in Sarah's eyes. The feeling of being an animal with its leg caught in a trap, but still thinking it can get free if it only pulls hard enough. It's not until it bleeds out that it realizes the trap is forever.

CHAPTER 15

ADAM

*S*he sits in the front row with the rest of the Maidens, her head bowed as my father drones on about how all females in the church should be in "perfect obedience" to their husbands at all times. If a wife is having marital issues, personal problems, or so much as a runny nose, it is because she is not in perfect obedience.

The women in the crowd nod along, though some of them—the ones who wear sunglasses more often than not —keep their heads bowed. After all, according to the Prophet, their black eyes and concussions are due to their own faults as wives.

He still preaches the perfect obedience doctrine, even after one member of the congregation forced his pregnant wife to stand outside on the coldest night of the year. "If you are in perfect obedience, you will not be harmed," he'd told her before going to sleep in their warm bed.

The next morning, she'd lost four toes to frostbite and the baby from the trauma. This was, naturally, her own fault for not being in perfect obedience. At least that's what my father and the rest of the savages in this building would argue.

"... and the wife shall be blessed. The book of *Ephesians* tells us, 'Wives, submit yourselves to your own husbands as you do to the Lord.' There is no 'except when you don't feel like it' in there. Can I get an amen?"

A deeply male rumble of "Amen" rolls through the crowd.

"It doesn't say 'obey only when it suits you.' It doesn't say 'obey unless you have a headache.' The scripture is quite clear on what is required of a wife."

"Amen." The crowd affirms the Prophet.

I don't give two shits what these sheep believe, as long as they pay their tithes on time. My eyes are drawn back to Delilah, her face hidden from me. But I can recall it easily, just like the rest of her. My cock stirs, awakening at the thought of her spread out beneath me, the way her breath hitched as I stroked her tits. It was an act of acute control not to take one of her nipples in my mouth, to finally taste the pale, warm skin that taunts me even now.

Noah walks up beside me, both of us hidden by the stage curtain as my father gets deeper and deeper into the pit of misogyny that leaves his congregation slobbering for more.

"We got a job tonight." He crosses his arms over his chest.

"What?" I intend to spend my evening with Delilah, teasing her until she begs me to eat her pussy.

"Enforcement."

"Fuck." I sigh. "Who?"

"We got word that a couple of the deacons have been talking about starting something new. Taking off with a handful of followers. They've been doubting the Prophet in secret meetings."

"How many?"

"No more than twenty."

"Who's the ringleader? Davis?"

"Yeah, how'd you know?"

"Gut feeling." I peer into the crowd and stare at one of the Heavenly police officers, Lieutenant Chris Davis. I've never spoken to him, but something in his bearing, the way he doesn't show the deference required for the Prophet—all of it has pinged on my radar a time or two. He's one of our newest deacons, a lower cog in the Heavenly machine that keeps everything running smoothly. But now he's out of rhythm. It's my job to make the necessary adjustments to keep this operation singing.

I'm up for it. "Jump him after Dad's finished blowing smoke?"

"Yeah."

I glance at my brother. Usually, he might scold me for a negative reference to our father where others might hear. This time, though, he's stone-faced. My father's easy condemnation of Noah's pet Gregory seems to have wised him up a bit. Or maybe he's just tired of trying to fix me when I'm too far gone.

We stay at the edge of the stage for a few more minutes, my gaze always drawn back to Delilah. No veil today, her hair is roped up into a prim bun at the crown of her head, just like all the others. As if she can feel my stare, she lifts her head slightly, her eyes glinting as she looks right at me.

Nothing crosses her features to give her away. A blank slate, or perhaps a mirror reflecting back nothing more than what it sees. Slowly, she lowers her gaze back to her folded hands.

"I'm telling you there's something off about yours." Noah elbows me.

"She's just another stupid fly caught in our father's web." I shrug off his words, though of course, I silently agree with him. "Let's go give that shit-talking cop a surprise."

My fist vibrates as it crunches into Davis's nose. His bones break, mine merely sing a jolly tune as I swing again, this time grinding my knuckles into his eye socket as he screams.

He's defenseless, though it took a good bit of work to get him this way. He put up a fight when Noah and I pushed him into the back of a Heavenly Mercedes.

"You can't manhandle me like this." He fumed in the backseat.

I held up his service pistol. "I suggest you shut the fuck up."

"Your father won't let you—"

I chambered a round, the action smooth and as natural as breathing to me. "The more you say, the worse it's going to get for you. Besides, I suspect you've already said enough. When was the last meetup, Noah?"

"Two nights ago, at his house. He had a handful of other deacons over."

I turned around and grinned at him as he blanched.

"H-how did you—"

I tapped the side of the barrel to my temple. "Psychic."

We'd taken him to a gravel circle on the backside of the property, the one with the three sturdy crosses on one side. No one would hear us. And Davis would have nowhere to run.

He'd been a challenge at first, all swinging fists and aggression. I let him wear himself out, then went in for the kill, tackling him to the ground. Once I had him pinned, I went to work. Noah began recording with his phone as Davis's blood coated my knuckles, his cries rising into the night air but never making it to God's ears.

Each hit sends a jolt of satisfaction through me. Something akin to arousal. And I know it's fucked up and wrong, but pure violence is one of the only things that can make me feel alive. My thoughts flicker to Delilah. Something new there. She gives me a taste of what I'm feeling now, too. Adrenaline, pleasure, and the primal need to dominate.

"Adam!" Noah shoves my shoulder, and I realize he's been calling my name for a while. He points to the crosses. "Should we ..."

"No. This is enough." I stand and shake some of the blood off my fists, then address the camera. "Davis will live... This time." I kick him in the ribs.

He howls and curls into the fetal position. Blood oozes from his mouth in a long string of crimson.

"Unless you're even dumber than I think, you'll see that this is a warning. We know who you are. We know your wives and your children. You have a nice house? It can be gone just like that." I snap my fingers. "Do you think your wife will stay with you if the Prophet casts you out? Think again. Do you think Judge Proctor—who *never* misses a Sunday—will grant you custody of your children when your wife leaves you for another man who is obedient to the Prophet?" I turn back to Davis and drop down on my haunches. "You understand, don't you Davis?"

When he doesn't respond, I grab a handful of his blond hair and yank his bloodied head back. "I said, *do you understand*?"

"Yes!" A red bubble pops on his lips as he screams the correct answer.

"Good." I rise and pull a handkerchief from my pocket to wipe my hands. "I think we all know the score from here on out."

Noah stops the recording and pockets his cell phone. We walk to the car in silence, get in, and drive away.

"I'll send someone to pick him up." Noah lets out a deep sigh. "I hate doing this."

I can't say I hated it. The ache in my knuckles reminds me I'm on top. I'm the one walking away from that scrap without a drop of my own blood spilled. "Davis should have known better. Disobedience has consequences." That is a truth both Noah and I know all too well. A memory of my mother howling in pain threatens to surface, but I drown it, pushing it beneath the dark waters until nothing ripples along my surface.

"Right." He drums his palm on the steering wheel. "I know. Fuck."

"Drop me at the Cloister."

He glances at the clock. "Kinda late for that, isn't it?"

"Just drop me." I've already had my violence for the night. Now I need another type of high. And there is only one person that will do.

CHAPTER 16

DELILAH

*H*e didn't come. I brush my hair out and stare at myself in the mirror. *Why didn't he come?*

I should have been happy, ecstatic that I was able to spend the evening unmolested, but a nagging itch at the back of my mind kept me from breathing easy. He'd been watching me during the evening service, his eyes dark pools of malice. And I couldn't keep myself from glancing at him every now and then. Maybe there was enough of a connection between us that I could use it somehow. He could be the key to me finding out what happened to Georgia and getting vengeance. But if he doesn't show up for my evening "training," how can I get close to him?

I shake my head at my reflection. Smoothing the soft waves in my hair is impossible, so I give up after another few moments and toss my brush down with an admittedly self-indulgent huff.

The dormitories are quiet, the earlier smattering of crying now silent. Some of the girls have it far worse than I do. The Protectors—the cruelty of calling them that isn't lost on me—all seem to have a sadistic streak. Even Noah, Adam's younger brother who often looks at me with kind, if curious eyes. His Maiden doesn't sport bruises, but she's quiet and withdrawn. Then again, being thrust into this vicious world when you thought you were going to be treated with kid gloves can do that to a person.

I sit on my bed, the rough sheets and lumpy mattress my favorite haven. With one more glance at the door, I lie down and adjust to the quiet. Despair seeps through the cracks in the walls, under the door, and coats every filament in the room. I can't hear the whimpering, but I know there are Maidens crying. They always cry at night.

Heavy footsteps in the hall set me on high alert, and I jolt upright. My lock clicks, and the door swings open so fiercely it bangs against the wall.

The devil strides in, blood on his white shirt and coating his hands.

I can't scream, my lungs frozen, as he slams the door behind him and stalks to my bathroom. My water turns on, and I turn to find him stripping his suit coat off, quickly followed by his shirt. Gauze wraps around his torso, as if someone started making him a mummy and got distracted. When he holds his fists under the water, a low grunt of pain, or perhaps satisfaction, lofts from him.

"Fuck." He leans on the sink, his head hanging.

Taut. Dangerous. But in the low light, I see something else. It's unexpected. I think for a moment I'm imagining it, or maybe I'm willing it into existence. But it's there. And when I recognize it, my lungs drag in air, and I throw my blanket off and creep over to him.

He fills his hands and runs the water through his hair, the dark strands dripping onto his shoulders as his breath heaves in and out. Something happened. Something bad.

"Adam?" My voice is small compared to him, to how he fills the room, my mind, and every molecule of air.

He simply stares at himself in the mirror. Hatred pours from him in waves.

It takes every ounce of courage in my body, but I reach out. Slowly. As if I'm trying to test a wild animal and see if I come away with my hand intact. My heart slows, and everything stops when my fingertips make contact with his shoulder.

He stills. Every bit of tension in him drawing tight, so tight that it might snap and break both of us.

Then he turns and grabs me, yanking me to him and taking my mouth. His kiss isn't soft. It isn't a request. Or even a demand. It's a total and complete annihilation of me, and the creation of *us*. He wads my dress in his fists, pulling the fabric tight around me as he presses me against the doorframe.

The scrape of his skin against mine is rough, vicious just like him. He sucks my bottom lip between his teeth and bites down until I open my mouth at the sting of pain. His tongue darts in, taking advantage and owning me with sure strokes. When he slides his hands down my sides and grips my ass hard enough to hurt, I gasp. He doesn't stop, just lifts me with ease, forcing me to wrap my legs around his hips as his mouth destroys me and remakes me into something new. Something that needs and needs and needs.

I open my mouth wider, giving myself over to that emotion, that all-encompassing desire for him that's just as wrong as it is irresistible. He slants his head over me, his hands massaging my ass and sliding closer to my center. I grip his shoulders, his skin slick and hot, and dig my nails in. His groan courses through my veins, ending in the growing wetness between my thighs.

His lips are brutal, and I can't get enough. My tongue wars with his, but mine is a grazing offensive. A paltry defense to his overwhelming force. I give him what he wants, what *I* want. Like an animal, he senses when he's won, when his prey has finally given in and given up, ready to offer up its own blood to the hungry victor. With a low growl he, presses his body into me, his clothed length hard against my bare center.

I press my legs against his hips, anything to ease the ache he's stoked in me. His hands slide lower, and when he strokes my wet center, I moan. I can't breathe, my world is spinning, but I don't want this to stop. He thrusts against me, his cock aligned with my clit, his fingers rubbing my hot flesh and teasing at my entrance.

When he breaks our kiss, I inhale deeply. When he bites my neck, I can't stop the obscene sound that flows from me.

"Again," he grunts against me, then bites my shoulder, clamping down like an alligator. I want him to drag me down, to drown me in him. I run my hands through his wet hair as he licks his bite then sucks my throat. His fingers continue to tease. I roll my hips along with him, not caring that I'm getting my arousal all over his pants.

I drag my nails down his shoulders, but the gauze around his chest stops me from going farther. When I touch it, he freezes, as if that white strip is the third rail.

"Adam." I don't recognize my voice, or the girl pressed up against the wall who wants nothing more than to be dominated by the monster holding her close.

"Stop." He puts me down and steps back.

The tension is back, his shoulders tight. Whatever world we'd just made together crumbles right in front of me.

"Ada—"

"Go to bed." His voice is a steady snarl, but his eyes hungrily trace the lines of my body.

I step toward him, trying to get that connection back.

"Go." He grabs my wrist and squeezes until it hurts. "Now."

I wince and pull my hand away. He's changed. The monster is back to the fore, his violence no longer promising pleasure.

Backing away, I keep my gaze on him as I slide under my blanket. He slams my bathroom door. A roar comes soon after and my wall shakes. I don't dare get up. Not when he looked at me as if I were his enemy.

He opens the door right as a Spinner barges in.

"What was tha—"

"This was my fault." He pushes past her, his shirt on but unbuttoned. "No punishment for Delilah or there'll be hell to pay." He disappears into the dormitory hall as the Spinner hurries into my bathroom.

"Oh, dear." She wrings her hands. "The Prophet won't care for this at all."

I get up and follow her into the bathroom.

"Your dress." She points.

Crimson hand prints appear at my hips like a grisly tie-dye.

But that doesn't take my focus. My mirror is smashed, a bloody smear in the center of the shattered reflection. I stare, half of my face looking back at me, a crimson gash across the image.

Broken.

It's what I saw in him earlier. His truth that echoed inside the darkest parts of my soul.

Just like me, he's broken.

CHAPTER 17

DELILAH

*T*raining the next day comes with a new set of lessons. Ones that—even though I knew what the Cloister was—never occurred to me.

"Some men—" The Spinner walks back and forth in front of the group, a plastic sheet crackling under her feet. Her hands are clasped behind her back, the knuckles turning white. If I didn't know better, I would think she's nervous, perhaps uncomfortable. She clears her throat. "Some men prefer what is referred to as 'water sports.'"

Half the maidens groan; the other half has no idea what she means. Now the plastic sheet makes sense. *Jesus.*

"In particular, the current governor of Tennessee, who is married to one of our former Maidens, is very much into this particular practice. It's far more common among powerful men than you'd think." She can't seem to stop clearing her throat. "So, this is something that we need to add to our curriculum."

"You want us to get peed on?" Susannah blurts.

"Susannah!" The Spinner stomps her foot on the plastic-covered wood floor, which makes only a dull thump noise. "You need to be in perfect obedience to your husband at all times. If this is what he requires, you must do it."

"But what if I don't?" Susannah adds sass to her tone.

I look around and, thankfully, the Head Spinner isn't in the room. If she were, Susannah would already be yanked up and taking a beating.

The teaching Spinner turns red, her round cheeks seeming to expand. "If you aren't in perfect obedience to your husband, you will get cancer, you will lose your ability to bear children, you will get fat, and your children will sicken and die. Any number of horrible outcomes can be thwarted if you are in perfect obedience to your husband." She shakes her head in an attempt at motherly disapproval. "Being in harmony with your husband and obeying him in all things are the keys to living a happy, healthy life. And, as the Prophet teaches, the only way to enter His heavenly Kingdom."

Susannah opens her mouth to speak again, but Sarah pinches her.

The Spinner, emboldened, continues, "Now. We are going to have a demonstration. Do I have two volunteers?"

No one says a word or so much as blinks.

The Spinner scowls and points to me. "Delilah, let's have you. And Eve, you too."

My stomach turns—though I'd thought there was nothing left in it after this morning's colonic. I try the first thing that comes to mind. "I can't. I don't have to pee right now."

The Spinner smiles. "Then you can be the receiver."

Shit.

Eve stands and walks over to the Spinner. She's already lost weight. And she has two black eyes instead of one now.

I don't want to do this. But I have no choice. This Spinner is only forgiving to a degree, and Susannah's backtalk has already pushed her closer to the boiling point. As if to demonstrate my thought, the Spinner reaches for her black baton.

"Okay." I rise and walk over

"Good." Her fingers stop their flirtation with the weapon. "Delilah, lie on the floor. I want you on your back. We've found that men who enjoy this type of thing often like to be the receiver rather than the giver. This means that each of you need to be able to go on command. Eve, this will be your turn."

I sink onto the piece of clear plastic and lie down, my gut churning and my gorge already threatening to rise.

"Now, Eve, I want you to stand over her. Straddle her, feet on either side of her elbows."

I close my eyes as Eve follows the instructions, her shadow falling across my face as she stands over me.

The plastic crackles as the Spinner steps back. "Whenever you're ready, just let it go. Now, girls, keep in mind that sometimes, they would like you to do this in their mouths or perhaps directly onto their genitals. God created each man different, but we are bound to obey them in accordance with Scripture..."

She continues prattling on about pleasing men as I wait for the warm humiliation to fall on my chest. My throat tries to rebel and force me to gag, but I don't. I lie still, hoping Eve is dehydrated.

After a few more minutes where the Spinner has to have said "perfect obedience" a dozen times, she snaps her attention back to us. "Eve!"

"I-I can't."

I open my eyes.

Eve shrugs. "I thought I could go, but I can't."

"You must." The Spinner reaches for her baton, pulling it from her belt with wicked efficiency.

"I can't." Eve's voice fades to a whimper.

"Eve, it's okay." I can't believe what I'm saying, but I say it anyway. "Really. Just do it. I can take it."

Her eyes water as she looks down at me. "I can't."

"You can."

"Eve." The Spinner steps closer, her baton at the ready. "Do it."

"I'll do it." One of the other Maidens, Mary, speaks up. I've never spoken to her, never had a reason to.

But when she stands, her red hair flowing over her shoulders and a placid smile on her face, I recoil.

"If the Prophet requires us to perform these tasks to walk more closely with the Lord, then I am happy to do it."

"Jeez," Sarah says under her breath.

"I'll deal with you later." The Spinner pushes Eve away from me and motions for Mary to come over.

Mary stands above me, taking Eve's position. I try to look into her eyes, but she stares straight ahead, not the least bit concerned that she's naked, I'm naked, and she's about to pee all over me.

"Good, now do what the Prophet has commanded."

"With pleasure." Mary smiles, and I realize she isn't acting. She's a true believer.

I clench my eyes shut, but hear my name on a familiar tongue.

"Delilah!" The Head Spinner calls.

"Wait." The teaching Spinner puts a hand on Mary. "What can I do for you, Grace?"

"I need to see Delilah." Her tone could cut ice. "Now."

The Spinner sighs heavily, then snaps her fingers. "Mary, move. Up, Delilah."

Mary steps away, and I scramble to my feet. For the first time since I've been here, I feel the urge to thank the Head Spinner. That urge dies when I see the tempest raging in her eyes.

I grab my dress from the hooks by the door and pull it on.

"Come." She's already walking away as my head emerges through the fabric.

I hurry to keep up with her rapid pace. We pass the dining hall, the kitchen, and then she turns down a corridor I've never visited. At a set of double doors, she enters a code on a digital keypad. The doors swing open silently. Her swishing black skirt almost brushes the shining wood floors as we pass some closed doors, then come to the end of the hallway.

She enters another key code and opens a heavy wooden door. Pushing inside, she walks around a dark mahogany desk and sits down in a plush leather chair.

"Close the door and sit." She leans back and threads her fingers together.

I close the door and try not to gawk at the nice furniture, thickly-paneled walls, chic lighting, and the elaborate video display at her back. A dozen screens show various views of the Cloister; some of them frozen on one view, while a handful of the screens cycle through live images of the dormitory rooms. I notice my room is on a stationery screen in the very center.

"I said sit."

Her voice spurs me to the nearest chair. She stays silent for an increasingly uncomfortable length of time. I don't meet her gaze, mainly because I assume she'd take it as impertinence. From the way she'd pulled me out of training, I can already guess I'm in trouble. Again. My stomach churns and pressure rises in my throat. Being here like this is a million times worse than the one time I was called to the principal's office in high school. Likely because in high school, they weren't allowed to tie you to a torture cross and leave scars.

I fidget in my chair and want to look at the screens again, maybe get an idea of where all the cameras are so I can pass that information to Sarah. She's hell-bent on escape, and I'll help her if I can. Maybe she can start over out there, be free from this place.

"I can't figure it out." Her voice cuts through my thoughts of freedom with the sharp, metallic clang of incarceration.

I glance up. "What is that, ma'am?"

She peers at my face, searching each curve and line, before finally focusing on my eyes. "Why you?"

I assume she'll explain, likely with painful detail, so I stay silent. After a few moments, she opens her desk drawer and pulls out something shiny, then sets it on the mahogany surface. "What happened here?"

Leaning forward, I see it's a shard from my mirror, the blood no longer crimson but a dried brown. "I ... don't know."

Her eyes narrow. "What did you say to Adam to make him do this?"

I shake my head. "I didn't make him do anythi—"

"Liar!" The word lashes out like a whip.

I jump at her sudden fury, but hate myself for doing it.

"Tell me the truth." She taps a short fingernail on the shard. "What did you do?"

"Nothing." *I touched him. I saw him. I felt how broken he was.*

Her lips thin even more, growing paler. I realize she must have been beautiful only a few years earlier. Could still be beautiful now, except for the twisted heart that shudders along inside her.

"Allow me to disabuse you of any notions you may have about Adam." She rises and pulls her baton free.

"I don't have any notions." I keep my back straight, though fear turns my thoughts to a TV screen full of snow.

"Wrong. You're lying again." She walks around the desk and points to its smooth, perfect surface. "Put your hand here."

I don't move. "Adam said if you punished me for—"

A burst of sparks explodes in my vision, and I'm not sure what happened. I slump back in my chair and put one hand to my aching ear. My fingers come away wet. She hit me there, busting my ear open.

"Hand on the desk, Delilah, or the next time I'll break your nose."

Shaking, I put my hand on her desk, the smooth surface cold against my bloodied fingers.

She uses her baton to separate my pinkie finger from the rest. "What happened between you? I want every word he said to you."

"He didn't say anything."

"Liar!"

I flinch as she raises the baton.

"One more chance to tell me the truth."

Tears leak down my cheeks even though I try not to cry. I shake my head.

Crack. I scream as she brings the baton down hard. Yanking my hand away, agony radiates from my knuckle throughout my hand and up my arm. I can't look at my finger. I don't have to; I know it's broken.

She hurries around her desk and fiddles with a remote beneath the TV screens. I can barely see her through the tears that well.

"This," she hisses. "Tell me about this!" She points her baton at the screen where the camera in my room captured a slice of my back against the bathroom door-jamb, Adam's hand barely visible on my ass. "You think I don't know what sort of harlot you are? Is that it?" She hurries back around the desk. "Put your hand out."

I shake my head and cross my arms over my stomach, tucking my injured hand away from her.

"I said, put your hand out!" She yanks at my elbow, trying to drag my arm free.

I lean away from her and duck my head as she digs her nails into me, a wild animal looking for my tenderest parts.

A bell rings.

Thunk. The baton lands on my shoulder, and the pain surprises me into an even louder scream. She must've swung with every bit of strength she had.

My mind short circuits, my mission erased, and I'm left with the bare need to survive. Escape. I have to escape. I'll take the baton from her and run for it. I steel myself for the assault. *Georgia.* I snap back to myself. I can't run. I won't.

A bell rings again.

She backs away, her animal fury receding.

I peek at her through my hair. She smooths her skirt and tucks a stray hair back into her black habit. Taking a deep breath, she adopts a placid expression, then presses a button under the edge of her desk.

The air in the room shifts and a slight creak from the door opening keys me up to run.

"I heard screams." Abigail's voice comes from behind me. "Wanted to make sure everything is all right."

"We're fine." The edge to the Head Spinner's voice cuts me down even further. "You shouldn't have interrupted."

I turn and catch Abigail's gaze, silently pleading with her to get me out of here.

She folds her hands in front of her skirt. "I think she's had enough."

"You don't tell me when anyone has had enough. *I* make that decision."

I crumble inside and wait for Abigail to obey. To my amazement, she doesn't budge.

"The Prophet has his limits. Even for you. He has twelve girls to help him do God's will. If you take one away or make her unable to fulfill his wishes, he won't appreciate it."

"Don't you threaten me with the Prophet." Her eyes narrow and she runs her baton along her palm. "He put me in charge. I'm Head Spinner. You are nothing but a used up old hag. The Prophet was too kind to turn you away, so he sent you here, to be a burden on the rest of us. I have half a mind to ask him to send you somewhere else. Maybe the Rectory."

"Oh, you could send me there." Abigail steps closer, and I'm distinctly aware of danger on all sides. "You surely could. But when I got out, I'd come right back here to you. And there would be nothing on heaven or earth that could stop me from repaying you in kind." She moves closer, her voice steady. "Now, you either let that girl come with me, and we forget this foolishness, or I inform the Prophet about your late-night jaunts."

The Head Spinners gasps. "What?"

"You heard me." Abigail reaches me and places a hand on my shoulder.

I whimper from the ache but don't dare complain.

"Get on up, Delilah. We're going."

Grace braces herself with one hand on the desk. "How did you know about—"

"There's plenty I know." Abigail helps me up. "*Plenty*. And a trip to the Rectory would be the quickest way to loosen my tongue."

I edge away from Grace, refusing to turn my back on her. She switches her focus from Abigail to me, and I can feel the fury oozing from her like crude from a ruptured tanker. *This isn't over.* She doesn't have to say the words —I can feel them deep in my gut.

Once we've made it to the hallway, Abigail pulls the door closed. I'm finally able to breathe again. If I'd gone another moment with Grace, I'd have made a mistake. Tried to escape. But that's what animals do when they're caught in a snare.

Abigail hurries me out into the main corridor and toward the dorms. Everyone else is still in the training room. A strangled laugh erupts from my throat.

Abigail arches a brow at me.

"It's just." I wince as my finger twinges. "I thought 'at least I didn't get pissed on.'"

"You'd have been better off. What did she do other than the ear and the finger?" She pushes me through to the dormitory and then into my bedroom.

"She hit me in the shoulder, but I think it's just bruised."

"Sit and strip." She points to my bed, then disappears out my door.

I sink down and glance up at the camera. She's watching. I can feel it. At least there's no sound. That's one thing I discovered in her office of horrors. None of the live feeds had audio. With effort, I pull my dress over my head, being as careful as possible not to aggravate my finger. It's already swollen to twice its size, the skin tight like a sausage casing. I rock back and forth—anything to distract from the mounting pain in my hand.

Abigail returns with a black bag and hastens to the bed. "Let me see the finger first."

I hold it out. "It doesn't look crooked. Maybe she didn't break it?"

A strand of iron-gray hair falls against her temple. "It's broken all right. And she managed to bust the blood vessels under your nail." She digs in her bag and retrieves a needle.

"What are you going to—"

She guides my hand to the nightstand and flattens it. It's so similar to what Grace did that I gag. "Hold still."

Pressing the needle to the base of my fingernail, right above the cuticle, she applies pressure.

I can take it at first, but as she pushes harder, the pain switches to white hot agony.

"Almost got it." She grips my wrist, holding me steady.

"Please, it hurts." Tears stream down my face.

"There." She pulls the needle away and blood spurts in a thin jet, marring the bedspread and leaking down the sides of my finger.

I stay still and let out my breath. It's working. The pressure is still agonizing but somehow more bearable.

"You don't want to lose the fingernail." She sits back and digs in the black leather bag again. "The Prophet wouldn't like that. It'd grow back, but you'd have to wear gloves until it did. That would lead to questions, and could even get you sent to the Chapel before you've had a chance to prove yourself."

"What's the Chapel?"

She stuffs some gauze around my finger to soak up the blood that's still running from the tiny hole in my nail. "Never you mind about that." Laboring to her feet, she leans over and peruses my shoulder. "Going to have a mighty bruise here." Her warm fingertips probe the area. "But nothing broken." She pushes my hair behind my ear. "The ear bled something terrible, but it's not that bad. Won't even need a stitch. Once the finger is bled out, I'll do you up a splint." She sets about to cleaning my ear.

In the silence between us, something grows inside me. Nerve. The need to push, and more importantly, to know what was going on. But I have to play it just right.

I keep my voice soft. "I still don't know what I did."

"You didn't do anything." She dabs alcohol on my ear, and I grit my teeth. "Well," she huffs, "Other than getting Adam as your Protector. That's where you went wrong, I'm afraid."

"Oh." I press down on my injured fingertip, oddly gratified when more blood oozes free. I cast my line out a little further and wriggle the bait. "I didn't know they were together."

"Together? No." She shakes her head. "Spinners aren't allowed to be in a relationship with anyone other than our mighty Prophet. And why would you want to be?" She dabs at my ear. "Other men are fallen. The Prophet is the only man I ever desire to be in perfect obedience to."

I shrug. "It just seemed like, from her questions, maybe she was jealous? But I guess that can't be it."

"That's it, all right." She returns to my finger, cleaning up the blood and peering at the knuckle. "I'll clean it a little more, then do the splint." She walks me to the bathroom and runs my finger under the tap. The cold water is a revelation and a hell, all at the same time. Once the blood has slowed to an intermittent trickle, she leads me back to the bed and has me hold my finger out as best I can while she wraps it with gauze. "Fingers heal fast. That's the good news."

I need to get her back on topic. On Grace or Adam, or anything that will clue me in about what's really going on.

"I don't think I said thank you." I hiss as the gauze touches my knuckle. "So, thank you. I don't know what would have happened if you hadn't shown up."

"More of this." She scowls at my broken finger. "That's what. Grace gets out of control when it comes to Adam. She can't see straight. So much of the time she—" She stops herself and shakes her head, as if an internal scolding is going on, then continues her work in silence.

"I won't repeat any of what I heard, you know." I stare down at her gray hair as she wraps the splint. "Not a word."

"You shouldn't have heard any of that."

"I suppose a lot of things go on here that I don't know about." I teeter out onto a limb. "I'm sure you've seen plenty of stuff over the years. Lots of Maidens."

She chuckles. "I've seen them all. Remember each one. Well, most of them. Some from the earlier years are getting fuzzy in my old brain, I'll admit."

A sizzle of excitement rushes through me. Georgia. She *must* remember Georgia. Her sparkle had always been unforgettable. But how to ask?

"Did you have any favorites?"

"Favorite Maidens?"

"Yeah."

"I don't like to play favorites." She finishes with the splint.

"Surely, some of the girls must make a lasting impression?"

She glances up, a furrow forming between her bushy gray brows. "What do you mean?"

Shit. I have to back off, even though it hurts me far deeper than anything Grace did to me. I shake my head and twitter, "Oh, I'm just talking to try and get my mind off the pain."

"I don't blame you. Grace really did a number on this finger." She stuffs her supplies back into her bag. "She just needs to let him go. That's all there is to it. That's when this madness will stop." She gestures to my hand as she rises.

My mind shorts out, then returns to focus in on her words. "Wait, so Grace and Adam *were* together?"

"Together? No." She hefts the black bag up to her thick shoulder. "She was his first Maiden."

CHAPTER 18

ADAM

*W*e drive down the rutted road, Noah keeping the Land Rover in check as I survey the construction along the back acres of the compound. Houses are going up, each of them with a basement that connects to the other houses, creating a subterranean world—yet another one of my father's ideas.

"I didn't realize it was going to be this big. He's building enough houses for the entire congregation and then some." Noah points ahead to the roads that had been bulldozed onto the ridge ahead of us, the red Alabama dirt snaking off in several different directions.

"That's the plan."

A whole new world created at the will—and existing at the pleasure—of the Prophet. He calls it the "Promised Land." I see it for the prison it really is. Constant monitoring, families under scrutiny, children in the Prophet's schools, any deviation from the norm stamped out. The Prophet's police force will patrol these streets, and no one will be able to come in or out without Prophet approval. Even so, hundreds of families have signed up for a spot in one of the modest homes being built here, all of them desperate for the protection and guidance the Prophet appears to provide. Idiots.

We stop where a construction crew is digging a basement.

I roll my window down and wave the foreman over to me. "Tony."

He's a tall man, broad, used to play for the Crimson Tide until he got injured—and then he got something worse. Religion. My father's brand in particular.

"Hi, Adam!" He bounds up, full of energy. Not the brightest, but he doesn't lack for enthusiasm.

I hand him an envelope. "For supplies."

He takes it, then pulls a rough-sharpened pencil from behind his ear and writes "supplies" on the envelope, as if he couldn't remember what is was for otherwise. "You know, the Caldwells have been giving me some trouble about buying all our roofing stuff in cash."

"Caldwells?"

"Yeah, they got a store off Gray's Mill Road. Go to church and everything, but they always squawk about my cash payments. Am I doing something wrong?" He scratches his chin, his red beard full and ridiculous against his thinning blond hair.

"Not wrong. You're doing fine." I try to give him something verging on an encouraging smile.

He flinches. "Okay, then. I'll just get on back to work."

"Sounds good," Noah calls before I can respond, then eases down the muddy road. He chuckles as he turns the SUV around.

I scowl. "What?"

"You scare the shit out of him."

"I was polite."

"Sure, but you still scare the bejesus out of him and he's what, six-five, two-fifty?" His chuckles grow louder. "Like, when you tried to smile, I thought he was going to piss himself."

"I smile."

"No, you don't." We head back toward the heart of the compound.

I change the subject. "I guess this means we need to head over to the Caldwells.'"

"Ugh." His laughter stops. "I hate to do that."

We bump up onto the black pavement as a white work truck passes us.

"We have to. That kind of talk can lead to trouble. The Caldwells need to learn to take the cash and shut the fuck up. The last thing we need is the IRS getting wind of any irregularities."

We wind through the property, both of us assiduously avoiding turning to look at the low gray cinderblock building buried deep in one of the hollows. The Rectory.

"Fine, we can go." Noah runs a hand through his hair. "But just don't hurt anyone, okay? I don't think I can take it today."

"Still pissed about Gregory, huh?" I pop my knuckles.

His mood sours even further. "I can't believe Dad would make me do that."

"Gregory lived to fight another day. All's well that ends well." I lean back against the head rest.

"Where did you get those bones?" He cuts me a sideways glance.

"I have my ways."

"Seriously, man. I mean, it's great. I'm glad we didn't have to off Gregory. But why do you have a secret bone stash to pick from?"

"Maybe I'm the psycho that Dad always wanted." I point toward the front gates. "Let's get this over with. Drive."

"You really aren't going to tell me?"

184

"Nope."

"Jerk." But his grumble is only half-hearted.

A secret stash of bones? No. A knowledge of where the Heavenly PD dump all the roadkill they find on the property? Yes.

The guard at the gate that separates the private compound from the huge Heavenly Ministries Church building waves and opens for us. The wrought iron slides sideways, and we roll out into the wide parking lot, and then down the hill to the highway.

"It's a left. Over near where the creek splits by the shopping center the tornado hit."

"Aw yeah, I remember that. Had a great Chinese place before then."

"That was a long time ago." When we were still kids, when Heavenly Ministries was nothing more than a vast plot of acreage. When our father was up and coming, not clinically insane. And when we were "normal" kids who went to a religious school and had a preacher for a dad. "Mom took us one time."

"Yeah." He swallows hard and drives, the sound of the wind whooshing through our dark thoughts.

We pull into the shopping center and park in front of Caldwell's, a mom and pop hardware store with a respectable lumber yard out back.

"Keep it level." Noah has always been the peacemaker. But sometimes, peace isn't an option. That's where I come in.

"As long as they do the right thing." We walk in, and a small bell at the top of the door chimes. The shelves are in neat rows, the merchandise front-faced. The Caldwells take pride in their establishment. Good. That's something I can use.

"Can I help you boys find something?" A middle-aged man with salt and pepper hair leans over the cash wrap to my right. His cordial smile and John Lennon glasses give him a friendly air that suits him perfectly.

"Mr. Caldwell?"

"That's me. Say, don't I know you?"

I stroll down the aisle with the nails and screws as Noah leans against the front door, blocking it. Snagging a hammer from a rack, I grip up on it, feeling its heft, then return to the counter.

By now, Mr. Caldwell is standing straight up. "You're the Prophet's boys, aren't you?"

"That we are." I amble over to him and set the hammer on the nicked wooden counter.

"Need a hammer?" He glances down.

"That depends."

He fidgets with the pockets on his khaki apron imprinted with Caldwell's on the front in green letters. "Depends on what?"

"You."

He stops fidgeting. "How do you figure?"

I don't want to hurt this man. Not like I wanted to hurt Newell. But I will.

I run my fingertips along the hammer's wooden handle, but keep my gaze locked with his. "I hear you've been complaining about the business you've been getting from the church. You don't appreciate—"

"Now, wait a minute. All I said was that—"

I hold up one finger. "Shh. This is the part where you listen."

The blood drains from his face, and I haven't even raised my voice.

"When our guys buy anything from you, they will pay with cash. You will not have a problem with this. You will take our money and you will say thank you. Do you understand?"

He nods.

Someone knocks at the door, but one look from Noah has him backing away.

"If I hear of any more problems—" I lift the hammer "—I'll have to come back. And I really don't want to." I make a show of looking around. "This is a nice place you've got here. Neat—loved, even. I can tell you take pride in what you have. So keep it looking nice. Keep your doors open. And keep taking our money while your mouth stays shut. Are we clear?"

"Y-yes, sir." He swallows audibly.

I drop the hammer onto the wooden counter with a thud, and he jumps.

"Noah, we're done here." I back away, then turn toward the door. "See you at Sunday service, Mr. Caldwell."

A flyer in the window catches my eye. A missing persons poster. I pause and peer more closely, only to find Delilah's gray eyes staring back at me.

Grace perches on the edge of the wide conference table, her blue eyes focused on me as I strip off my suit jacket and drape it over the back of a leather chair.

"Nice of you to join me." Her tone is silky, deceptive as always.

"Let's get on with it." I drop into one of the chairs, the back springy with disuse. I suppose the Spinners didn't find much use for this part of the Cloister.

"That's the only hello I get?" She purses her lips in a faux pout.

I rub my eyes, my knuckles throbbing from the damage I'd done just the day before. "What do you want from me, Grace?"

She walks around the table and leans next to me, her ridiculous black habit covering her from head to toe.

"I remember when you used to be happy to see me." She slides her fingers up my bicep and gives me her best come hither look.

I knock her hand away. "I'm here for business. Nothing else. What did you and that idiot Newell cook up for the winter solstice?"

"So easy for you, isn't it?" she snarls. "Just throwing people away?"

"There's the Grace we all know and love."

"The Grace *you* made me."

"I didn't make you into anything." I don't want to rehash the past. Not again.

She hikes her skirt up and throws one leg over my lap, the lace of her black thigh highs peeking from beneath the dark folds of fabric as she straddles me. "Have you forgotten us?"

"There isn't an us." I turn away from her, the monster I created.

She digs her nails into my jaw and pulls me to face her. I let her. Knocking her on her ass would be easy and satisfying. But she's clearly put some effort into her theatrics this time. May as well let her get it out of her system.

"Is it because of her?"

"Her who?"

"Your new slut?" She grips harder. "Delilah?"

"Leave her out of this."

She lets go and pulls her habit off, her blonde hair falling around her shoulders, reminding me of the stupid kids we used to be. They are dead and gone.

"It can be good again, you know?" She leans forward and whispers in my ear.

I grab the arms of the chair to keep myself from shoving her off and cracking her skull on the table until she stops moving. It would be so easy to break her neck. A slender, delicate thing, requiring less force than I'd ever needed before. The final snap would play like a blissful amen at the end of an aria from hell.

She lowers her lashes. "I can be your baby girl."

My hand is at her throat before I can stop it. I squeeze. Hard. It feels good. When her eyes widen, and she claws at my hands, I enjoy the acrid scent of fear that colors the air around her. I want her dead. If she didn't know it before. She knows it now.

"Keep your fucking claws to yourself." I shove her away from me. She pinballs off the office chair to my right and lands on the floor, her chest heaving as she drags air into her lungs.

When she looks up at me, hatred burning in her eyes, I want to spit on her. "Did you think we could just pretend nothing happened. That *she* never happened?"

She flinches. "That was so long ago, and—"

"Shut the fuck up." I snap my fingers. "Give me whatever shit you had planned for the solstice, and I'll take it from here."

"We're supposed to work together." She pulls herself up and straightens her dress. "That's what the Prophet wants."

"And we always do what he says, don't we?" I snarl.

Her ire drains away and tears shine in her eyes. "Adam, please. If the Prophet finds out I didn't do what he wants on this..." She takes a deep breath. "Please, let me work with you. I won't try anything else. I swear. Just business, okay?"

I wrestle with my annoyance, but I give her a short nod. "Fine. Show me the plans."

CHAPTER 19

DELILAH

I know the sound of his footsteps. When he enters my room, I'm on my knees, my dress laid across the foot of my bed.

He drops a paper bag next to the door, then strides over and sits in front of me. His scent wafts to me, some sort of soap mixed with the outdoors. I forget that I haven't truly been outside in almost a week. Other than the short trips around the campus in the white bus, we don't spend any time outside the Cloister.

"What are you thinking?" His voice is silky.

I meet his eyes, already acting like his trained dog. "About how it would be nice to go outside."

"Why?"

I shrug. "I don't know. It sort of gets claustrophobic in here, I guess."

"If the Prophet let you roam around outside the Cloister, the wolves might get you. All the men who want to hurt you, the fallen world that wants to corrupt you." Sarcasm twists each word into a different shape. "You're ever so much safer in here. With me."

He reaches out and strokes his fingers through my hair. Leaning forward a bit, his gaze strays lower—to the injury I'm trying to hide.

"What's that?"

I pull my hand between my thighs. "Nothing."

He grabs my chin and yanks my gaze to his. "What did we agree about trust, little lamb?"

Shit.

"Show me." His eyes narrow as I lift my hand. "Broken finger." He runs his hand along my shoulder, pushing the hair away. "And someone hit you. Hard. Who?"

"I had an accident—"

He tsks, his dark eyes sparkling like obsidian. "Trust, little lamb. If you lie to me, that trust is broken. And once it's broken—" He lunges forward and yanks me up.

I squeak as he throws me on the bed and crawls on top of me, his hands gripping my still-sore wrists and pinning me beneath him.

"As I was saying, little lamb, if you break that trust, your body is mine. And I'll do everything I want to it. To you.

It would be a pity for you to misinterpret what's going on here." He squeezes my wrists harder, bringing back the singe of pain from that day on the X. "I have ultimate control over you. And there's nothing you can do to stop me. But—" He drops his lips to my ear "—I've given you a chance to keep me at bay. If you lie..."

I bite my lip to keep it from trembling as he meets my eyes again. His hunger is palpable, and I shiver knowing I'm the meal he desires most. I fear Grace and her punishments. But, as he stares down at me, I realize I fear him far more. There's a darkness in him that seems to have no bottom.

"Last chance, little lamb." He squeezes my wrists.

"Grace." The dread in me comes out in the shape of that one word.

"Tell me what happened." He relaxes his grip and slides his hands down my forearms.

Goosebumps rise in the wake of his touch. "She pulled me out of class—"

"What was on the teaching schedule today?" He nuzzles my throat with his nose.

My face flames. "It was... They were, um..."

He laughs softly, darkly. "Yes?"

"A pee thing."

"Watersports day so soon?" His dark hair tickles along my cheek. "The Spinners are starting early. So, did you get pissed o—"

"No." I shake my head. "Grace called me out. So I went to her office."

He tenses. "Then what?"

"She locked the door and asked me about you."

"What about me?"

"About the mirror."

"Ah." His lips brush along my throat, and heat pools between my thighs.

"And you told her what?"

"Nothing. That's why..."

"Why she hurt you."

"Yes." I let out a deep breath.

"Thank you for being honest with me, little lamb." He eases off me and rests on his knees between my legs, he pulls my hand into his. "How badly broken?"

"At the knuckle, though Abigail says it should heal straight."

"Good." He lays it softly on the bed. Such a contradiction —one minute threatening and the next, gentle. "Then it shouldn't hurt your chances any."

"My chances?"

His jaw tightens, but he doesn't respond, just runs his fingertips down my thighs, circles my knees, then back up. He pauses at my hip bones, stroking back and forth with his thumbs, his palm spread along my hips. "I'll deal with Grace. She disobeyed me when she hurt you. I'll make her pay. Now, where did you tell your mother you were going when you joined the Cloister?"

The question jolts me out of whatever spell his touching weaves. "My mother?"

"Where does she think you are?"

I swallow hard. Adam is dangerous, and the last thing I want is him anywhere near my mother. But why was he asking?

"Remember, little lamb. Trust." He smooths his hands along my inner thighs and spreads me open wide. Completely exposed.

"I told my mom I was joining the Cloister for a year-long study program."

"Did she have a problem with this?" His fingers trace the groove where my thighs meet my hips.

I gasp at the intimate touch. "She-she didn't like it. Didn't want me to do it."

"Why?"

I can't tell him the full truth about my mother. So I tell a half-truth, and hope that he doesn't catch the deception. "She said it's a cult. And dangerous."

His fingers graze along my skin, igniting everything they touch. Catching my breath becomes difficult, and my nipples are so hard that they tingle and ache. "Right on both counts." His smirk kinks something inside me, force-fully turning my fear into need.

"Why?" It's the only word I can get out as his maddening fingers continue their circuit, stroking so close to my center. I bite my lip at the thought of him feeling my wetness, knowing how I react to him.

"I need you to do something for me." He leans down, his breath whispering across my bare flesh.

I grip the blanket. "What?"

He inhales, and it's as if something inside him clicks out of place, a record bouncing from its intended groove. "Do you have any idea how much I want to devour this needy cunt?"

A tremor rushes through me.

"I think about it sometimes. Today, when I was having lunch, I thought about how much I'd enjoy running my tongue along your wet slit and pushing inside you. Tasting every bit of you, sucking on your clit until you scream."

Everything inside me spirals out of control, and for one desperate moment, I consider lifting my hips the slightest bit. Pressing myself to his mouth, giving him permission to do every wicked thing that comes to his mind.

"Does that bother you, Maiden? That I want to own your cunt and wear your taste on my lips for as long as it lasts?"

"Please…" I don't know what I'm asking for.

"Please?" He blows on my clit, and my entire body shudders. "Please lick your cunt? Is that what you're asking?"

Yes. No. My voice is frozen, trapped inside a maze of mixed emotions.

"I think you don't want me to stop." His dark eyes promise hell, oblivion, the sort of sin that will never wash off.

I'm teetering on the edge. One more warm breath from his lips will send me plummeting over.

A scream rips through the dorm, followed by a cry for help. Sarah's voice. I snap out of the haze as Adam sits up. She's still screaming, but her cries are muffled, and then a rhythmic banging adds to the sound.

I scramble off the bed and reach for my dress.

Adam pulls me back down onto his lap. "Where do you think you're going?"

"I have to help her."

"You can't." His arms are like steel around my ribcage.

"Let me go!"

Sarah's cries are tearing me apart.

"There's nothing you can do, little lamb."

"I can go in there and—"

"And what? Confront her Protector, challenge him to a duel?" He wraps his hand around my throat. "He'll hurt you, just like he's hurting her. And then I'll have to kill him. Is that what you want? More blood on my hands?"

"No." A sob threatens. "I just want him to stop."

"He won't. None of us will. That's part of your training. The Prophet will keep you safe from the wolves, but there's no stopping his lions from ripping you apart. And the sooner you accept that, the easier this will be for you."

"Is that what you want?" I claw at his hand. "For me to break?"

"I'm going to break you. It's only a matter of when I choose to do it."

"Fuck you!" I dig my nails into the back of his hand and struggle against his hold.

"There's that spirit I saw in you the very first day, by the fire." He splays his fingers along my ribs and keeps me tight against him.

"Get off!" I try to break free, but he is solid, like a sheet of molten steel.

"You aren't leaving this room," he growls in my ear, and my fight is over. There's nothing else I can do except listen to the screams and the degradation of the banging bed.

He sighs, his breath tickling past my ear. "Let's get back to the conversation we were having before I was so rudely interrupted by the scent of your wet cunt."

"You can help her."

He shakes his head. "I'm afraid not."

"You could go in there and—"

"*She* is none of my concern. You are."

He shifts beneath me, then pulls a folded sheet of paper from his pocket. Shaking it open, he hands it to me. I see my face staring back at me, my mom's information printed below it. "Have You Seen This Woman?" in huge, stark letters across the top.

My hands shake as I try to make sense of the flyer. The screams die down and stop along with the banging bed. Sarah's ordeal is over. No one helped her, not even me.

"I found this not far from the Compound. Why would your mother be searching for you if you told her you were safe and sound in the Cloister?"

"I don't know."

"No idea?"

"No." My mom didn't want me to go. Not because she feared for my safety, but because she'd lose her last chance at scaring up drug money. One of her many boyfriends introduced her to heroin while I was away at college. She hadn't been the same since. Only a ghost of the mother who used to care about me, who was so proud when I got a full scholarship.

When Georgia died, I even thought maybe it was a good thing Mom was out of it, insulated from the grief. But the day I buried my sister, my mom showed up in a black dress more fit for a night club than a funeral. Her hair in disarray, days-old mascara smudged under her eyes. Even so, I was glad to see her, to feel the faded warmth of her embrace. She pretended to grieve, even held my hand as I watched Georgia's casket being lowered into the cold, hard earth. At least she waited until we walked away to ask me for money. I gave it to her.

Later, I had to see her again, to tell her the outline of my plan to find Georgia's killer so she'd play along. She agreed to keep my secret, to give perfect answers if anyone from Heavenly Ministries came calling, and I only had to give her what was left of my final student aid check to make it happen.

If I tell Adam her weakness, he'll use it, maybe crack her open until she spills all my secrets. I can't have that.

"You left just then. Something's going on in here." He strokes my temple, then moves back to my hair and grips hard. "Are you being honest with me, little lamb?"

"Yes." The roots of my hair sting as he pulls my head back until I meet his gaze.

He stares, as if measuring the truth in the grayness of my eyes, then releases me. "Get the bag by the door."

I scramble off his lap. The bag seems innocent enough, but I open it slowly, wondering what fresh torture lies within. I recognize the blue first. Reaching in, I pull out my favorite sweater, a navy cable-knit, and then my favorite pair of jeans. I hug the clothes to me as if they're an old friend. Somehow, even though I've only been at the Cloister for a week, it feels like years have passed since I've had a glimpse of my old life.

"Put them on." He watches me, the dark eyes telling me nothing of the thoughts within.

I pull the sweater over my head, the ghost scent of my old body wash lingering on the fibers. The jeans don't fit as well as they used to. I suppose a week of Cloister cuisine has cut off almost five pounds.

He pulls his cell phone from his pocket and unlocks it. "Sit on the bed, act normal, and record a nice little video for your mother." Rising, he points to where he'd been sitting.

I follow his instructions and sit, folding my hands in my lap and trying to school my features.

"Tell her you're safe, happy, and there's nothing to worry about. That you'll see her soon." He focuses on my hand. "Hide the splint."

I tuck it beneath my other hand. "I'm ready."

"No tricks." He glowers at me.

"I won't." I shake my head, trying to look earnest. I'd never rehearsed some sort of code word with Mom so she'd know I was under duress, and it's not as if I'd use it. More to the point, she would probably be too strung out to notice. She must have had help with the flyers.

"All right." He taps his screen. "Go."

CHAPTER 20

ADAM

*S*he speaks right into the camera, her big gray eyes sparkling as she lies to her mother, telling her she's safe, well taken care of, and not harmed. I play it on a loop, her soft voice washing over my bedroom like calming waves.

She lies to me, too. I let her. I don't know what she's hiding. Maybe I like the extra bit of mystery. I take a drag from my joint and blow the smoke up and out, taking care not to obscure my view of Delilah.

"... was my choice to come here, Mom. Please respect my wishes..." Her eyes convey so much when she says that part, as if there's another layer of meaning I simply can't grasp. Even though I strip her bare every night, she still hides from me.

"Fuck." I stub out the joint. This obsession of mine has to end. It grew overnight, a pale white mushroom, perfect as it reaches toward the gloomy sky and hoping for the sun.

Maybe she can be my sun.

"... I've never felt safer. I have a Protector who watches out for me at all times and..."

I'll have to edit that part out. My father wouldn't want the inner workings of his fucked up menagerie getting out to the masses. The Compound runs on secrets, concentric circles of them, all with the Prophet in the center.

I rub my eyes and suspect my brain is fried from blue balls and this new strain of weed that we've been pushing.

Having her the way I want isn't an option. That's the one rule that can never be broken. Fucking a Maiden is a sure way to get kicked out of the Compound for good. And for me, the price is far, far higher. But I can do other things.

I watch her mouth form tender words, ones not meant for me, and I free my throbbing cock from my shorts. Pretending—that's the key to surviving here—is something I am exceedingly good at. Lying, dissembling, cutting the corners off the truth.

Delilah doesn't have to pretend. No matter what words spill from her pale pink lips, she is my truth.

I stare at her mouth, knowing what delicious secrets it holds. How her tongue slides against mine. How her breath hitches when I touch her. How her soul tries to wrest itself from my grasp before she gives in and opens for me, showing me all of her with ruthless honesty. With hard, curt jerks, I bring myself to climax with her as my only thought.

"Bigger." I point to the ring of trees surrounding the clearing. "I want these gone."

"That's going to be one hell of a bonfire." One of our groundsmen, Chase, scratches his head. "Don't reckon we've ever had one that big."

"Good." I grab a shovel and score an area in the center. "Start stacking the pallets out to here. Add whatever wood from the trees to the center at the bottom. It's too wet to burn well, but once it catches, it'll smolder for days."

"All this for Christmas?"

"You think our lord and savior Jesus Christ deserves less?" I thrust the shovel back at him.

Chase's bearded mouth drops open. Doubting devotion— that's the one wound that no member of Heavenly Ministries can bear.

"Of course not, sir. The bigger the better. He died for our sins. I'll build it higher than the tower of Babel if that'd please the Prophet."

I clap him on the back. "Good man." If I told him the real reason for the fire, he'd probably die of shock. Only my father's inner circle knows that he serves two masters. The God above and the one below.

"I'll get right on it." He heads off toward the row of white trucks and whistles at his workers. "Chainsaws, boys!"

I stride back toward my car, the winter wind shaking the last vestiges of dry leaves overhead. Out here on the western side of the property, one spot of land calls to me. But I can't go out there. Not today. Not when everything inside me is already so raw. Dealing with Grace and fighting the inextricable pull of my Maiden is destroying what little composure I still have left.

My phone buzzes. I answer and drop into my car. "What?"

"Got another problem."

I want to yell until my lungs burn. Instead, I ask what the fuck is wrong this time.

Noah sighs. "Just get up to the house. Dad wants to see us."

"Fuck." I throw my cell into the passenger seat and gun it down the lane. Leaves fly behind me, and a squirrel narrowly misses its date with destiny as I wind through the hilly terrain until I pass the Cloister, then slow as I approach the public-facing areas.

Parking at the back of the Prophet's mansion, I step out of my car as Noah blows a thin stream of smoke.

"You still haven't quit?" I hold my hand out and he passes the cigarette. I take a drag, then flick it to the ground.

"I did." He shrugs. "But sometimes I can't help it."

"No judgment." I'd leave that to my father. It was his forte, after all.

"What are we in for?"

"Not sure. Something about one of the Maidens."

"Fuck." I wonder if he's caught wind of the flyers around town.

"Let's get it over with." He climbs the stairs ahead of me, his step jaunty despite the weight of our father's impending bullshit.

We enter through the back hall, our footfalls echoing on the perfectly polished marble. Smoke wafts from my father's office and carries the distinct scent of marijuana.

"Maybe he's baked and it'll all be one big laugh?" Noah's hopeful tone is worn thin.

I walk in first. Castro sits at the small secretary table in the corner and rolls a joint. My father stares appreciatively at the one between his fingers. "This one goes down so damn smooth. We should up the price."

"That strain? Sure. We'd get it. It's pretty popular in Mountain Brook."

"If the rich kids love it, they'll pay for it." He drops it into an ashtray, then turns to us. "Boys, sit down."

We take seats across from his desk, even though I itch to move, to walk around, to indulge in the fantasy that I'm not tied to this place, my father pulling my marionette strings.

"It's come to my attention that a woman from Louisiana has been visiting the congregation for the past few days and asking questions about her daughter."

My hands go cold.

"Now." He leans forward and puts on his 'I'm a reasonable man' mask. "I understand that her daughter is your Maiden, Adam. So, I expect you to solve this problem. We usually have excellent relationships with the parents of all our Maidens, and—" he grins "—Orphans are even better."

Sick fuck.

"But yours has a meddlesome bitch for a mother that needs to be taken care of."

"I'll handle it."

"How you going to do that, son?" He's trying to start a fight.

I put on a bored tone. "I'll speak with her. She must be staying in town. I'll go to her, explain the situation, and send her back to Louisiana."

"You seem confident." Poison rolls off his tongue. "You think just going and explaining's going to do the trick?"

"Yes."

"What if she won't go?"

"I'll tell her all the lies she wants to hear." I glance at him. "I learned from the best after all."

His expression sours. "Your smart mouth is going to earn you some more lashes. Or maybe you need more convincing to stay in line? Maybe the lash isn't enough for you anymore?"

"I'll go with him." Noah, claps his palms on his thighs. "Make sure it all goes down smoothly."

My father leans back and opens his top desk drawer, his gaze flickering between my brother and me. He seems to come to some sort of internal decision, but only says, "Castro, that shit is a little too mellow for me." He pulls out the cross-shaped box for another hit of his favorite candy.

"I'll get on it." I stand.

"Did I say you could go?" My father's tone hovers at the brink of a jagged cliff.

I re-take my seat and wait as he arranges two lines and snorts both. Once he's done, he wipes his nose and checks a mirror.

"How are the winter solstice preparations coming?"

"Fine."

"You get with Grace?"

"Yes."

"Yes what?"

A brief vision of me hurdling his desk and strangling the life out of him as Castro tries to pull me off flashes across my mind. Through gritted teeth, I reply, "Yes, *sir*."

"Good." He waves a hand at us. "Get the fuck out of here."

CHAPTER 21

ADAM

Twenty Years Ago

"*That* is so fucking lame." I laughed as Brody, my best friend, did his best attempt at a skateboard trick.

"Shut up." He grabbed his board, a wide grin on his face. "You try it, asshole. You're the chosen one and all."

I shook my head. "No, that's my dad." Taking the board from him, I walked up the street toward the cul de sac. We lived right off the campus of Briar Baptist Church in a row of houses reserved for clergy. A few curtains twitched in the low brown houses that lined the way.

Taller at twelve than anyone else in my class, my newfound height made me even worse at skateboarding than Brody, but I had to try to show him up. Noah sat on our front porch, his honey-colored hair flipping up in a light breeze as he played with toy cars.

I dropped the board with a clatter on the street. Thunder boomed to the west, another warm front coming to shake the spring into existence.

Stepping onto the board, I kicked a few times, then rode with both feet down the slight hill toward Brody. He stood with the same grin, his arms crossed over his bird chest. Noah stopped to watch, his mouth hanging open, the car race forgotten.

I bent my knees and jumped, trying to kick the board over as I went. It flipped, but not far enough, and I flailed for a minute with my too-long arms before falling and banging my chin on the curb. Lights out.

"...be in so much trouble if he doesn't wake up." Brody came into focus. "Oh, shit. He's awake."

I blinked and sat up. My chin ached, and Noah cried beside me, big fat tears rolling down his chubby cheeks.

"I'm okay." I squeezed his shoulder. "It's okay." Gingerly, I touched my chin. My fingers came away bloody.

Brody made a show of wiping his brow. "Jesus, man. You scared the shit out of me."

"I thought I had it."

He laughed. "Not even close. Thank God you didn't die. I'd never live it down. I can see the headline now 'Brody

Clevenger, Devilishly Handsome Young Man, Accidentally Kills Adam Monroe, the Preacher's Son.'"

"You're an idiot." I struggled to my feet, the world going black for a second before coming back into focus with a boom of thunder.

"Seriously, I felt like Neville when he thought he'd killed Harry Potter."

"We aren't supposed to talk about those books." Noah had stopped crying.

"You see any parents around, kid? Any invisi-parents waiting to arrest us for enjoying a little Hogwarts in our spare time?"

"That's the work of the devil. If you watch that, you'll go to hell." Noah had gone solemn, a perfect mirror of my father.

I ruffled his hair. "Nobody's going to hell." I didn't believe in hell. It seemed like an idiotic concept, but I never dared say anything like that out loud.

"Speak for yourself." Brody grinned. "I just got tickets to the Rock Roundup at the Amphitheater. KISS is headlining."

"Seriously?" I couldn't tell if he was telling the truth or I was concussed.

"I wouldn't bullshit you about music." He punched me in the shoulder. "You know this. And yes, I've got an extra ticket for you. But you'll have to tell dear old dad that you're off to Bible study or something equally holier-than-thou for this to work. You in?"

At a concert? A real one, not the lame ones we have with only Christian music and chicks who wear too many clothes? "I'm in."

Noah frowned. "Daddy won't—"

"What Dad doesn't know won't hurt him, big guy. Keep this between us, okay?" I held my hand out. He gave me a reluctant five.

"That's my Noah." I smiled, and he couldn't help but return it.

The first drops of rain began to fall, the scent of water on asphalt wafting around us.

"I've got to get to piano practice." Brody held out his fist. His father was the music director for Briar. "Go in and put about ten Band-Aids on that, and you'll be fine. Or maybe just rub some dirt on it."

I met his fist with my own. "See you tomorrow."

He waved and headed up the street, jumping on the grass as a line of cars sped through the sleepy neighborhood. I recognized my dad's SUV at the head of the line. Noah and I watched from the porch as Dad pulled into the driveway and the other cars parked along the street.

Dad hopped out and hurried over to us. "Boys, I've had a revelation. I told the elders at Briar about it, but they turned against me. Against God. Against their Prophet."

"What's a Prophet?" Noah cocked his head to the side as he stared up at Dad.

"A man who has spoken to God." He knelt down and gripped Noah by the shoulders. "God revealed to me our path. He told me what we need to do, where we need to go, and the ministry we need to build."

"What do you mean, you spoke to God?" I couldn't follow anything he was saying, and not just because he spoke with a crazed inflection.

He stood and gripped my arm, a too-bright light in his dark eyes. "You'll see, son. All these men—" I cast a glance to the yard and found two-dozen men assembled there in the now-pouring rain, listening intently to my father "—they know the truth of my revelation. They're coming with us. We leave tonight."

Lightning flashed, the thunder coming a few seconds later.

"Dad." I shook my head. "There's school. I have homework. Noah just learned how to read. We can't—"

His face hardened, and my skin crawled. "We can, and we will. We are here to do the will of God."

"I thought that was what you *were* doing? You're the preacher, so—"

"No!" He shook his head so hard his neck popped. "I am leading a pack of heathens who have lost God's favor. We will build a new Eden, a new church, a new safe haven for believers." He leaned closer, so close that I couldn't see his eyes, which set the hairs on my arm standing on end. "And I know this because of my vision. Not only did God come to me, so did the Father of Fire." His whisper ended in a triumphant note.

"The *devil*? I don't know what you're talking—"

"You don't have to know, son." He stood straight up again, the fervor still coursing through him like a high electric current. "You just have to follow me, your father, your Prophet. Believe in me, and you will live in paradise on earth and in heaven. It has all been shown to me. You'll see. All of you will see." Turning to the men on the lawn, he motioned them to come inside.

They walked past us, filling our home with low voices as Noah and I stood on the porch—me, dumbfounded and Noah, lost.

"What's wrong with Daddy?" He took my hand, his little one cold and clammy.

"I don't know. Maybe Mom can talk some sense into him."

Noah's chin trembled. "I don't want Mommy to talk to him. He..."

"I know." I squeezed his hand. He didn't have to say it. Whenever Mom got too "mouthy" as Dad called it, there were consequences.

"You're still bleeding," he offered, his eyes downcast.

My father hadn't even seemed to notice the blood on my chin.

I turned and stared down the street at the direction Brody had gone. It was as if he'd walked away and taken "normal" with him, a cape attached to his back, fluttering in the rain with a somber wave goodbye. Because nothing would be normal. That time had come to an end, right along with my childhood.

Both Brody and "normal" were gone. I never saw either of them again.

CHAPTER 22

DELILAH

arah walks into the training room, the bruising on her face a mottled blue and purple. She doesn't look me in the eye, even though I'm silently pleading with her to keep her chin up.

She climbs up on the nearest table, assumes the position on all fours, and waits for Abigail to hook up the inevitable enema.

I edge closer to Sarah as the other Maidens follow a Spinner toward the wall of pain as she explains the intricacies of various nipple clamps.

"Are you all right?" I keep my voice low, but the running water nearby helps muffle the sound.

"No." She hangs her head. "No, I'm not. First, I got pissed on, and then last night—" The word cracks as she spits it out.

I swallow, my mouth dry. "What happened?"

"What did it sound like?" She finally meets my gaze, her left eye bloodshot, the center of a ruined flower.

I clamp my teeth together to keep my lip from trembling.

"You know, he made me suck his cock for the past few days. And, I didn't want to, but I can disconnect. I can go somewhere else." She shrugs. "I don't have to be there, on my knees, getting my face fucked by a smelly beast. I can close my eyes and go wherever I want. But last night—" Her voice doesn't crack this time; it shatters.

Abigail flips off the water and steps over to Sarah's backside. "Lord almighty, what a mess." She mumbles angrily under her breath and doesn't seem to notice that I'm speaking to Sarah out of turn. Placing a bedpan under her, Abigail squeezes a sponge of what I hope is warm water.

Sarah flinches, and the water that pours off her body is tinged pink.

"Too rough." Abigail keeps mumbling. "Supposed to be training them, not injuring them."

"Everything's going to be okay." I stroke Sarah's hair, a movement as forbidden as it is natural.

"No, it's not." She winces as Abigail makes another pass. "Not until..."

She doesn't have to finish her thought. It's not safe to finish it, anyway. She won't be okay until she's gone from here, free of the Cloister.

"Delilah!" The teaching Spinner finally notices my absence.

"Go." Sarah lets her head hang again, dark hair creating a wall around her.

I join the other Maidens and get a sharp glare from the teaching Spinner. She glances at the splint on my finger and perhaps decides I'm not due for punishment again quite yet. At least that's what I hope is going on in her mind.

"Eve." She gestures for the girl to step forward. "You'll be our first to demonstrate."

Eve moves to the front of the classroom and turns to face the rest of the Maidens. Her eyes downcast, she doesn't move as the Spinner attaches a metal pincher to each nipple. A chain runs between them and dangles down toward her belly button.

"These are on the lowest setting." The Spinner gestures as if she's a model on *The Price is Right*. "I would recommend they stay on that level if you're just, I don't know, trying to please a man by looking the part. The pain is minimal. But—" She pulls on the chain, and Eve exhales roughly. "The mechanism works by pulling here. Each pull will squeeze tighter. Now, plenty of men enjoy this done on their own nipples. It's up to you to follow his lead, look into his heart, and discern what types of activities he enjoys."

"What if I don't want a man?" A strawberry blonde at the back of the class, her voice soft as silk, speaks up.

The Spinner drops the chain. "Who said that?"

The girl, her chin high despite the tremble in her hands, steps forward. "I didn't sign up for this. I don't want this. I want to go home."

My heart sinks into the acid vat of my stomach. The first few days, there were several outbursts like this. Girls who actually thought this was a safe place. But they died down after the beatings. The Spinners' batons could do wonders for any Maiden doubting her role at the Cloister.

"Get back in line, Sharon."

"No." She crosses her arms over her bare stomach. "I want to go home. Let me go."

The Spinner pulls her baton free. "You need to reconsider."

"No." She darts to the wall and grabs a cane.

The other Maidens back away from her.

I stand, transfixed. This little slip of a girl, one who'd never so much as pinged on my radar, is ready to fight for her freedom.

"Abigail!" The Spinner calls. "Lock the door."

The old Spinner looks up from her work on Sarah. "What in the world is going on?"

"Do it!"

She hustles to the door and pulls out a key ring from a skirt pocket.

Sharon swings the cane back and forth, warding off the Spinner. "Let me go!"

"You are safe here, Sharon. You are loved." Menace laces each word from the Spinner's mouth.

"Fuck you! I'm not some whore you can train and sell to whatever sadistic freak pays the Prophet!"

The air leaves the room as Sharon shouts the truth to the rafters.

"Those are lies whispered in your ear by the devil, child." The Spinner tries to move closer, but Sharon keeps swinging. "The Prophet loves, cherishes, treats you as holy above all other women."

Abigail is still fumbling at the door as Sharon backs to it, the cane swishing with each of her steps.

Wings unfurl in my heart, the tips brushing against each chamber. Hope. I can't escape, but maybe Sharon can.

I stand next to Sarah who watches the scene with wide eyes.

"Sharon, this is your last chance to accept the Prophet's teachings. Don't follow Satan down his familiar path. Don't let the filthy world twist your—"

"Shut up!" Sharon screams and shoves Abigail away, the keyring skittering across the wood floor. She wrenches the door open, then glances at the keys.

Get them. I would throw them to her if I could, but I'd have to get past the Spinner to do it.

She swings again, not running, knowing she needs that set of keys if she has any chance of making it.

"The keys," Sarah hisses.

Sharon lunges for them, right as the Spinner swings her baton, missing Sharon as she snatches the keys. The Spinner is thrown off balance and crashes to the floor.

"Run!" a host of voices cry. Mine among them.

She turns for the door, takes two heady steps toward freedom, and then Mary rushes forward and grabs a handful of Sharon's hair. With a vicious yank, she rips her down onto her back, the flat *smack* of skin on the hard floor ugly and painful. The cane flies from her grip and lands in the hall.

I squeeze Sarah's hand, having taken it at some point during the scene. The Spinner scrambles back to her feet and rushes to Sharon as other Spinners enter the room and surround the rest of the Maidens.

What ensues is a beating that makes my knees weak, and I struggle to keep from retching. Sharon's cries and screams echo throughout the Cloister, but the Spinners guarding us show no emotion, though some of them join in at intervals. They grant Sharon no mercy, and eventually drag her away.

The Head Spinner enters the classroom, her baton bloody on one end, and takes center stage. "The devil is always at work. Even here in the Cloister. Sharon is evidence of this. Maidens, you must guard your hearts against the darkness, against the evil of the outside world. Here, you are safe. Here, you are loved. Sharon has fallen from the Prophet's light, dragged down by demons, no doubt. Do not follow in her footsteps."

We huddle together, a mass of naked women, trying to find some sort of comfort in each other. Except Mary, who stands proudly with the Spinners.

"That's enough for today. Spend the rest of the morning in prayer." She turns on her heel and leaves.

"You heard her." The teaching Spinner herds us to our dresses, then escorts us back to the dorms.

I sit on my bed, everything inside me cold and brittle. Sharon's cries still play in my mind, along with the *thunk* of each baton, each kick to her side as she lay helpless and curled in a ball on the floor. Where is she now?

My door cracks open. I forgot to lock it. Chastity enters and closes the door behind her.

"Are you all right?" She sits next to me, but spares a glance for the camera.

"I don't know. Are you?"

"I have to be." She shrugs. "This is the way of the Cloister, the way the Prophet has instructed."

"Do you ever..."

She looks at the camera again, then whispers, "Question the Prophet?"

"Yes."

"No." She shakes her head, the scar on her forehead more visible when she turns toward me. "He is anointed by God. You'll see. At the winter solstice, you'll see why he is special."

"What happens at the winter solstice?"

"I'm afraid this wasn't just a social visit." She turns on a dime. "I have a certain chore to do today, and the Head Spinner has instructed I take you with me to do it."

"It must be a bad chore, then." I eye her warily.

She shifts, crossing her ankles beneath her skirt. "It's not my favorite, no. But it's necessary." She clears her throat. "The Head Spinner also wanted me to deliver a message along with this assignment." A blush creeps into her cheeks, and her discomfort trickles into me. I cross my arms over my breasts, as if this tiny defensive move can stop the Head Spinner's wrath.

"Go ahead."

Her kind eyes turn apologetic, but she follows her orders. "She says that you should 'take note of the Chapel and how its whores act, since you'll be one of them sooner than you think.'"

CHAPTER 23

ADAM

The sun angles harshly on the motel room door, obscuring the faded numbering scheme for the rooms. But this is the right one. Heavenly Ministries owns a stake in most of the establishments clustered around the nearest interstate exit to the property, and Motel Rapture is no exception. The woman at the front desk gave me the rundown about Delilah's mother, including her dirty little habit.

I knock and wait. Shuffling sounds from inside, and then the door cracks open. Blue eyes meet mine, though they are bloodshot and sagging around the edges. "What do you want?"

"I'm from Heavenly Ministries."

Something like a smile splits her face, though it turns into more of a grimace. She's only 54 years old, but she looks more like 70. When she swings the door inward, I finally get a sense that she really is Delilah's mother. The same slight frame, a certain way of carrying herself—not too stiff, but with her shoulders back.

"Make yourself comfortable." She points to the double bed that's still made, then wraps her pink bathrobe tighter around herself as she sits on the other mattress.

I keep my body language open, resting my elbows on my thighs as I lean forward. "I'd like to start by saying that your daughter is safe."

Her eyes narrow. "I don't believe you. Your cult has gone and brainwashed her."

"I can assure you that's not the case."

"Then why isn't she here? Tell me that, smart guy." She reaches for a pack of cigarettes on the nightstand.

"The program she's in is an intensive, year-long immersion in biblical living." I try to keep some sort of warmth in my tone, even if my words are robotic lies. "We take care to ensure that each of the program participants is given the chance to experience the Word of God first-hand, on their own terms, and within the safety of Heavenly Ministries."

"Sounds like a lot of bullshit to me. Anything that needs that many words is bullshit." She lights up, taking a deep pull, the wrinkles on her upper lip appearing like crevasses in the side of a prehistoric mountain. How did this woman create the otherworldly creature back at the Cloister?

I lean back, watching her watch me. "Let's cut to the chase. What is it that you're after?"

She blows smoke at me in a direct puff, but doesn't have the lung capacity to finish the insult, and the smoke doesn't make it all the way to me. "I want to know my daughter's safe."

"She is."

"I want to see her. I need proof."

I pull out my phone, tee up the video, and play it for her. Just hearing Delilah's lilting voice soothes me. I want to see her, but I keep the phone held out as her mother scrutinizes every word.

"That's her." She waves the screen away, not even waiting until Delilah is done speaking.

"See? Safe just as I told you."

She laughs and takes another long drag from her cigarette. I can actually see the flame eating away at it in record speed. Then she grabs another, lights it from the dying one, and blows a smoke plume to the ceiling.

"You think I don't know my own daughter? The girl I nursed at my breast, the one I raised, the one I slept with in my arms?"

The one you let your husband prey on. I swallow my indignation; I have no right to it.

She continues, "I see her. She looks fine. But she doesn't look *right*. Something in her eyes, the way she holds herself. You've done something to her."

"She's where she wants to be."

"Oh, I don't doubt it." She laughs, a raspy, sickly sound. "She's exactly where she intended."

"So you'll leave this alone, then? No more flyers?" I pull the one from my pocket and toss it on the floor. I've already had two other Protectors scouring the city for the rest.

"That depends."

Here it comes. I've known plenty of addicts. Her ploy is no more sophisticated than any other. I stare at her, waiting for the inevitable ask. Like every addict, she has no idea how far down the rabbit hole she's gone—with the drugs or with me. A junkie from Lousiana with no ties except her most recent good-for-nothing boyfriend, she could disappear right this second and no one would care. I could wrap my hands around the crepe-like skin of her neck and squeeze. She wouldn't be able to make a sound. I know right where to press, and how the blood vessels in her eyes will blow, and the way her body will tense and finally, finally go limp. And when I let go, the air that got trapped and festered inside her will come out in a death rattle. More blood on my hands. Another unwilling sacrifice to the Father of Fire. How the fuck did I get here?

"Are you even listening?"

I return my attention to Delilah's very-much-alive mother. "No. Start over."

"Asshole. I *said* you can keep my daughter there—" She raises a finger "—*unharmed*, and I won't make a stink about it. But I'm going to need some funds to carry me through these months without her."

There it is. Selling her daughter to the devil as long she gets her next fix. Maybe all parents are like her. My father certainly is.

"How much?"

She nibbles the end of her cigarette. "One hundred thousand ought to do it."

I turn the number over in my mind. Is that what Delilah is worth? A measly sum. Thirty pieces of silver.

"I could get greedy, you know." She shrugs, a piece of ash falling to her robe. "But I'm trying to keep this reasonable."

I rise, suddenly feeling the need to get out of this room, away from this faint, profane shadow of Delilah. "Fifty-thousand, and you don't set foot in this state again. Ever."

"Seventy-five." She puts out her cigarette.

"Sixty. Take it or leave it."

She holds out a leathery hand. "Deal."

I turn my back on her and stride to the door. "The money will be delivered within the hour. I want you across the state line before sundown."

"I will be." She follows me. "And one thing."

"There are no more things." I open the door and inhale the cool air on the catwalk.

"Don't kill her." Her voice softens. "Not like you did that other one."

I still. "We didn't kill anyone."

"Fine, whatever you say. Just don't kill my daughter." It's the only motherly thing she's said, though her request sets the bar pretty low. "Promise me?"

"What is my promise worth?" I grip the railing as a pigeon lands a few feet away. "Should I knock another five thousand off your price?"

"No. We agreed on sixty." She answers too quickly, and I'm disgusted with her all over again.

"Then I'll do with your daughter whatever I please. Stay out of Alabama or face the consequences." I turn and scowl at her.

She shrinks back into her room. "Please don't kill her. Like you did Georgia." She closes the door, and I hear the lock being thrown.

Georgia—the murdered Maiden. I eye the door. She must have done her research, reading about the scandal and connecting it to Heavenly, despite our heavy payoffs to the local police and media to keep it quiet. *Fuck.*

I could kick the door down, drag her out by the hair, and no one would say shit as I pulled her screaming down the stairs. But I don't. Not because I have any care for her. She's just another non-parent, someone who should have been trustworthy but turned out to be empty, rotten from the inside out.

Instead of taking vengeance on the woman, I keep walking away. It isn't worth it, I tell myself. I refuse to believe I let her live so Delilah wouldn't be needlessly hurt.

After all, hurting Delilah is my calling.

CHAPTER 24

DELILAH

*C*hastity shoulders a backpack as we walk out of the Cloister and into the blustery afternoon. The sun is out, and I've never felt such a delight from the simplicity of soaking in the bright rays.

"Let's go." She sets off down the sun-dappled lane, and I keep up, drinking in the smells and sounds of the woods.

Though Grace clearly intends this trip to be some sort of punishment, my spirits lift as I see blue sky between the overarching tree limbs and hear birdsong. I'm never taking these things for granted again. But I have to turn my thoughts earthward, to Chastity. This may be my only chance to speak to her without any listening ears around.

"So, how did you come to the Cloister?" I tuck my hands into the too-big white coat she'd handed me before we left.

"We aren't supposed to talk." She crosses her arms over her stomach as a breeze rushes down the curving road.

"Oh, I just thought—"

"No talking." She gives me a stern glare, then glances behind us.

I follow her gaze and find a Protector ambling up the road, an assault rifle slung on his shoulder. *What the hell?*

"Grace," Chastity whispers and picks up her pace.

That's the only explanation she needs to give. Even walking through the open air on the Compound, we're watched.

We walk in silence for another ten minutes, and I try to focus on the world around me to temper my disappointment. But my thoughts stray back to Georgia, and then to Adam. His darkness is deep, seemingly complete, but he killed Newell to save me. That single event—even though I'm not allowed to speak of it—tells me that there's light left in him somewhere. Maybe buried beneath an avalanche of gloom and horrible deeds, a sliver of hope remains. Or, it could be that I'm delusional and looking for things that aren't there. But if that were true, why would he want me to trust him? Is it just another mind game meant to break me down?

We top another rise, and on the downslope, a church sits off to the right. It reminds me of country churches I'd pass on the highway when driving from Louisiana to

Alabama. In my drone surveillance, I just assumed it was an old worship space, maybe the first Heavenly Ministries Church before the huge stadium sanctuary was built.

Chastity moves to the edge of the road, heading straight for the white church with the steeple reaching ever heavenward. A couple of Compound jeeps and golf carts, along with an out-of-place black limo are lined up in the gravel parking area beside the structure.

The Protector with the rifle follows at a distance, more of a warning than an immediate threat.

"Is that the Chapel?" I keep close to Chastity, our elbows bumping.

"Yes."

"What is it?"

She hefts the backpack higher on her back. "Hell."

My gut sinks as we crunch into the gravel parking lot. The sharp-edged rocks press into the bottoms of my white flats, likely leaving stone bruises in their wake.

"Just follow my lead. Don't talk to anyone." She walks up the peeling wooden steps, the white paint wearing off to show graying boards beneath, then opens one of the front double doors. Warm, perfumed air flows out as we enter the vestibule. The first thing that strikes me is purple. The carpet, the walls, the doors—everything is done in varying shades from lilac to eggplant.

An armed guard sits in a chair to the right of the next set of double doors leading to the sanctuary. He chews on a toothpick and plays on his phone, giving us a simple grunt and cocking his head toward the sanctuary.

My stomach churns as faint noises make it to me through the wood-paneled walls. Sighs, moans, masculine laughter. We shouldn't be here. I want to turn and rush out the door into the sunlight again, but the Protector who'd been following us walks in, blocking the exit.

"Let's go." Chastity leads the way across the too-plush purple carpet and enters the worship space.

But it's not a sanctuary at all. The narrow center aisle creates a corridor where, on either side, scaffolding has been erected to create two stories of rooms, all open. Some have gauzy curtains hanging in front of them, others are bare. Inside each is a woman. Some on the second story sit on the catwalk along the front of the rooms, their bare legs dangling. Others lounge in beds or chatter with each other while sending us inhospitable looks. Most are naked, young, and hostile as I follow Chastity down the row of what has to be two dozen women stacked in open cubes.

We pass one on the right with two women inside, a gray-haired man grunting and thrusting into one while the other plunges a thick dildo into his ass.

I put my hand to my mouth and speed up, almost stepping on Chastity's heels. But she's slowing down. I peek around her and see a man in a suit standing in the aisle, watching three women in one cube lick and grind on one another. He's in the middle of taking off his tie as we try to pass.

He holds out his arm, blocking us in next to the narrow stairs leading to the upper level. Mid-thirties, blond, handsome—but nothing warm lives in his light blue eyes. "Are you two on the menu?"

"No, sir." Chastity shakes her head, eyes downcast.

"I think you should be." He takes my hand and pulls me toward him.

I dig my heels into the purple carpet. "No."

"No?" He laughs and yanks me close. "You're going to say no to a U.S. Senator?"

All the blood drains from my face, and I can't seem to breathe. He leans close, as if he's going to kiss me.

I shove away from him and try to retreat down the aisle, but his grip on my wrist is like a vise.

"Look who's back." A woman in a black bustier and stiletto heels walks down the rough wooden steps from the top catwalk. "I'm sorry Senator Roberts, but those two belong to the Prophet. If you'd like more company—" She snaps her fingers, and three more women exit their rooms and hurry toward us. "I've got you covered."

He finally loosens his grip enough for me to wrench my wrist away. I wonder if he's re-aggravated the healing skin, but everything seems fine.

He smirks. "A Maiden, eh?"

I try to shrink, hunching my shoulders forward and clutching my elbows.

"I'll be seeing you." He winks and returns to the debauchery in front of him.

"Come." The tall woman in the bustier walks ahead of us, her hips swinging and her hair falling behind her in a straight, dark slash.

She passes through a door and up a few shallow stairs to the old church's altar. It's been converted to a lounge area, couches and a desk filling the space. An area to the right is walled off with a door leading to a separate bedroom. The baptismal is filled in with dirt, exotic plants with deep green leaves unfurling in the colored sunlight streaming through the stained glass. Two bronze birdcages hang on the branches of a lemon tree, the birds inside oddly silent and watchful.

Sinking onto an ornate wooden chair with gold cushions, which could have been original to the church, she crosses her legs at the knee. "Take a seat."

"We have work to do." Chastity pulls her backpack off and sets it on the desk.

"Can't spare me a moment?"

At first I thought she was older, but looking at her in the light filtering through the stained glass, I can tell she's maybe late twenties. Beautiful, her bare breasts don't need the bustier's help to sit up and demand attention. I study my fingers, but glance up at her when I think she's not looking.

"I'm just here for the swabs, Jez, nothing else." Chastity's voice turns harder than I've ever heard it.

Jez reaches out and touches Chastity's skirt. "How's the scar?" Something in her face seems to crack, the overdone makeup unable to hide her sorrow.

"It doesn't hurt." Chastity pulls out an array of long swabs, like extra-large Q-tips, each enclosed in a sterile blister pack. "Can you call the girls?"

"Can we please talk? Just for a minute?" Jez's eyes water, the deep brown glistening like melted chocolate.

Chastity shoots a glance to the upper front corner of the sanctuary. I follow her gaze and see a camera, the red light flashing, pointing right at us.

"We can't."

Jez lets her hand drop and retreats into the golden chair, but she never takes her eyes from Chastity. I appreciate being ignored as I try to take it all in. A whorehouse on the Compound. Then again, what is the Cloister but a whorehouse-in-training?

"What's wrong with you?" Jez glances at me.

"The Maidens. We come here? This is where we end up?"

Jez grins, the warmth she'd shown to Chastity draining away as she looks me up and down. "You too good to spend some time at the Chapel?"

The word "yes" lights up in my mind and pops like old-timey flashbulbs. "I-I—"

"We're ready." Chastity hands me a pair of medical gloves, then frowns at the broken finger. "Just be careful not to touch anything with your bare hand. I'll hand you the sample. Each one goes inside one of these." She sets an array of long glass vials onto the counter. "Before you place it inside, you'll need to write down the girl's name. I'll either say it or ask her when she comes in." Pulling a Sharpie from her bag, she gives it to me without looking at me.

"What exactly is it that we're doing?" I eye the long swabs.

"This one talks too much. I thought Maidens weren't allowed to speak unless spoken to." Jez shrugs. "Maybe rules have gotten lax since my time at the Cloister."

I glance to Chastity, who continues with her work as if she hadn't heard me. I try again. "So, we're doing what?"

"STD testing." Jez smirks. "We can't have the girls passing shit to the fine, fine gentleman who frequent this establishment, now, can we?" Her tone tells me she'd be more than happy if every man who visited left with herpes.

"What about HIV?"

"More questions, Maiden?" She looks me up and down. "You're an interesting one. We give blood samples every six months. But our clients are more worried about the clap than anything else."

"Oh." I say 'oh' as if that clears everything up for me. As if a whorehouse on a religious compound makes total sense. As if I don't have questions about how Maidens end up here. I do some quick math and reassure myself it's impossible for every Maiden to be in the Chapel. There isn't enough room, and I didn't see that many women on the way in. Not to mention, I know some get married off to important or wealthy men. Some of the others return to the congregation or their parents, but very few.

"Go ahead." Chastity motions to the door, and—with one more long look—Jez walks over and opens it.

When she turns her back, her dark hair brushing to one side, a row of scars appear. Small circles sprout in a row down her spine and disappearing into the bustier. Though I can't be certain, they look like cigarette burns.

She swings the door open and calls out, "Girls, time for the check. Get on in here if you aren't busy. If you are, come when you can."

"I'm already coming," a man yells from down the corridor. Some of the women laugh. Others silently exit their cubicles and make their way toward us. Most are nude, which has become frighteningly normal for me. I'm more often naked than clothed at the Cloister.

"Here we go." Chastity lowers herself to her knees.

The first woman comes in, her mascara already streaked and dried down her face. Her ribs protrude, and she looks ten years older than she probably is. She gives Chastity a glare, then turns her gaze to me. Something like molten fury passes across her face. She steps toward me, but Jez grabs her too-thin arm and whips her around. "Get it done."

"Cherry," Chastity says.

Cherry bends over and spreads her cheeks.

"*Cherry*." Chastity gives me a pointed look.

"Oh, right." I grab the Sharpie and write the woman's name on the vial.

Chastity takes a clean swab and gently inserts it into Cherry, then pulls it out and hands it to me. I place it in the vial and press the top on.

"Is it in yet?" Cherry laughs, but there's no joy in it.

"You're done." Jez motions for the next woman to come inside.

We spend the next few minutes taking samples. It's demeaning, but none of the women seem to mind. They walk in dead-eyed and leave the same way. Most of them verge on emaciated, though a couple are large, as if they've been treated differently to please certain clients' particular desires. It isn't lost on me that Chastity seems to know most of their names.

When we're done, Chastity collects the vials and places them in the backpack.

"That's it, then?" Jez speaks with too much force, but volume can't hide the vulnerability in her eyes.

"Until next month." Chastity hefts the backpack. "I'll send these off to the lab as soon as possible."

"So efficient." Jez steps closer to Chastity.

"Jez—"

She touches Chastity's face so softly that I suddenly feel out of place, a spectator to an intimate scene.

"They'll see," Chastity hisses, but leans into Jez's touch all the same.

I turn my back and side step until I'm standing in front of the camera. The angle is tricky, but maybe I can shield them, at least a little bit.

"Does it hurt?" Jez's voice is soft, the venom gone.

"Not anymore."

"I'm sorry." Jez's voice cracks just a bit, a hairline fracture.

Chastity lets out a breath. "It's not your fault."

"It's not yours either."

"We have to go."

"I know."

I can't tell if they embrace, but then Chastity is tapping my shoulder. "Come on. We need to get back."

I catch Jez's eyes, the tears that threaten, and she covers her mouth with her palm to stifle a sob.

Chastity walks out, her long skirt swishing on the garish carpet, and I follow her past the grunting senator and some other scenes of depravity. Skin slaps on skin, women moan loudly, and I focus on getting out of here. Keeping my eyes ahead, I stay in step with Chastity until we push out the doors into the vestibule. The guard doesn't look up as we pass, and a rifle leans next to the outer doors. It wasn't there before. For a second, I consider grabbing it. But the foolishness of the idea keeps me walking. It would accomplish nothing, and after all, I was in this until the end—until I found out about Georgia.

The cool air washes over me as we exit into the sunny day, and it's as if I can finally breathe again. No more cloying perfume or the thick scent of sex.

As we start walking the road back to the Cloister, I glance behind us. No guard. That must have been his gun by the door. He's still inside the Chapel, one of the many faceless users I'd heard as I walked through.

Chastity hurries up the rise. I almost have to run to keep up, and I want to ask her to slow down, to enjoy the freedom for as long as we can, but when we're out of view of the Chapel, she whirls on me.

Grabbing my coat, she pulls me face to face. "You will say *nothing* about what you saw and heard today."

"I wouldn't." I try to square this fierce Chastity to the meek one from the Cloister. "I'm your friend." My words aren't a manipulation. They're true. Ever since the night with Newell, I've known that Chastity was different than the other Spinners. I just didn't know how different until I saw her interactions with Jez.

She loosens her grip. "It's just, I don't want Jez to—"

"Get in trouble. I understand." I grip the back of her hands and put my heart into my words. "I'd never do something to hurt you." She'd already been hurt enough, judging by the scar on her forehead and the feelings she swallowed when we were in the Chapel.

"Thank you." She releases me and steps back, then lets out a shuddering breath. Playing the heavy isn't her style, but she definitely gets her point across when she wants to. "We better go."

We walk elbow to elbow, not hurried but not slow, down the tree-lined road back to the Cloister.

"Can I ask you something?"

She tenses.

"Not about that." I jerk my chin toward the Chapel. "Something else."

"Sure." Her answer is guarded, but I take what I can get.

"When were you a Maiden?" If she was in Georgia's "class," I may finally be able to get some answers.

"Three years ago. Why?"

Shit. She was one year before Georgia. "So, when your year was up—"

"That's not something I want to discuss."

My heart sinks farther, deeper, and flirts with despair. "I was just wondering about a Maiden that was here after you. The one that got hurt..." I take a deep breath. "Got killed."

"We are forbidden from speaking about her." Her words are curt, signaling the end of whatever confidences just passed between us.

The Cloister comes into view, the prison bars beckoning us closer. We walk in silence, heads down, and the breeze loses some of its clarity, the landscape no longer giving me heart to go on.

When we're a few yards from our jail, Chastity puts out a hand and stops me.

I turn to her, the blue of her eyes brilliant even against the backdrop of the azure sky. "What?"

She chews on her lip, then says so softly that I almost miss it. "She talked about you."

"Who?"

The door hinge creaks, and the Head Spinner walks out of the back of the Cloister, her raptor-like gaze landing on us with eerie focus.

CHAPTER 25

DELILAH

"*R*ight where you belong." He walks in and tosses his jacket to the floor next to me before sitting on the bed.

This isn't where anyone belongs, but I swallow my criticism. "You're late."

"Am I, little lamb?" He pulls my face up to his. "Does this mean you missed me?"

"No." Had I missed him? I shake off the question. "I mean, I was wondering if you sent that video to my mom, is all."

He turns his neck and cracks it with unnerving precision. "I did."

"And?"

"Why so worried?" He peers down at me, a furrow forming between his dark brows.

"I just—" I shrug and come out with the most plausible explanation "—I know how Heavenly deals with outsiders."

"Oh, I see." He smiles, slow and poisonous. "She's alive and well. On her way back home."

"Really?" I didn't expect my mom to give up so quick. Then again, if Adam spoke her language... "Did you pay her to go?"

"Of course. She's an addict. Something you failed to mention." His nostrils flare.

My insides crumple that she caved, but relief tempers the disappointment—she seemed to have kept her mouth shut about Georgia. Adam wouldn't be in such a good mood if she'd spilled.

And maybe I'm making progress. I haven't been able to speak to Chastity since this afternoon, but I have to believe that she meant Georgia when she'd said 'she talked about you.' I've been holding onto that flame of hope, letting it fuel me for the rest of the day. I snap my attention back to Adam. Not that it's difficult. He looks like some sort of dark CEO in his deep gray suit and tie. "Heroin makes her a different person. I didn't want you to know."

"Embarrassed?" He strokes my too-warm cheek.

"Yes." My voice is barely a whisper. I hate to admit I'm ashamed of my own mother, but it's true. And maybe, for just a moment, I wondered if she gave a shit about me again. The flyers, coming here, trying to find me—but it was just a charade, a different sort of shake-down. I ignore the stinging fact that a simple payoff is enough for her to abandon her only daughter.

His fingers stray lower, to my neck. "You should have told me. Trust, remember?"

I shiver at his soft touch and the leashed violence it suggests. "Yes." I want to argue that he never asked, that it wasn't important. But I know it won't matter. The tight tone of his voice tells me that much.

"You know I have to punish you." He tries to feign regret, but doesn't quite manage. His hunger is still there, beneath the surface, claws waiting to catch and rip and destroy.

I can't respond.

"On hands and knees." He stands and unbuttons his shirt, revealing fair, muscled skin with a trail of dark hair leading south.

I swallow hard and crawl onto the bed.

"Did you go outside today?"

I turn to look at him as he stands behind me.

"Yes, how did you—"

"I spoke with Grace." His hands curl into fists, but then he shakes them out. "Told her you were to be allowed out."

"Oh." I don't mention the nature of the outing—visiting a whorehouse wasn't what I'd had in mind—but I'd take it over staying locked up inside the Cloister. "Thank you." I face the headboard again, and it occurs to me that I'm having what could pass as a normal conversation while I'm completely naked, on all fours, and about to be punished by a man who treats me as a pet rather than a person. And I just *thanked* him. "No." The word rockets out before I have a chance to stop it.

"What?" He approaches me and strips off his shirt, tossing it to the floor.

I sit back on my heels. "No. You aren't going to punish me."

He smirks. It's hard and cold, like his eyes. But heat courses through me all the same.

"Is this how you want to play this evening?"

"I'm not playing." My voice shakes and I scoot off the bed and stand. "You aren't punishing me. I'm not a—"

He hurdles the bed and has me in his hard grasp before I can even form the thought to run. I'm slammed onto the bed face first, his weight on my back, his bare chest pressing against me.

His mouth at my ear curls my toes. "I think we may have a slight misunderstanding between us, little lamb." He grabs a handful of my hair with one hand and slides the other down my side. "You see, I'm the one who calls the shots where you're concerned. I own you."

"Stop." I try to push up, but it's no use against his lean muscle.

"I can't. Not until you understand. This is a lesson you need." His hand slides beneath me. "And one you *want*."

"No."

"You've wanted it since the first night I saw you. Fire at your back. Hell in front of you." He presses his fingertip against that one super-sensitive spot between my legs.

I gasp.

"This body, this mind, even this soul—all mine. I've already killed for it. I'd do it again a thousand times over." He strokes slowly, heat sizzling through the deepest parts of me. "And I'll do whatever I want with you. I won't force you. That's not what this is." His finger slides lower, delving into my wetness, and then back up again, circling my clit. "This is a lesson." His thick length presses against my ass, and dark sparks burst in my mind. "One that I should have already taught you." He bites my earlobe, and an unbidden moan rises from my throat. "Pleasure and pain. I offer both. You will *take* both. And you will trust me to give them in whatever amounts I see fit." His teeth migrate to my neck, biting down like a wild animal holding its female in place.

I struggle to catch my breath as he stops circling and starts strumming my clit. His cock grinds against my ass, his hips moving in time with the maddening strokes of his fingers. Everything inside me tightens, twirling around him. I've come before, to my own fingers, but it has never been like this. A punishing need for release, a desperate rush toward ecstasy.

"Please."

He bites harder, almost breaking the skin, and I cry out, unsure if it's pleasure or pain that gives me voice. My mind stops and focuses on the building tension, the intense need, the primal craving to let go.

But then his fingers disappear.

I let out my breath in a huff. He still grinds against me. "Do you want me to make you come, little lamb?"

Everything goes blank, my body chasing after what he'd offered. I hate myself, but I don't lie to him. "Yes."

His weight lifts. "Turn over."

I push over onto my back and stare up at him, a dark god with hell in his eyes.

"Spread your legs."

I'm damned to obey. No, I *want* to obey.

"Good lamb." His lashes lower, and he drops to his knees. Gripping my hips, he yanks me toward him. "Tell me you want me to eat your virgin pussy."

I bite my lip, the truth stuck in my throat.

A jolt and a sting rush through me. I yelp and try to sit up. His wide palm on my chest pushes me back down.

"You slapped me." I grip his wrist. "You slapped me *down there*."

Smack. I jump and squirm as he slaps me again. A heady feeling, one that shoots me even higher than his fingers, rushes through me.

"This is for disobeying." He hits me again, right on my clit.

I try to close my legs, but his broad shoulders prevent it.

"This too." Another slap.

I'm writhing, desperate to escape or something worse, to surrender.

"Tell me you want to come on my mouth." He rears back and delivers a stinging slap that brings tears to my eyes.

His gaze burns into mine as he rears back again.

"Yes." I choke out. "Yes, please."

With a guttural noise he leans forward and opens his mouth wide. I jerk when his tongue licks me from bottom to top. It feels wrong, overwhelming, and utterly addictive.

"Adam!" I grip the blanket.

He slides his tongue up and focuses on my clit, that little bundle of nerves that seems to light up my entire body. "Eyes on me."

I stare down at him, my breasts heaving as I try to catch my breath and fail. His tongue is a weapon, one he wields with delicious efficiency. He slices through my modesty, my fear, and goes straight for the kill. I can't separate myself from this moment, can't escape his clutches, and I don't want to.

My hips move as his fingers dig into my skin. He isn't gentle, doesn't give me any reprieve from his lashing tongue. Wet noises bounce off the walls, and I'm too high to be embarrassed. High on him.

When I thrust my hips against his mouth, he groans, the sound vibrating through me, adding to the maelstrom of tension between my thighs. I've never felt arousal like this. It's so intense it hovers on the verge of nausea.

I close my eyes, but gasp and open them when he pinches my clit with his teeth.

"Watch me." He licks his lips. "I want to see your face when I tear you apart."

"Oh my—"

He focuses on that one spot of white heat, his tongue whipping faster. My legs shake, and everything shrinks—all of my thoughts and emotions folding in on themselves until I'm nothing more than a pulsing kernel of need. And he knows just how to make me pop.

I can't hold it back, my entire body tensing. My pleasure bursts on his tongue and floods my body like a tidal wave. I thought I'd come before. I never had, not until Adam Monroe was between my thighs. Thoughts disappear as I let out a raw cry, my body contracting and relaxing to the tempo of his tongue. My orgasm isn't linear. It's a roller-coaster, loops and drops that rob me of my balance and keep me guessing. I can only breathe again at the end when the train returns to the station, slow and languid, it's occupants sated and exhilarated.

"Naughty little lamb. Next time I'm going to record those obscene noises you make." He gives me one more lick and stands, gazing down at my boneless body with animal satisfaction. Leaning down, he runs his fingers along my slit. I shake at his touch, the sensation too much. He brings them to his lips and smears my wetness there, then licks the rest from his fingertips.

Oh my god.

My eyes travel south to the bulge in his pants, and I swallow hard. For the first time in my life, a thrill goes through me at the thought of pleasuring a man with my mouth. But Adam isn't just any man. I know that now.

He's my weakness, the one thing that could derail my search for the truth.

"Do you want it?" He runs the heel of his palm along the thick ridge.

"I-I—"

"I'll tell you what I want. My cock so deep in your mouth that you can't breathe, that you can't do anything except suck and pray that I pull back before you suffocate." His guttural voice strokes the jagged parts of my desire. "Tears in your eyes, your hands gripping my thighs, and fear. So much fear."

I sit up, my body trembling. "You want me afraid?"

He tilts my chin up so I meet his gaze. "Fear that you love it. Fear of how filthy you are when you're on your knees for me. Afraid of your own wants. Afraid of how far you'll go to please me and yourself. That's what I want to see. What I *will* see." Dropping his hand, he stalks around the bed and snatches up his shirt and jacket.

When he leaves, slamming the door behind him, I stare after him. His footsteps quiet and disappear, and the girl I share a wall with cries quietly on the other side. A chill sinks into my bones, and I yank up the blanket, wrapping it around me and trying to understand everything that just happened.

He gave. I shake my head. He didn't take anything from me. Not like I expected. Not like in the past. Adam had pushed me, showed me the extent of his control, but instead of taking advantage, he *gave*.

I lie back and stare at the beams in the ceiling, though Adam plays like a movie before my eyes. When a scream cuts across the hall and dies out, I try to shake myself out of it. This place is hell, and Adam is just another one of its devils.

Maybe he gave tonight, but he's a taker. They all are. It's just another mindfuck. He doesn't have to do these things to me, to anyone. He enjoys it. He's a sadist just like all the rest. I close my eyes and curl into a ball.

My mind repeats the sins of this place, of Adam. But my body is forever changed and so, I fear, is my heart.

CHAPTER 26

ADAM

*S*unday's church service begins with the usual prayer and exhortation for the Holy Ghost to inhabit the space as the Prophet takes the stage. The sanctuary is bedecked in Christmas finery, huge garlands hanging from each level of balconies and draped across the front of the stage. Heavenly Ministries spares no expense for the season, setting up a live manger scene out front that runs around the clock every day, replete with a crying or sleeping baby.

The seasonal décor only reminds me of the impending winter solstice. Preparations are underway, but three weeks isn't much time. Newell was half-assing it, but I can't do the same. My father expects me to fail, to go small. I intend to knock his fucking block off with the spectacle. Not that it will bring me much comfort. But, for once, I have something in common with normal father-son relationships. Or, at least I think it's normal to want to blow up the old man's shitty expectations. Maybe it's twisted, too.

Delilah kneels in her customary spot, eyes down, hands folded. Ghostly in her white gown, she seems to hesitate between this world and the next. An ephemeral spirit, one I will slowly darken with each touch of my hand, each word from my lips. I am the poison that will drain her spirit, the wolf that will rend her limb from limb.

Those cold facts didn't stop me from tasting her last night. I shift from one foot to the other as my cock wakes up. She does that to me, just the thought of her, the way she looks on her knees. It took all my self-control to tear myself away from her after I feasted on her cunt. I made it home, only to jerk it for all of thirty seconds before spending on my stomach as I lay in bed, the video of me between her legs on replay. I wish I still had her taste on my lips. But I'd get my wish this evening.

"—in the coming war." I cock my head as my father goes off script.

"You see, there is a war coming, my friends. One that we haven't prepared for. But it's one we must win."

Noah elbows me and mouths *what the fuck?*

I shrug. This is new. The teleprompter is stopped on the words "We must pray to our Heavenly Father for a prosperous..."

Those words don't come from Dad's mouth.

"The fallen of this world will seek to destroy us. The good people here—the heathens out there want you dead."

Some voices of agreement rise from the packed house. The rest of them are silent, staring wide-eyed as my father preaches the end times.

"Terrorists, feminists, Jews, atheists, Muslims, illegal immigrants, socialists, Black Lives Matter, communists, baby-killers, the godless who are so depraved they won't even say the words 'Merry Christmas' anymore, and even worse, transgenders who mutilate themselves and want to do the same to your children, the gays who prey on the weak—"

More angry shouts echo in the sanctuary, and the hackles on my neck rise.

"All of these are forces of evil. Every single one of them wants to hurt us. To hurt *you*." He points to the congregation. "Bobby Williams. Your daughter, Ivy. Right now, there are men out in the fallen world who covet her. Who look at her 15-year-old body and think lascivious thoughts."

I stifle a dry laugh. My father has coveted Bobby's daughter since she was twelve.

He points to another congregant. "Penny Barnes, you're a widow raising three kids. How can a single mother possibly be able to fight off the demons of this world when she's out there alone?"

Penny shakes her head and bursts into tears.

"That's right, Penny. The world breaks us down, tears at our souls. It isn't godly. They say being conservative, being Christian, is a sin. Well I say they will burn in hell, and we will go to the Lord's promised land."

Shouts of approval shake the stage. Noah gives me a look that carries various shades of "oh, shit." I turn to Delilah. Her gaze is on me, her gray eyes wide as my father continues slinging fiery rhetoric to an increasingly agitated crowd.

But my father is a showman. And he can work a crowd like a ventriloquist with one hand up the dummy's ass.

His voice softens, his tone growing calm. "God has spoken to me."

The crowd relents as if the tempest has abated, the surface of the water growing still, rapt.

"As the Gospel of St. James reminds us, 'The wisdom that comes from heaven is first of all pure; then peace-loving, considerate, submissive, full of mercy and good fruit, impartial and sincere.'" My father looks skyward, one hand raised to the God he imagines above the clouds. "But God has told me of the wicked beyond our gates who have no love for peace. He has told me that destruction is coming, and that we must prepare. Just as he told Noah, He's warned me of the flood of sin, evil, and worldly terrors. But He also told me there is one way we can fight this. Only *one* way."

A reverent hush has fallen over the crowd, all eyes turned toward the stage or one of the many huge screens projecting the Prophet.

"We must stand together, my friends. We must be as one. Only by joining with each other and holding the line can we beat back this darkness. Pooling our love and our resources—"

"And there it is," I whisper. "The money grab hidden in prophecy."

"...in this together. We must stick together to fight the evils of this world. That's why, as some of you know, we are constructing our own community. Monroeville will be built in phases, and the first one is estimated to be completed in only two months' time. This will be a place where your children can play in the street, stay out catching fireflies in the twilight hours, and you will never have to worry about one of the godless stealing them away from you, hurting them, or worse. You will be safe. They will be safe. And the best part? The housing is free."

A cheer swells through the masses. I hold onto Delilah's shock as she glances at the Prophet and then back to me as if to say 'did you know about this?'

My father's tone brightens further, light through a dense dark cloud. "Anyone who wants to live in Monroeville, can. We will build until all the faithful are safe inside. Our schools will grow, our people will thrive, and we will be a shining beacon to the rest of the world. Christ is alive, and He is here, in us, in *you*."

As the crowd roars with approval, Noah says, "I thought we weren't rolling this out for a while."

I shrug. "I guess he wants them paying their dues sooner rather than later. And, at this point, they won't even balk at turning over half of their earnings to Heavenly."

"Ah, the fine print." Noah wrinkles his nose. "Maybe they'll lose faith when they see that little addendum."

"It won't matter to them. Hell, a lot of them already double tithe anyway. They'll sign on the dotted line, and then Heavenly will own them." Just like it owns Noah and me. I return to Delilah, always drawn back to her light. Even though I know that Heavenly owns her, that my father owns her, I still entertain the fantasy that she's mine. That I can keep her safe from everyone but me. It's a fiction, but one I indulge in even now as she searches my face for some sort of reassurance. She believes that I can give it, and I want her to believe it, even though it's a lie as big as the ones my father is telling.

"They'll be broke, living on property they don't own, but they'll be ever so *safe*," Noah sneers.

Sometimes, he reminds me of me, and in those moments, I worry about him. But at least maybe he's waking up to the rising bullshit.

"All I hear is more shit for me to do." I'd started working on the contracts for the housing with our lawyer, but as my father is already setting the process into motion, I'll need to front-burner that. I'll also have to move some money around to make way for the new "donations." Heavenly is a perfect conduit to launder money since it's a non-taxable church, but large influxes of cash can still raise eyebrows. I'll need to prepare new accounts to accept the tithes, keep the trail clean, and funnel most of it into my father's off-shore accounts. I pinch the bridge of my nose as a tension headache threatens.

The Prophet finally moves on to follow the teleprompter, smoothly picking up where he left off. The crowd falls right into step with him, never sensing that the walls are building up around them. They'll be closed in, buried alive, and beholden to the Prophet for their next mouthful of food or breath of air.

Delilah studies the floor once again, head down in what looks from most angles like reverence. Even though I can sense her mind is racing, replaying my father's words. Maybe she's impervious to his spell, but it doesn't matter. She's still just another lamb to the slaughter, and I'm the one who'll wield the blade.

CHAPTER 27

DELILAH

*I*t's TV Tuesday, and the Maidens spread out in the ratty recliners and couches as the screen flickers to life. Abigail keeps her muttering to a minimum this time, seeming to have gotten the hang of how it all works.

I glance at Sharon's empty chair, and foreboding falls over me like a shroud. Where did they take her? My stomach turns as I imagine the sort of tortures they might visit on her for her rebellion. I wonder if Georgia was like Sharon—brave, ready to fight for her freedom. Or was she docile, accepting of the constant shit shoveled by the Spinners and the Prophet. Who was her Protector? Adam's face flashes through my mind, but I push it away. Whether he was or wasn't doesn't matter. What matters is who took her life. But progress on that front is slim. I have even more questions than I did when I walked into this mindfuck.

The light blinks, pulling me from my thoughts. A younger Prophet appears on screen, his posture relaxed as he sits on a brown leather couch. He smiles and gives off a Mr. Rogers vibe as he invites us to "sit and have a talk" with him about life at the Cloister.

"Now I know some of you may be having doubts."

Sarah snorts.

"But I'm here to assure you that everything is going according to God's plan. The things you are learning from the Spinners and your Protectors are the guideposts that will lead you through your life as a lamb of God. You are the future, the purest hopes that Heavenly Ministries has for a bountiful life on earth as well as in heaven..."

I tune him out, my mind once again floating to his son. Adam hasn't been back to my room. Two nights have passed with me waiting on the bed, wondering which one of him will come through the door—the tormentor or the lover. And when he didn't show up, I hated the disappointment I felt. To assuage the self-loathing, I tell myself that it's natural I take comfort in him. He's the only one that's truly allowed to get close to me, so it makes sense that I want him. But, of course, this is just another part of the mindfuck that is the Cloister. The conditions force you to cling to your abuser, because there is no one else. I've only been here a little more than a week, and my mind is already a swamp of regret and confusion.

My attention fades even further as Chastity walks into the room and whispers into Abigail's ear. I need to get alone with her again, to question her, to find out if she was talking about Georgia. She *had* to be. Abigail nods along with whatever Chastity is telling her, then both women walk out together.

Once the door clicks, Sarah hops up and walks to the front of the room, her face lit by the projector light. "Enough of this propaganda bullshit." She waves at the board behind her. "We need to discuss what we're going to do about this hell we're in."

"We are where we're meant to be." Mary's gentle voice overlays with the Prophet's.

"Okay, Mary's a goner. I knew that from the second she pissed on me."

Susannah claps her hand over her mouth to stifle a laugh.

Sarah's tone hardens. "And I know right this second, in your little faith-addled brain, you're thinking about telling on me. But, darling Mary, if you do, I promise I'll do much worse to you than a golden shower."

Mary fidgets in her seat, but says nothing.

Sarah moves to the side, the Prophet's crotch superimposed on her face. "We didn't sign up for this. None of us. Not even Mary over there. We're being abused, raped, and broken so the Prophet can sell us off to the highest bidder or worse." She runs a hand through her dark hair.

"I don't know what the worse is just yet, but I'm assuming that going home with some rich prick is like, the grand prize. The opposite end of that, well, I can't imagine."

I know where we go. The Chapel. But I'm not about to stop Sarah's forward momentum.

"So, does anyone see Sharon in here? No. They took her after she tried to escape. Does anyone know where they took her? I can assure you it's not somewhere any of us want to be. And if we stay here, we'll only get more and more damaged. That's what they want." She glances at the door. "They'll be back any second. Look, if you aren't with me, fine. But if you are, you don't have to say anything. Just let me know one way or another. Keep yourselves safe. And if anyone is even *thinking* of ratting me out—" She glares at Mary "—just know that I will find out who it was, and I will visit so much pain on you that you'll think I'm a Protector." She darts up the steps as the door opens and Abigail returns to the projector.

"These lessons are necessary and set you apart from the godless whores who thrive outside Heavenly's gates..." The Prophet's voice comes to the fore once again, promising reason and protection in a place that has neither.

We don't have lunch. A few of the women grumble as the Spinner leads us past the dining hall without stopping.

We walk straight to the training room and disrobe, then spend two hours taking turns with a flogger. Unfortunately for me, I get paired up with Mary.

Sarah raises a brow at me as I drop to the floor and the Spinner instructs Mary—over the rumble of my stomach —how to hold the flogger and swing from the elbow.

I flinch as the first strike whips across my bare bottom, but am relieved to find that Mary is a light touch with the leather. She swats me several times, the pain faint and bearable. I think about how I would feel if it were Adam holding the flogger, abrading my flesh again and again until I begged for the soft touch of his tongue. Heat seeps into my veins, and I switch my concentration to something else, quick. Bad things—like the women at the Chapel, their degradation, and the senator there who grabbed me. My blood cools, and I take the hits without complaint.

"Swap." The Spinner claps her hands, and the row of Maidens stands and switches.

Mary hands me the flogger, but the Spinner walks down the row and switches them out with fresh ones. At least hygiene is important, if dignity isn't.

"Get to work." The Spinner claps her hands.

I use my wrist to fan the leather strips along Mary's backside. She tenses at first, then loosens her shoulders when I go easy on her. A few more hits, and I'm getting into a rhythm, focusing on my movements and ignoring the gnawing hunger in my gut. Down the row, one of the Maidens is going to town on poor Susannah. Even the Spinner tells her to take it down a notch, because "more intensive training comes later, once we all have the technique correct." Naturally.

The training room door opens, and the Head Spinner walks in. Her hands are joined in front of her as she strolls along the row of Maidens. I silently will her to keep walking past me, to ignore that I'm even here. But, no. Of course not.

She stops right behind me. "Poor form, Delilah."

My arm falters, but I swing anyway.

"Pathetic, really." She moves to my back, her starched dress pressing against my skin, and grabs my wrist. "Like this," she hisses in my ear. Pulling back, she swings my arm forward, the leather slapping against Mary's backside. She jolts but doesn't make a sound.

"Harder." Grace pulls my arm back farther and swings even harder.

Mary lets out a cry as red streaks appear on her pale skin. This is nothing like the other Spinners taught us.

"That's what I want to hear." Grace releases me and steps back. "Hit her again."

Mary is tensed, her back quivering from the strain. I strike her, but nowhere near as hard as Grace. The room is quiet now, all eyes on me.

280

"I see." Grace retreats to the wall and drags down a short whip. "Either you do this right, or I'll *show* you how."

Blood rushes to my head and sound becomes thick in my ears as I imagine the damage that whip could do.

"Hit. Her." She slides the leather through her palm, her light eyes on me.

I pull back and put a little more force into it. Mary jerks, but doesn't make a sound.

Grace clucks her tongue. "I'm afraid that won't do. Step back and I'll—"

"I can do it."

Her blonde brows furrow, then smooth out. "Go ahead."

Mary glances at me over her shoulder. I mouth "I'm sorry" to her, but she doesn't respond, just lets her head hang between her shoulders.

Bile churns up my throat, but I swallow it down and draw the flogger back. With a vicious swing, I land the leather with a resounding slap.

Mary screams.

Grace smiles. "Again."

"But I—"

"Shall I do it?" She threatens with the whip.

"No." I fight the tears that try to well, and look down at the raw, red skin along Mary's backside. *You're saving her*, I tell myself. The flogger is better than the whip. It has to be better than that.

I swing again. Mary's cry cuts through all my layers and draws blood from my soul.

"Much better." Grace returns the whip to the wall. "Proper form is important, ladies." With that, she leaves the room and locks the door behind her.

I drop to my knees next to Mary. "Are you okay?"

Her tears make soft *plop* noises onto the mat. "I'm okay. It's for the Prophet, so it's worth it."

I take no comfort in her words, and remorse threatens to choke me. It only gets worse when I look up and find several sets of eyes on me, distrust glowing in them like dark embers.

After training, hungry and exhausted, we make our way back to the dorm. A Spinner reminds us that we're expected to be on our best behavior for our weekly night with the Prophet, then tells us to shower and pray.

I enter my room and stifle a yell when something moves on my bed. Flicking the light on, I find Adam stretched out, his hands behind his head, his dark eyelashes fluttering open.

"Close the door." His voice is thick with sleep.

"How long have you been here?" I push the door closed and walk over to him, sitting next to him instead of on the floor. "And where were you last night? And the night before that?"

"So many questions." He grabs my arm and yanks me next to him, my body crashing against his as he wraps his arm around me.

"Unf." My face rests on his chest, warmth bleeding from him and into me. I'm too tired to protest, and I inhale him —some sort of tobacco mixed with a hint of soap.

"I've been busy, little lamb. My father is moving fast on getting the faithful onto the Compound. He makes quick decisions based on his vision from God. I do all the fucking legwork to make his *prophecy* come true."

His hand snakes down my side and rests on my hip. "Miss me?"

"No."

"Liar." He squeezes my ass.

"What was training today?"

I close my eyes and try not to see the welts across Mary's backside. "Flogging."

"One of my favorites." His hand slides back and forth across my ass, then his fingers begin to crinkle the fabric, inching my dress up bit by bit. "Did you enjoy it?"

"No."

"You will when I get my turn." His bare hand touches my skin, his fingertips skating across my surface.

"And when is that?"

"You already want my pain. I knew I made the right choice when I picked you."

"I was just asking a question."

"You ask far too many questions. Even Jez told me so."

I stiffen. "She told you about that?"

He laughs, the sound low and dark and pulling me down like a lure at the bottom of a cold lake. "There isn't a move you make that I don't know about."

Chills ripple across my skin, but I can't tell if they're from his words or touch.

"What did you think of our little Chapel?"

"I hate it." Honesty is stupid and will get me into trouble. But a few truths here and there can't hurt. At least that's what I tell myself.

"I thought you might."

"Will I end up there?"

"No." His answer is quick, his grip on my ass verging on painful. "Don't worry about that."

"What makes them different? Why do some of the Maidens go there?"

"You can't ask questions like that, little lamb. It'll get you disciplined."

"You want to discipline me?" I dance across the thin ice, aware of the frigid water underneath.

"Yes." He pulls me on top of him and hikes my dress up to my waist. "Straddle me."

I relax my thighs and my legs spread around his narrow hips. When my bare pussy touches his hard length through his pants, I dig my nails into his abs.

"I don't just want to punish you." He grips my hips and rubs me back and forth against him. "I want to fuck you raw," he grits out. "I want to take your virginity and wear it like a fucking badge."

My hips move along with him, grinding against his cock, pink flooding my cheeks as I realize my wetness is darkening his pants.

"Take it off." He yanks at my dress.

I pull it over my head. His hands are on my breasts before it hits the floor. He leans up and claims one nipple in his mouth as I continue riding him despite knowing how wrong it all is. I can't stop. I want this one release, this ecstasy that only Adam can give me.

He lies back and slaps one of my breasts. I'm surprised, but when he does it again, my toes curl.

"My lamb likes the pain." He twists my nipples, sending desire ricocheting through me.

I gasp, and he grips my hips, dragging me up his body until I'm on top of his face. When he licks me, I grip the headboard, unrestrained need spilling out of me in a moan.

He slaps my ass and buries his face between my legs, his dark stubble rubbing against my sensitive skin as his tongue tours every secret spot I have. Another slap on my ass and I'm moving my hips to his rhythm. When I try to let up on him, fearing he can't breathe, he hits my ass harder and yanks me down.

"Adam!" I can't breathe when he goes after my clit, his tongue wicked and perfect and too much but not yet enough.

I grind on him recklessly, letting my hips tell me what to do. Each surge sends pulsing heat between my thighs. When they begin to shake, he slaps my ass again, hard. I thought I had time. I don't. The pain crosses with the pleasure, and I fall into it, my orgasm shaking me as the waves roll and roll and roll until I can finally take a breath. My hips still, my body languid, and my mind buzzing, I sit back toward his chest.

He grabs me and throws me down, then nestles between my legs. "Fuck." He stares at my bare, wet pussy and reaches down to unbuckle his belt.

We aren't supposed to be doing this, and I shouldn't want it. Shouldn't want *him*. But when he frees his cock from his pants, I lift my hips, needing to feel his skin.

"Don't." His low voice, barely scratching through his throat, carries more tension than a high wire.

He sits back, the pulse in his neck rapid-firing as he surveys my body, then holds my gaze. "Don't move. Don't make a sound. If you do, I'll fuck you. I'll have to fuck you or I'll lose my goddamn mind. But I can't." He strokes himself slowly.

I stare down at it, the smooth head, the way his hand wraps around the thick shaft.

"Fuck, little lamb. I can feel your eyes on it."

In that moment, I want him inside me. I want to feel him surging so deep that I can't think of anything except him.

He strokes faster, his fingertips playing along the bottom of his length, while he balances on his other fist. "I'm going to coat you in me."

I spread my legs wider, and he groans. "Don't fucking move!"

He strokes a few more times, then lets out a low grunt. Hot come splashes against my bare flesh, and he empties himself on me, his low noises sending sizzles of heat burning through me.

When he sits back, I look down at the aftermath, the obscene, erotic view of his mark on my innocent skin. He can't seem to look away either. We both come down, our breaths slowing, our hearts thumping instead of racing.

He leans over and uses my dress to wipe me clean, and then himself. Zipping up, he rises from the bed and fastens his belt.

"You're going?" I can't process my feelings. The hunger, the exhaustion, the fear—all of it has screwed my judgment.

"Have to." He turns his back and strides away. "See you at the Prophet's audience."

When the door slams, I turn over on my side and curl into a ball. *What am I doing?* That question echoes back and forth across my mind.

Even when there's a knock at my door telling me it's time to see the Prophet, the question still has no answer.

CHAPTER 28

ADAM

I took it too far this afternoon. It was too close. *I* was too close to the point of no return. But fuck, I was strung out from two days straight of bullshit, no sleep, and no end in sight.

Noah joins me at the entrance to the Temple. He looks almost as bad as I do, the golden boy glow faded, his clothes rumpled, and his eyes bloodshot. "I really don't want to sit through this shit right now." He unbuttons his shirt as we walk.

"Skipping isn't an option." I wish it was. Watching my father lord over his crop of Maidens isn't at the top of my 'for shits and giggles' list. Then again, I want to see what he does to Delilah so I can cover over every touch from him with one of my own. If I could have left my seed all over her virgin cunt, I would have. It would be perfect to see the look on my father's face when he realized what I'd done. But that would have resulted in discipline for both

Delilah and me. I can take as many lashes as my father can toss at me, but Delilah doesn't deserve punishment, especially if it meant she'd be sent to the Rectory.

"Wake the fuck up, asshole." Noah thumps me on the upper arm.

"Do you need a Snickers?" I unbutton my shirt. "You miss your afternoon snack or something?"

"I'm not hangry." He shrugs. "Okay, maybe a little. But I'm just tired of this shit."

"Welcome to the club."

"But we should, you know, follow what Dad says." His tone loses some of its edge. "He's the Prophet and all."

"Still got that faith, huh?" I don't like to fault my brother much, but that one thing—his misplaced belief in our father—rankles.

"I have to hold onto something, man. Otherwise..."

Otherwise he'd let himself feel the heat around us, see the fires of hell closing in, and smell the scent of our burning flesh. I couldn't argue with that.

"Let's get it over with." We follow Protector Gunn into the sacred circle, my father already flying high on his throne in the middle of the room. His coke habit is out of control. Good. I hope it kills the bastard.

I take my spot and kneel. The other Protectors are already here and in position. Good little lapdogs, each of them. But why wouldn't they be? They get treats all the time, fresh young girls in white, a new one each year.

"Why are you looking at me like that, son?" My father glowers at me.

I didn't realize I'd been looking at him at all. My subconscious probably had me staring daggers. "No offense intended."

"None intended, huh? Is that right?" Belligerence lives in his voice. "Well, I took offense. What do you have to say about that?"

Noah rocks forward. "Dad—"

"I'm not talking to you, Noah. I'm talking to the son-of-a-bitch you call your brother."

My fingers curl into fists as he says it, and I know Noah is just as angry as I am. Our mother is the gentlest soul on this godforsaken Compound. And she's paid dearly for it.

The doors open, and Grace struts in, her gaze glancing off me before landing on my father. "We are here for your blessing, Prophet." She even does a little curtsey.

"We'll finish this later." My father's icy demeanor melts as he turns toward the doors. "Bring them in, by all means." Now jovial, he opens his arms in welcome. A spider welcomes the fly with the most perfect of manners.

The girls walk in, already stripped bare. I search through them to find my little lamb. So pale, she's striking even in the midst of a dozen other beauties. They're warier this time, but sit in front of my father as instructed.

When the Spinners bring the poisoned food, only one among them reaches for the fruit. Delilah looks at me with wide eyes. She'll try to resist, but it won't work. The Spinners starved them today to ensure a good audience with my father. They will eat, because they have no choice.

"My darling Maidens." My father stands and walks among them. "I welcome you here once again for our weekly congress. How I've missed you all."

He sits next to one with dark hair, bruises darkening the light brown skin on one cheek. "You are blessed among women. What's your name, child?"

She remains still, her face impassive. "Sarah." No inflection in her tone, but something in her eyes tells me she's a bit cagier than the others.

"Lovely Sarah." He strokes down her arm, then cups her breast. "I've been waiting for you. And you are safe here with me. Always." He rubs his thumb over her nipple, and her expression hardens even more, an impenetrable shell. "Now, eat."

She finally looks him in the eye, then gives a slight shake of her head.

"Oh, shit," Noah breathes. "Oh *shit*."

"He won't do it here." I watch as my father's mask remains in place. He reaches for a plate of grapes and plucks one, then forces it between her lips and into her mouth.

A single tear rolls down her cheek as my father waits for her to chew and swallow. When it's done, he releases her and turns to the other Maidens. "Eat and drink. It is my gift to you. I love each and every one of you. Everything about you is holy to me. Your beauty—" He rises and continues to walk among them "—your grace, your perfect obedience."

They all eat and drink, giving in to their hunger and the sheer power that the Prophet wields over them. Even Delilah succumbs, her eyelids growing heavy as the LSD seeps into her bloodstream and clouds her mind. She lies back on the pillows, her gaze focused on the gilded upside down cross above the throne. A symbol of our obedience to the Father of Fire, the emblem glitters in the low light.

Noah leans toward me. "Is he going to pick one this time?"

"He already has." I watch the dark-haired girl who'd denied my father. Her fate is sealed.

The Prophet stalks among them, then sits again, a Maiden on either side of him.

He pulls them close, then positions them so they face each other. "Nothing is sweeter than the purest fruit." With my father's urging, the Maidens kiss. He watches for a while, then takes their hands and places them on each other. Before long, moans rise from their throats and they lay on the pillows, tangled in each other.

"At least we get some entertainment this time." Noah sits back on his haunches when Dad isn't looking.

Pleased with his work, my father moves to another set of Maidens and encourages the same behavior, even pushing one onto her back and urging the other to eat her out. I tense when he reaches for Delilah, pulling her into a sitting position. He kisses her forehead, then motions another Maiden over to her.

Everything inside me tenses as Delilah receives a kiss from another Maiden. My father moves along before urging them to baser acts, but Delilah allows the Maiden to lay her down, still kissing her, one of her hands roving across Delilah's breasts. My cock becomes painfully hard as I imagine it's me doing the exploring, the touching. I know how heavenly her skin feels, how soft her breasts are, the nipples perfect for biting. The other Maiden runs her hand through Delilah's hair, and I want to yank the harpy away from my little lamb. But I can't. Just as with everything else here, I'm forced to stay in line.

I watch them for ten more minutes until the other Maiden is pulled into a threesome and Delilah is left to herself on the pillows. Relief pulses through me, but it's short-lived. These orgies are a weekly occurrence, and Delilah can't escape every time. She'll be drugged and defiled, and there's nothing I can do to stop it.

She lies still for a moment, then cranes her neck until we make eye contact. I hold her there, as if my gaze is some sort of force, until her lashes fall and she tumbles into sleep.

The scene continues for another hour, until my father wants their attention back on him. He calls them up to his throne so he can prey on each Maiden individually. I'm relieved when he doesn't give Delilah any special attention. It just means he hasn't noticed that this one is different to me. If he ever did ... I decide to save those violent thoughts for later.

When each one of the Maidens is looking at my father with dreamy eyes, seeing the Prophet instead of the man, he is satisfied and allows them to return to the Cloister. It's genius, really. Ensure that the Spinners and the Protectors abuse them every waking moment, then bring them to the Temple where the Prophet offers food, love, and empty promises that sound filled to the brim with hope and solid as a block of granite.

"Grace, I'd like to meet with Sarah alone," he calls as the women are exiting.

"Yes, Prophet." A smirking Grace pulls Sarah aside.

The girl is still in the warm bubble of the drug, her limbs heavy as Grace walks her back to my father.

I don't close my eyes. It would be so easy to do just that. But I don't. Because I'm here, and I'm not going to do a thing to stop what's about to happen. I deserve to see it, to hear it, to fucking feel it deep in my gut—the wrongness of it.

My father pushes the girl onto the pillows on her stomach. I can't see her face, but I watch her anyway. Because it's what I deserve. Grace stands just in front of her, ready to grab her if need be. He pulls her hips up to him.

When she cries out in pain, I keep watching. Grace grabs her hair and shoves her back, keeping her still while my father ruts on her like a goddamn beast. I keep watching. When he finishes, stands, and then kicks her in the stomach, I keep watching. When he spits on her, I keep watching.

"You are nothing but a filthy whore. All women are. You don't say no to your Prophet. You do what I say, when I say it. Perfect obedience to me is the only way a bitch like you can get into heaven. You will obey, or you will burn."

Already in the fetal position, she doesn't say anything. But she knows what just happened to her. The same way I do.

I am tainted by her violation, and I feel it. Another stain on my soul. Another reason to hate my father.

"And you." He turns to me, his robe still in disarray. "I'm not done. Your willfulness has guaranteed that I pay your mother a visit this evening."

"Dad, please—" Noah tries to get to his feet.

"Sit down!" His voice thunders around the room. "I will do what I must to keep this ministry alive. To keep my oaths to God and the Father of Fire. You will *obey* me, damn you!"

He's left no room, no way to stop whatever horror he intends to visit on our mother. Noah and I are supposed to accept it as an appropriate punishment for whatever slight my father feels—whether real or imagined. Just as with the women, he expects perfect obedience from his sons. I bow my head and pretend to give it.

What he doesn't know is that I'll kill him for this. For all of it.

CHAPTER 29

DELILAH

First thing the next morning, we all settle into the TV room for more edification from the Prophet. My mind still has a thin film coating it from the drugs. I try to remember everything that happened the previous night, but all I can see is sparks of light, neon travelling from me to the other Maidens, and a straight line of white-hot energy shooting across the crimson floor and binding me to Adam. I'd never done drugs before the Cloister, and I already wanted to stop. But if the starving us on Tuesday was any indication, we would be forced to partake in the weekly ritual.

Abigail flips on the projector, and we're greeted with Miriam Roberts in a white skirt suit with red-bottomed heels and a too-white smile. "Maidens, it is so lovely to be able to speak with you today. The Prophet was kind enough to ask me to share a few words about my wonderful experience at the Cloister." A woman in black maid's attire sets an iced tea on the small table to Miriam's right, then hurries away. "Now, I realize the first few weeks are the hardest. You feel like you're in the wrong place, or perhaps that the Prophet has forsaken you. But I can assure you that this couldn't be further from the truth." Another poised smile. She blathers on, and I cast a glance at Sarah's empty chair.

Where is she? I try to recall last night. Was she with us on the bus back to the Cloister? Try as I might, I can't remember.

"...your education is preparing you to be in perfect obedience to your husband. This is the way to please the Prophet and God. The world is a terrifying place. The Prophet is the only one who can keep you safe, so give thanks to him at every opportunity." She sips her drink. "Now that you've fully invested in what we do here at the Cloister, it's time to talk about your future."

I perk up at this.

She smiles again and folds her hands in her lap. "Being a Maiden is more than just learning how to be in perfect obedience to your future husband. That is important, of course." She leans forward, looking directly into the camera. "But your relationship to the Prophet is far more important than any other in your life. Pleasing the Prophet is your reason for being here, and he's the reason you are chosen above all other women." She nods, agreeing with herself. "There are many ways you can serve the Prophet. The Prophet will decide the correct one for you when the time comes. But, no matter where you go, you must always remember that the Prophet is the head of your life, the head of your household, and the head of your heart. Whatever information you learn from the people around you—even if you find it trivial—must be reported back to the Prophet. And this is doubly important for Maidens such as myself. Powerful men hold even more powerful secrets. The Prophet needs to know these secrets in order to keep you safe."

Ideas begin to click into place as she continues her propaganda. I already knew that some of the Maidens went on to marry politicians and rich businessmen, but I didn't realize the Prophet was using these connections as a clandestine spy network.

I lean back, digesting this information and trying to decipher what it might mean about Georgia's fate. Did she cross the wrong man in a quest for information? I'd originally suspected the Prophet of her murder, especially given the ritual desecration of her body, but could it have been a smokescreen to hide an even more insidious plot?

We sit through her smooth propaganda for an hour or so —the cogs in my mind clanking and spinning the entire time—then break for the training room. It's my day on the table, so I assume the position as Abigail applies the enema. I don't even feel the humiliation anymore. I just accept it. Maybe all the brainwashing is working on me.

"Hey," Susannah whispers from beside me.

"Yeah?"

"Do you know where Sarah is?"

I glance back at Abigail who is busy at the sink. "No. Haven't seen her." And I'm ashamed to admit that I was too preoccupied with thoughts of Georgia to focus on Sarah's absence.

"Shit." She props her head on her hand. "Something's happened."

The same gut-churning worry I felt when she didn't show up for TV time reappears. "Do you remember last night? I can't."

Her cheeks flame. "Yeah. You don't remember anything?"

"Just light."

"You don't remember kissing me?"

My jaw drops. "We kissed?"

"Yeah."

"Why aren't we in trouble?"

"The Prophet made us do it. All of us were—" She falls silent as Abigail putters around behind us, then returns to the sink. "Doing stuff together. Like, forbidden stuff. But it was all okay. Because—" She shrugs "—he told us to do it."

"Sarah?" I clench my teeth together as Abigail pushes the warm liquid inside me.

"Squeeze, dear. Just keep it in for as long as you can." She pats my ass, which isn't helpful, then moves on to the Maiden on my left.

"Her, too. But when we left, she stayed behind."

My stomach drops. "That's bad."

"I know." She clams up as another Spinner walks over and eyes us.

I try to plot a way to see Chastity. She'll know what happened to Sarah, and maybe she can finally tell me what she knows about Georgia. Maybe if I can sneak out of my room during afternoon prayers—

The double doors swing open and Grace strides in. Sarah follows, her usual white dress now embroidered with a red cross over her heart. *What the*?

"Sisters, rejoice for Sarah who has received the Prophet's gift."

"We rejoice for you and your blessing." The Spinners say it as one, and chills race down my spine.

Sarah doesn't look up, her usual spark gone, as she shuffles in and sheds her dress.

"Okay, let it go." Abigail pats my backside.

I release and sag from the relief, but my gaze returns to Sarah. She kneels on the floor next to one of the Spinners who's instructing a Maiden on breath play, her hands wrapped around the girl's throat.

Abigail uses baby wipes on me, and once I'm clean, she points to the training floor and motions another Maiden to take her turn.

I walk over to Sarah and sit next to her. I can't say anything, not with a Spinner right there, but I reach out with my fingers and brush her thigh. She flinches away from me, her eyes huge.

"You two, let's practice." The Spinner releases her grip on the Maiden and lets her roll out of the way. "Delilah, you get on your back. Sarah, you will play the man."

I obey and remain still as Sarah straddles me. The faraway look in her eye is something so different than her usual fire that I want to reach out to her again. But I don't. She's shaken, fearful, and somehow vacant.

"Now, apply light pressure." The Spinner takes Sarah's palms and presses them to my throat.

Sarah squeezes lightly.

"You need to stop her breath. Control her." The Spinner leans over me. "Don't press on the front, use the sides of your hands. That also stops blood flow, which leads her to the edge of passing out. That's what we want."

She doesn't change her grip.

"Sarah!" The Spinner's cross bark cuts through the room. "Do as instructed."

I reach up and pat her waist to let her know it's okay. As soon as my fingers brush her skin, she grips tighter, leaning forward and using her weight on my windpipe. "Don't touch me. Don't you ever touch me again."

"Sarah," I try to say, but I can't get the word out.

"Too much." The Spinner furrows her brow. "Sarah." She grabs her forearm, but Sarah shoves her off and returns her hand to my throat.

"Don't you *ever* fucking touch me again." Her eyes are wild, and she isn't seeing me.

I grip her wrists as my lungs begin to burn.

"Sarah!" Susannah yells and runs up behind her, wrapping her arms around her torso. "Let her go. It's Delilah!" She yanks as the Spinner finds her feet and draws her baton.

Sarah won't let go, and my world fades.

The familiar *thunk* of a baton hitting flesh adds little sparks to the black dots flooding my vision. Another *thunk,* and Sarah falls beside me. I drag in some ragged breaths and struggle to sit up.

"Sarah." I reach for her but stop.

Tears pool in her eyes and leak down to the mat, and now she seems to see me. "Delilah? I'm sorry."

"It's okay." I tentatively stroke her hair away from her face. "I'm getting used to chokings these days." I do my best attempt at a smile.

Sarah doesn't return it. "I'm sorry," she whispers.

"It's okay. Really." I touch my neck. The damage isn't nearly as bad as it was with Newell. "I'll heal right up. Are you all right?" I don't know where the Spinner hit her.

"No touching, Maiden." The Spinner sticks the baton in my face, and I drop my hand.

"I'm sorry," Sarah whispers again.

"I promise I'm fine."

The baton knocks me on the temple, but not hard enough to really hurt. "No talking either."

I sit back as Sarah's tears continue to fall.

"Get back to training. Susannah, on your back. Delilah, you are in control of her breath." The Spinner doesn't bother Sarah, just leaves her where she fell. The Cloister is full of little blessings.

Adam bursts into my room like a tornado. I jump and slide to the floor, pulling my dress off as I go. He strides to me, yanks me up, and throws me on the bed, then crawls on top of me. Burying his face in my hair, he inhales and wraps his arms around my back.

I can barely breathe, but I'm afraid to move. "Rough day at the office?" I eek out.

He laughs low in his throat. "You could say that." He nuzzles my neck. "How about you? Any good training today?"

"I almost got choked out again, so yeah."

He pulls back and peers at my throat. The spots where Sarah pressed too hard are swollen, but otherwise none the worse for wear.

"She didn't do it right." He draws his tongue along one of the sensitive areas.

"I know. I think..." I gasp as he fastens his lips to the tender spot just beneath my ear. "I think something happened to her. And she's, I don't know, not thinking straight."

"Sarah?" He nibbles my ear.

"How did you know?"

"Wild guess."

"Why does she have the red cross on her dress now?"

"Didn't we already discuss that questions aren't allowed?" He kisses down my chest.

"I just thought—"

"Don't *think*. Not right now."

"Hey." I grab his shoulders. The starvation and the drugs and the utter desolation of this place well up inside me, blotting out my mission and my reason and forcing a raw scream from my throat. "Hey! You can't just come in here and treat me like a fuck toy." I try to wriggle out from under him, but he grabs a handful of my hair.

"Do we need to go over who's in charge here again?" He leans down and bites my nipple until I cry out. "Because I'm more than happy to teach that lesson as many times as needed for you to get it. You *are* my fuck toy, and I'll use you whenever I want you."

"Stop!" I grip his hair and yank.

He growls and snatches my hand away, some of his hair still in my palm. Crawling up my body, he pins my hands over my head.

His dark eyes are cold waters, a monster lurking in their depths. "Why do you beg for punishment?"

"I don't. I want answers."

"What you want doesn't matter and never will."

I seethe and try to free my wrists, but his grip is as sure as iron manacles, and just as harsh. "Fuck you!" I yell in his face, knowing that I'm making a mistake. But I can't stop myself, not after what happened to Sarah, not after what happened to Georgia. I've gotten nowhere since I signed on for this madness. Any fleeting clue about Georgia disappears before I can even touch it, and now Sarah is being victimized right before my eyes, and there's nothing I can do about it. But I can scream. "Get off me, you sick fuck!" I rage and buck, using every bit of strength I have to fight him. "I hate you!"

He curses, but keeps me locked down, his body too much for me, his strength far too enduring for me to overcome. When I'm spent and go still, he lets go of my wrists and sits at the edge of the bed, his back to me.

I'm breathing hard and my body is shaking from the exertion. What little food they gave me at dinner is already long gone. And beneath the physical, I'm tired. My heart and my mind are already fracturing. I came here to destroy this place, but it's breaking me instead. Tears well, and I can't stop them this time.

He sighs, the sound heavy. "She has the cross because she's been claimed by the Prophet." He shakes his head. "*Fucked* by the Prophet, in common terms. Now her Protector will be allowed to partake of her body in all ways. The cross on her dress simply signifies that she's fair game, set apart, already sampled, no longer a virgin."

Stunned silence. It's like the Prophet read *The Scarlet Letter* and decided to put that puritanical bullshit into action.

I swallow hard. "Will that happen to me?"

"Yes." He scrubs a hand down his face, and I realize he looks haggard. Days of unshaven growth, tousled hair even before I grabbed it. His shoulders are still broad and strong, but they slump slightly.

"When?"

"I don't know. If he takes a Maiden this early, it's for a punishment. Sarah—"

"Wouldn't eat the poisoned food." Her moment of defiance comes back to me with crystal clarity.

"Exactly."

"But he'll eventually—"

"Yes. The Prophet will take each Maiden's virginity in due time."

"Including mine." I say it calmly, though everything inside me is twisting into a vicious knot.

"Including yours." His voice is low and almost thin, too worn and stretched.

I sit up and dry heave, but nothing comes up. I'm empty on all levels, hollowed out by how sick the Prophet is, how debased every single part of Heavenly Ministries has become. Was it ever a righteous place?

My thoughts run, each one stumbling over the last. There is no escape. I knew that when I started this, but I didn't know the cost. None of the Maidens did. The abuse, the brainwashing, the drugs—would I be here if I'd known? A flash of Georgia's blonde curls crosses the path of my thoughts. And I know the answer. Yes. I owe it to her to find the truth, to punish who hurt her.

I stare at Adam, and I'm looking into the broken mirror. He's on the other side, the jagged shards piercing his image just as they do mine. The Prophet is crushing him, maybe in different ways, but annihilating him all the same.

I let out a long breath. "I want it to be you."

"What?" He glances at me, his brows furrowed.

"I want you to take my virginity."

Fire ignites in him, the one that burns just beneath his veneer. "You don't know what you're asking."

I scoot over to him. "I do."

"No, you don't. The consequences are unimaginable. For both of us."

I slowly drop to the floor and wedge myself between his knees. "I won't let your father take it from me."

He cups my cheek, his thumb brushing over my lips. "It's no longer yours to give. When you joined the Cloister, you gave up the right to yourself."

"That's not true." I shake my head. "I'm still me. It doesn't have to be this way between us."

"We can't be together. I'm your Protector. I'm here to prepare you for the Prophet and, after that, for whatever man chooses you during the trials."

"Trials?"

He tenses even more. "No more questions."

"So, I get 'chosen' or I wind up at the Chapel? Is that it?" I can't keep the bitterness from my tone.

"There or worse."

Ice trickles through my veins. "There's worse than the Chapel?"

"Things can always be worse, little lamb. You should know that by now." He sighs and pulls me onto his lap so I'm straddling him. "Why do you fight me?"

"I can't help it." Honesty is the only thing my heart can give.

"You have to stop."

"You like it." I peer into his dark eyes, trying to see a glimpse of soul.

He smiles, a little lopsided, a lot perfect. "Maybe, but I can assure you the Prophet won't appreciate it."

I lean closer and whisper my lips across his. "Take me, please."

His hands slide up my thighs and around to my ass. He squeezes, pulling me closer until my bare breasts press against his dress shirt. "No."

I capture his bottom lip between my teeth and bear down.

He groans and kneads my ass. "You're going down a dark road." The warning in his voice comes out ragged.

"Are you waiting there to catch me?" I wrap my arms around his neck, and spread my legs until I feel his thick cock against me.

"Fuck." He claims my lips, rough and hungry. His scruff scratches along my smooth skin, and I breathe him in. His hands rove my back then settle low again, gripping hard and pulling me down on his rigid cock.

I am devoured. His kiss is ownership, more permanent than a tattoo and more scarring than fire. I open wide for him, his tongue seeking and finding mine. Dusky tobacco, hard whiskey, and him all dance along my taste buds.

Twining my fingers in his hair, I clutch the strands, pulling until he groans. I drop my lips to his throat, nipping and licking. Salty and sultry, his taste whispers in some primitive part of my brain, and I want to sample him everywhere.

He wraps his large palm around my shoulder and pulls, leaning me back until my breasts are upturned to him. Lowering his head, he kisses down the valley between them, then licks around one nipple over and over until I'm squirming and desperate. As he claims the stiff peak in his mouth, my back arches and a quivering moan escapes my lungs. He lashes my nipple, sucking and biting, then performs the same torture on the other one. I scrabble at his buttons, but he yanks his shirt apart, shucking it off, then pulling me to his chest. Skin to skin.

"We can't do this." He claims my mouth again, his kiss even more insistent, the need in him matching my own.

I reach down and unclasp his pants, pull the zipper down, then slip inside. He tenses as my hand wraps around his shaft. Soft yet hard, the skin is so warm. I rub up and down, the same way he did when he came on me. Just the memory of him coating me in his release spurs me to grip him harder.

He rocks his hips, meeting my hand as it slides up and down. I want more. The need inside me won't relent, and I follow the twisting path it takes. Sliding to my knees I lean forward, my mouth so close to his wet tip.

"You shouldn't." He grips my hair. "Not after what happened to you when—"

"This is different." I dart my tongue out, touching the salty wetness. "I want this."

His mercy evaporates, replaced with animal hunger. "Then take it." He tangles his fingers in my hair and pulls me onto his cock. Opening my mouth wide, I take him in as far as I can. I gag, back off a bit, then try again. He groans, his hips pumping into my mouth. My gag reflex dies down, and he's able to slide deeper. I take him, using my tongue to caress the soft skin as his head presses against the roof of my mouth.

I suck and lick, not caring if spit runs down my chin. His grunts and labored breaths funnel to that sweet spot between my legs, and I'm soaked for him.

Pulling back, I lick his head. "I want you inside me."

"We can't." He glances at the camera, his face tortured.

"Bathroom." I bob down onto his cock again, and his hips jerk. Then he's pulling me to my feet and shoving me toward the bathroom.

I stumble and then hurry through the door.

He follows and slams it behind us, then lifts me onto the sink. "Fuck, I shouldn't be doing this." But his voice is strained, as if my begging is breaking him.

"Please fuck me." I lick my lips. This started out of spite. My bird finger to the Prophet. But the more he looks at me, the more I see how close he is to breaking again, to shattering. And this time I want him to do it inside me.

"Spread," he grates.

Looking down, he watches as I open my wet sex for him. He drags his fingers across my clit, then licks them. Dropping to his knees, he gets a direct taste, licking up my wetness. I grip the sink as he presses a finger inside me.

"Please." I can barely get the word out.

"Such a tight cunt." He's gone, his voice turned into rough gravel as he tastes me. "I'm going to hurt you, little lamb." He licks me again, from opening to clit. "I'm going to hurt you so much."

My thighs shake as he plunges another finger inside, stretching me as he tongues me.

"Adam." I lean back against the wall, the broken mirror no longer there. My pleasure is building with each stroke of his tongue, each plunge of his fingers. Everything in me tightens, and he senses it, fucking me harder with his fingers and whipping his tongue.

I shatter, the orgasm coming out in a choked scream. It rolls over me as his fingers continue to work in and out. I shake, my body unwinding in steady waves until only aftershocks remain. He stands, my wetness on his lips, and kisses me. I taste myself, my desire.

Opening my thighs even wider, he nudges his head at my opening. The tension begins again, twisting in my belly.

"Relax, little lamb." He kisses me again, swallowing any protest I may have offered. But I have none.

He pushes inside me, then waits, every muscle in him rock hard. Then he pushes farther and stops, as if encountering some resistance. "This will hurt, but then I'll make it feel good. Trust me?"

I nod and grab his shoulders, holding onto him as he takes the only thing I can offer him. He claims me in another searing kiss and pushes all the way in. I cry out, but he keeps the sound, his tongue whisking it away as he stays inside me.

Full, so full. I'm impaled on him. My walls convulse around his thickness. He strokes my back softly, his mouth gentling against mine as he languidly gives me everything he promised.

When he pulls out, I gasp. He plunges back in, his cock moving smoothly until he's fully seated.

"Look at us." He watches as he pulls out again, then pushes until we're completely joined. "Your pink pussy taking all of me. A perfect, greedy cunt."

I shiver at his filthy words but want more of them. All of them.

"It's mine now." His dark eyes meet mine. "You belong to me. I don't care what happens. You are mine." He thrusts again, harder this time. "To fuck. To devour. To hurt." Another harsh thrust, and I'm clawing at his back. "Do you understand, little lamb?"

"Yes." I match his gaze as he plunges in and out of me, our bodies communing on every level. He fucks brutally, each stroke hard and direct. He grips my hair and kisses me hard, his tongue working at the same tempo as his cock. I can't catch my breath, and he doesn't want me to, fucking me like it's the last time. Maybe it is.

"I can't go slow with you. Not this time. Can you come like this?" He grabs my ass and lifts me, pinning me to the door. It increases the friction on my clit, and sends him even deeper.

I gasp.

"Or like this?" He takes one thumb and presses it between us, rubbing my clit as he pistons into me.

I dig my nails into his shoulders as the pressure between my legs ratchets up. "I'm going to—" I can't finish the sentence. I hold my breath, and then see stars.

My hips lock and I'm falling. He pounds me harder, the door creaking under the strain, and then slides so deep it hurts. His low grunts mix with my moans as he empties himself inside me. I float along on the rolling waves, drowning in ecstasy as he pumps a few more times, then rests his forehead against the door beside me.

"Fuck."

I would agree, but words don't come. I'm sore and deliciously sated.

He bounces his forehead against the wood. "We shouldn't have done that."

His regret stings me enough to pull me from the clouds. I try to put my feet on the ground, but he doesn't allow it. His cock pulses inside me, still filling me with unexpected bliss. He indulges it and thrusts one more time, sending a sweet, sizzling ache through me.

"If you tell anyone, I'll kill you." He holds one hand in front of me, the knuckles still bruised. "I'll use these hands to do it. And I'll look you in the eye until your light goes dark."

I believe every word.

"I guess you'll have to trust me now," I whisper.

He strokes down my cheek, then rests his hand possessively around my neck while his dark eyes capture mine. "Once I do, I'll never let you go."

CHAPTER 30

ADAM

I sleep in the next day, trying to make up for all the lost time. For the first time in years, I'm able to slumber through the night, no dreams, no sweats.

But when I open my eyes to Noah looming over my bed, his face serious, I realize the torment was waiting for me to wake up.

"What?" I rub my eyes.

"Dad wants to see you."

I glance at the window. "It's the crack of fucking dawn."

"Get up." He throws the blanket off me.

"Fuck!" I sit up and swing my legs off the bed. "What's going on?"

"He suspects you broke the rule yesterday." He crosses his arms over his stomach and paces the length of my room. "Did you?"

"Did I fuck a Maiden?" I shake my head and look at him confused.

He relaxes just a hair. "I knew you wouldn't do that. I don't know why Dad suspects you all of a sudden."

And the Oscar goes to ... Adam Monroe.

I stand. "Come on, let's go up to the house and put this fire out." Walking into my closet, I pull on some fresh clothes. I don't bother glancing at the mirror; I already know I look like shit. Noah leads the way out into the second floor hallway. I pass the door on the left that hasn't been opened in four years. I don't look at it, but the truth of it is always there, like a dagger in my back that I can't reach.

We stride into the cold air, our breath puffing out in dreary clouds.

"Any idea what prompted this brand new dose of paranoia?"

"Nope. But he's summoned the rest of the Protectors."

Fuck. I keep up a long stride, rushing to meet my fate. If Delilah talked, then it would be over for both of us. But if it's just whispers from a Spinner or something circumstantial, I can talk my way out of this.

The house is warm and scented with cinnamon as we walk in. Mom is waiting by the back door.

"What are you doing here?" I scan the area and Noah closes the door quickly and flips the lock.

"He's on a tear. Coke all night long. Girls from the Chapel."

"What did he do?" I push the dark hair away from her forehead. A patch of gauze covers about an inch of skin. Murderous rage erupts inside me like a geyser.

"He's done worse." She glances around. "I just wanted to warn you. He says he's got video of you breaking his law. But I watched through a crack Castro left in the door. It's nothing." Her cheeks heat. "I mean, it's something, but it doesn't—"

"Mom, footsteps." Noah grabs her elbow and pushes her down behind the basement bar.

"The Prophet is waiting." Castro hits the bottom step from the main level, grinning and motioning for us to get on with it.

Mom stays put. If he saw us talking to her, there would be even more hell to pay. I haven't been that close to her in years, not one-on-one, anyway. An old, familiar ache cuts through my chest, but I ignore it and follow Castro to my father's office.

"Here he is, my prodigal son." My father glares as Noah and I enter. The other Protectors are already spread around the room, crammed on sofas or standing at windows.

"I have more contracts to work on, so if we could get to it, that would be perfect." I lean against the doorframe and cross my arms over my chest.

"You see how he flouts my law?" He looks around the room.

The Protectors nod as he pulls their pathetic puppet strings.

"My firstborn, the one who *should* be working to further the goals of Heavenly, who *should* be the example that all others live by. Instead, he turns his nose up at both God and the Father of Fire. And worse, at *me*."

I let him go on and on about how awful I am. Most of it's true, so there's no point arguing. When he finally gets to the point, I stand straight.

"And now, he's broken the one rule that we all live by. The *one* rule I enforce with unflinching certainty based on what God has revealed to me. He has fornicated with a Maiden."

The Protectors' heads turn on a swivel. They can stare all they like.

"Do you have any evidence?" I inspect my fingernails.

"I certainly do!" he bellows and scrabbles to grab a remote.

Castro hits a button on the wall, dropping a flatscreen from the ceiling. My father presses play, and video from Delilah's room appears.

A smirk spreads across my face as the scene plays out and she drops to her knees. "Mind if I narrate? I can tell you for certain that her tongue is soft as silk, and, thanks to my instructions, her gag reflex verges on nonexistent."

A couple of Protectors shift uncomfortably. I'd be feeling awkward too, if I was sporting a boner like they are.

"Here!" My father points as I push Delilah off screen and follow her into the bathroom. "This is where you broke my law." He fast forwards and stops, noting the time stamp when we exit the room. "Fifteen minutes. What were you doing in there for fifteen minutes?"

I smile. "She swallowed my first load, but dribbled some down her chin. I told her to go clean it up. You saw me shove her worthless ass. Then she sucked me off again, and swallowed every last drop in perfect obedience."

My father's brows are still pressed together. He must be behind on his botox schedule.

"You expect us to believe that?"

"Have you asked her?"

"I sent Grace this morning."

My stomach churns at what Grace would do to Delilah if she thought the allegations were true. "And?"

325

He throws the remote onto the desk, and the back pops off, sending batteries rolling onto the floor. "Grace!"

Soft steps across the marble at my back, and Grace appears. She must have been waiting in the sitting room.

"Yes, Prophet?"

"What did the girl say?"

She cuts her eyes at me. "I questioned her for an hour. Used a few tactics to make sure she was truthful. Her story matches his down to the last detail. I also performed the test—" she holds up two fingers "—but it was inconclusive as to virginity, given she admitted in her entrance interview that she was a filthy female who violated herself with tampons. However, I would like to investigate further."

"How?" My father finally sits in his chair, but doesn't take his eyes off me.

"If I may inspect Adam's manhood?"

I fist my hands, but don't give any other outward sign of wanting to beat her to death.

"By all means." My father waves a hand at me.

"Thank you." She faces me, a smile playing across her thin lips. Dropping to her knees, she unbuckles my belt, unfastens my pants, then pulls them down to my ankles. "No underwear?" She smirks up at me.

"Get on with it." My cock doesn't even twitch as she does her inspection.

Leaning in, she takes a big whiff, then settles back on her heels.

"Well?" My father raps his knuckles on the desk.

Grace stands. "He's clean. No scent on him."

"He must have showered," my father mutters.

I scratch the four days of growth on my face. "Afraid not."

"Get the fuck out of here!" He yanks open his desk drawer and pulls out his coke stash. "All of you!"

Noah lets out a deep breath and pulls me into the foyer. "Fuck, man."

"Come on." I hurry down the steps and out the back door, not even glancing at the bar. My mother may still be there, but I won't reveal her hiding spot.

I'm moving fast, thanks to the adrenaline exploding through me.

Noah is close on my heels. "That was close. Too close."

"I know." I shove my hands in my pockets and head for my house. My father is losing his already shaky grip on reality, and no one will do a thing to stop him.

"Dad is acting—"

"Like a psycho? Even more than usual?" I keep my voice low even though we're out of earshot of the rest of the Protectors.

Noah shrugs. "I guess he's just doing what God tells him, or the Father of Fire."

"You still believe that horse shit?" I hate myself for wanting to pummel him.

"You saw the flames. You saw what he can do."

I shake my head. "What we *thought* we saw when we were stupid kids doesn't mean anything. And it doesn't explain what he does to Mom, or you, or me, or anyone else in this goddamn pit." I whirl on him. "Wake the fuck up, Noah! Our father doesn't speak to God or the devil, or anyone other than his coke habit. This place is the farthest thing from holy. And he's planning on making it all worse."

His jaw clenches. "I don't believe that." He frowns. "Well, not all of it."

"Fuck off, Noah." I turn my back on him, then stop. Turning, I say, "Look, I—"

"No, I get it." He holds up his hands and backs away. "I'm fucking off. Forget that I came to warn you, that I always have your back, that I *always* take your side against Dad."

Regret punches me in the gut, but I let him go. I add the hurt in his eyes to my already-crushing problems.

CHAPTER 31

*A*dam doesn't come. I wait for him, wondering what he endured this morning. Grace questioned me, using her baton on me every time I gave her an answer she didn't like, and then violated me in an even worse way. I'm sore, bruised, but holding onto hope that Adam will know I didn't say a word. And I need to see him. Not because of what happened with Grace, or to find out what's going on, or even to ask about Georgia. I just *need* to see him.

I stand and walk to the bathroom, examining my injuries under the harsh bathroom light. My mottled skin will heal in time, and even my broken finger is starting to mend. I glance up at the newly-installed camera in the corner and feel sick. There's nowhere to hide. Not anymore.

Pulling my dress back into place, I return to my bed. Everything hurts, so I lie down and stare at the door.

Waiting. Maybe he'll never come again. The thought twists in my gut like a knife. Surely, he'd never tell them anything. Or would he give me up? I shake my head at the thought. He wouldn't. And if he had, I get the feeling I'd know it. Grace looks forward to punishing me more than her next breath. She'd take any opportunity to grind me down.

I try to calm my racing heart. Closing my eyes, I hear phantom footsteps that sound just like Adam. But they aren't him. The other Protectors have already come and gone. I'm alone. I pull my knees up and hug them. It's easier to make myself small now. Slow, methodical starvation does that to a person.

My eyes close, but I still listen for him. I can feel him inside me, the ache reminding me with every step I take that I'm different now. But is he?

A scratching noise at my door startles me awake. The moon is gone, the sky outside black—it's late in the night. The scratch comes again. I hurry out of bed and hesitate by the door.

"Let us in." Sarah's voice reassures me, and I open up.

"We can't go in the bathroom," I whisper as she, Susannah, Eve, and Hannah line up along the wall under the camera.

"Yeah, I heard you got a little extra hardware installed." Sarah puts a hand up to stop me from closing the door. "We're going."

"Right now?" The urge to run with them pulls at me like a strong undertow.

"Bitch is in the bathroom. This is our chance. Are you coming?"

I should say no, instead, different words come out. "I-I'm not sure."

"You better get sure." Sarah's dark eyes meet mine, and the intensity in hers brings me back to myself.

Sarah's right. I should leave this place. I've gotten no closer to finding out what happened to Georgia, and at this rate, I could end up at the Chapel in short order. The thoughts are all so reasonable, but my feet are anchored to the ground.

Georgia keeps me here—her ghost lingering in the dark halls, hints of her like cobwebs so fine they can only be felt, not seen. Leaving is failure. Giving up on her has never been an option. But is this giving up? Or is this finding the truth in another way?

"Ten seconds, and then we're out." Sarah peers into the hallway.

And now, it's not just Georgia that ties me to the Cloister. Adam—he's another reason to refuse this offer. My heart pulls toward him, demanding I stay right where I am. But

I can't trust that organ anymore, not when it's led me to this. Dying here, or something worse, is not what Georgia would have wanted for me. There *has* to be some other way. And maybe, I lie to myself, I can still be with Adam.

"Now or never." Sarah sticks her hand out.

I waver for a second, torn between everything I feel for my sister, my captor, and my freedom. With a shaking hand, I take hers.

"Smart girl. Let's go." She leads the way into the corridor.

I join the other three with her, falling into step as we creep across the dormitory floor. When she reaches the door to the rest of the Cloister, she pulls a keyring from her pocket.

"Where did—"

"Shh." She gives me a deadly glare, then turns back to the door.

The toilet in the small antechamber flushes, and we all freeze, except for Sarah. She keeps trying keys. The Spinner's footsteps are loud in my ear, one after the other as she walks across the bathroom floor.

Shit shit shit shit shit. We're going to get caught before we've even left the dorms.

Click. Sarah turns the key and the door swings open on a low squeak. We hurry through and close it right as the bathroom door begins to open.

"Stay close." Sarah takes the lead again down the long hallway that bisects the entire structure. We pause at intersections, looking both ways for something far worse than speeding cars. Sarah holds a hand out when we come close to the dining hall.

A faint snore vibrates through the air. Sarah points at her eyes and then down the hall. I'm guessing it means she sees someone. She eases across the open doorway that leads toward the Spinners' rooms. I follow, and see Chastity slumping in her chair, the source of the light snores. A pang of guilt stabs through me when I think about what might happen to her when Grace realizes we snuck out on Chastity's watch. But I can't dwell on that. I have to keep moving. My decision has been irrevocably made.

The last girl creeps past, and we turn right toward the back doors. The ones that require a code to open.

I grab Sarah. "Do you have the code?"

"No." She continues along the corridor.

I grab her again. "How are we going to get out?"

"We'll figure it out." She takes my hand and squeezes.

I stow the rest of my protests and follow, hoping that Sarah knows some sort of code magic to get us out of this prison. We have to have been caught on camera at this point, but no alarms ring. If someone is supposed to be watching, they're asleep at the switch.

We reach the back doors, and Sarah stops and pulls what looks like a shiv from a prison movie out of her dress. "Susannah." She hands it over, and Susannah pulls up her sleeve.

"Are you—" Susannah jabs the sharp end into her skin right where they implanted the tracker. Blood runs down her arm in a ribbon.

Sarah pulls another shiv, which looks like a sharpened toothbrush handle, from her pocket and stabs it under the cover on the keypad. Working it under the plastic, she digs in as far as she can, then yanks. The plastic splinters down the side.

"Here." I reach over and pull at it, the plastic cutting into my fingers as I help her leverage the cover off. It pops free and falls to the ground.

We flinch at the hollow sound the plastic makes when it hits the wood floor, then don't move for a few seconds. Running footsteps and angry yells—they never come. We all breathe again as Sarah pulls out the wires behind the panel.

"Do you know what you're doing?"

"I took some electrical courses at community college." She examines the wires. "So, no."

Eve hands me the bloodied shiv. It's my turn. I feel along my arm and find the implant. With as much courage as I can manage, I use the sharp end to cut into my flesh, leaving a hole that leaks blood. I'm used to pain now, but it still hurts.

"Let me." Susannah places her fingers on either side of the hole and squeezes as if she's popping an enormous pimple. I bite my lip to keep from crying out. A moment later, the implant is out and piled on the floor with the others.

"Sarah?"

"I already got mine out." She lifts her arm to show the red stain and continues to fiddle with the wires.

"Can you get it?"

"I don't ..." She pulls out a yellow wire, then a blue one.

I examine the door, trying to find where the lock is. Leaning down, I can see a metal bar through the crack that spans between the two doors.

"Give me the toothbrush." I hold my hand out, and someone slaps it into my palm. I try to shove it into the crack beneath the bar, but it's too thick. *Shit.*

"What is it?" Eve peruses the area.

"I think that bar may fall from one side or the other to lock the door. If we can find something thin enough to fit in there and strong enough to lift the bar, that might be our way out."

She squints at the crack between the doors, then darts off down the corridor.

"Eve," I hiss.

"What's she doing?" Hannah wads the skirt of her dress in her hand, then lets it go, then wads it again. "Ratting us out?"

"No way." Sarah has pulled several different wires free, but doesn't seem any closer to getting the door open.

I try to wedge the toothbrush in again, but it won't go, and there's no way to whittle it down.

Footsteps raise the hairs on the back of my neck, and I stare at the gloom until Eve reappears. We all take a breath when we realize it's her.

"I've got this." She kneels in front of the door and slides something in the crack.

"What is it?"

"Our good friend the dildo stick." A metallic clang sounds from the door when the ruler makes purchase on the metal bar.

"Smart."

She tries to lift the bar, but it either doesn't work that way or is too heavy. "It's digging into my hands, so I can't get any leverage."

"Here." I wad the skirt of my dress around my palm, then grip the part of the ruler closest to the door.

Eve holds the end.

"On three."

She nods.

"One, two—" We both push up on the ruler, and the bar moves, but not enough. It clangs back down. "Fuck." I pull my hand away, and Eve's shoulders slump.

So much time has passed. My hope is draining away, and I keep casting fearful glances down the dark corridor. If we can't get out this door, we're sunk. They could catch us any minute.

"We're never getting out, are we?" Eve looks up at me, her eyes welling with tears.

I have to stay calm, even though I'm going to pieces on the inside. "We are. We just need to—"

"What are you doing?" Chastity appears out of the dark hallway, her brows pinched.

I freeze. Dread whispers along my skin, like poisonous tendrils caressing me toward death.

Susannah sprints past me toward the Spinner. Chastity is too surprised to react. By the time Susannah wraps her arm around her and presses the bloody shiv to her throat, Chastity has no chance.

"Make a sound, and I'll stab this all the way through you."

Chastity nods, her eyes wide, as Susannah walks her over to us.

"Don't hurt her." I can't help my trembling words. Chastity has been good to me.

"I'll do what I have to." Susannah keeps the sharp end pressed to Chastity's neck.

"Do you know the code for this door?"

She nods again.

"The key pad is busted, Sarah." I point to the broken plastic on the floor. "Can you put it back together?"

"Fuck." She gets to her feet.

"So, no." I want to scream. Instead I turn to Chastity, "There's another door. The one we came in that first night. Do you know the code for it?"

She doesn't respond, and Susannah pushes the shiv into her skin, a crimson snake flowing down Chastity's pale throat. She flinches, then nods.

"Let's go." I take the lead, hurrying back to the main hall and turning right. We go as fast as we can, but still check each intersecting hallway. By the time we get to the room where the Spinners washed our feet, faint rosy light is beginning to peek through the windows.

"Enter the code." Susannah walks Chastity to the door.

Chastity enters four digits.

I practically hop from one foot to the other, adrenaline lighting up every cell in my body. Like a wild animal

338

fleeing the hunter, I can't stop. The urge to move and move and move hums beneath my skin.

The keypad beeps, but the door doesn't open.

Hannah covers her face with her hands. "We're going to get caught."

Susannah shakes Chastity. "Are you fucking with us?"

"No. I just did it wrong."

"Her hands are trembling. Give her a second." I eye the bar between the two doors.

"We don't have a second." Sarah points her shiv at Chastity's face. "Get it right or lose an eye."

Chastity enters the code, and with a pneumatic sound, the bar lifts.

"What do we do with her?" Eve asks.

Sarah looks at me, and I don't like the darkness I see in her eyes.

"We take her with us." I take Chastity's arm and drag her outside. "Close the doors."

The cold air hits me in the face, and I've never felt anything more wonderful. "We have to hurry." I keep Chastity at my side as we dash up the path toward where the bonfire was the first night. "Beyond this is another clearing, and after that, a few acres of woods before there's a fence." I recall the layout I'd memorized before coming here. "There's barbed wire on the fence, but we can pile our dresses on the top in one spot, climb over, and not get hurt."

The dead leaves crackle beneath us as we enter the trees. The branches and trunks give me some sense of security. At least we aren't out in the open.

"They'll catch you." Chastity stays with the pack, but like us, she's winded.

"No." Sarah shakes her head. "Not a chance."

"We'll be gone from here before they know it." Hannah hurries ahead.

"They will catch you." Chastity doesn't even need me to hold her elbow anymore. She's keeping up. "They always do."

Eve gives her a sharp glare. "And how would you know?"

"Because they caught me."

CHAPTER 32

ADAM

"*H*igher." I stand back as the small construction crane swings a set of pallets onto the top of the bonfire structure. Once it's in place, I motion for Tony to turn the machine off.

He walks over and whistles at the structure we built almost overnight. It's three stories tall, dry as a desert, and ready to go up in a rush of flames.

"Heaven won't be able to miss it once it's lit." Tony cocks his ball cap back on his head.

"That's the plan." I clap him on the back. "You can get on over to the development now. I think we're done. Put in for overtime and I'll see you get paid."

"No, sir." He peruses his work. "This is for the glory of our Prophet. I was happy to do it. Molly wasn't too happy when I told her I had a night job, but she got in line real quick." He winks. "We're big believers of perfect obedience at our place."

I wonder what part of Molly is bruised or broken before brushing the thought from my mind like dust off a mantle. "All right then. I'm going to stay and do some cleaning up on the back side. I figure we'll set up one of the pavilions over there."

"Yeah, that'd be a good spot. I'll call Gene and see if he can come on out and start working up the structure. Last time I looked he had a truck bed full of raw wood that would work for this. Anyway, see you later, man." He shakes my hand, then walks off toward his white work truck. Once he's bounced down the road toward the rear of the property, I'm alone.

I walk toward the back of the clearing to gather up my shovel and work gloves. The sun isn't up yet, the first rays lighting the tops of the barren trees. It's cold and lonely, and I'm more than happy to have a few minutes of solitude. As always these days, my thoughts stray to Delilah. I wanted to see her last night, but my father had different ideas. He piled more work on me, keeping me busy while they installed additional monitoring equipment in Delilah's room. Maybe he even sprang for audio. I plop down next to a chunk from a tree trunk and lay back.

The chill doesn't bother me. I let my head rest against the bark. It's green, probably thinks it's still alive, but I killed it days ago. Wind makes the tree limbs creak and knock, and I watch the ridge to my left. Any second the sun will show its face, bright orange granting color to the dingy winter woods.

Did Delilah worry about me? I can't stop thinking about her, about what Grace said about trying to get answers from her. *Grace.* I'd like to destroy that bitch, but for some reason, she did me a good turn. When she did her little perusal in front of my father, she lied. I hadn't showered since I'd been with Delilah, a mistake on my part. And a witch like Grace would be able to tell, but she didn't give me up. Why? I know it wasn't for Delilah's sake. She wants to ruin her, to send her to the Chapel as soon as possible. Then again, she could have scarred her by now, ended her run at being a Maiden of worth that's bartered off to the highest bidder. Any Maiden who's scarred or "defective" as my father calls them, are never allowed to marry.

I'll see Delilah tonight. The Prophet won't upset the equilibrium amongst the Protectors. He already tried that with the office showdown. I just need to lay low. And more than anything, I need to see *her*. She asked me to trust her, and I do. That's part of my problem, because now she's invaded my entire being. Trust is like a chain that binds us, and I'd like it to cinch even tighter.

Her trust is the only thing seeing me through right now. I had no idea how close I was to the void, to the edge, to despair, until I found her. Now I have hope that maybe we can work our way out of this place. Maybe we can have a future. Her belief in me can make all that happen.

Setting my plan into motion has never been so close, so real. But with her by my side, I can finally make this place right.

"Adam?" a man calls from the other side of the bonfire pile.

I stand and brush myself off, the solitude busted. Walking around the structure, I find Gene there along with the promised pickup truck full of lumber. "You got here quick."

"Tony radioed me, and I was already up on the main road. He said you're needing some stuff built." Gene is older, with crooked glasses and a warm smile. "My crew is right behind me. We can go ahead and get to work on this before we start working on the decks at the family houses."

"Yeah, sounds good. I can show you the spots." I lead him back around the side, and catch movement in the woods.

"Did you see that?" He stops next to me.

"Not sure." I change direction and head into the trees, Gene at my heels.

CHAPTER 33

DELILAH

"*I* definitely heard voices," Sarah whispers and holds a hand out.

We each duck behind trees. After a few moments, footsteps crackle from up ahead. Someone's coming. Have they already sounded the alarm? Surely not. There'd be more men in the woods beating the brush to try and find us. This is a coincidence. Has to be. Whoever it is will go away. They'll lose interest and just go back to whatever it is they were doing.

I try to breathe slow and even, but my heart is beating at a jackrabbit pace. We only have a handful of acres to go before freedom. We're so close.

Susannah has Chastity behind a wide pine tree, the shiv at her neck again. But Chastity stares at me with doleful eyes, as if she's already seen this drama play out and knows the ending. She's tried to escape before. Is that where the scar on her forehead came from? A punishment?

The footsteps grow closer, and I can't tell for certain, but it sounds like two sets. We have to stay still, hidden. Maybe they'll go back, maybe it's a deer, maybe it's nothing at all and we're just paranoid. I hope it's the latter, but I know it isn't. Someone is coming, and it won't turn out well if we're caught.

I grip the tree and rein in my desire to peek around the trunk and see what or who it is. This is our only chance, and we have to make it. *Go away, go away, go away.*

"I think I saw a woman, maybe." A man's voice, and he's close.

Shit. I look at Sarah. She's pointing toward the back of the property, toward our escape.

Run? I mouth. It's a bad idea. But the men aren't going away. We're almost caught.

Sarah nods vigorously and mouths it back to all of us. Holding up one finger, then two, then three. We all take off, fleeing from cover and rushing at breakneck speed over the uneven terrain.

"Stop!" the man yells, but we don't. We keep running.

Chastity is ahead of me, her black skirt flying behind her as she passes Hannah. She's one of us, desperate to live beyond the confines of the Prophet.

Seeing her dash for freedom gives me a second wind, and I hurdle a small fallen tree, my feet skidding on dead leaves when I land. I stay upright, barely, and barrel down a hill, my feet splashing in the cold water at the bottom of the hollow as I fall forward and dig my nails into the dirt on the other side, pulling myself up and out.

Eve yells behind me, and I turn to see her fall. Her ankle is caught between two roots, and she's fighting like a wild animal to free herself.

"Go!" she yells and wrenches her foot loose.

I climb the side of the hollow until it levels out enough for me to gain speed.

"Get off me!" Eve's scream chills me far more than the frigid water, and I don't have to look back to know she's been caught.

Sarah is ahead of me, Chastity is out of sight, and Hannah is struggling up from the bottom of the hollow.

I keep going, pushing myself even as my muscles burn and saplings scratch and pull at me. One foot after the other, my thin flats doing nothing to cushion my footfalls against the cold, hard earth

Shouts erupt from behind me, more men coming after us. I have to make it. Down the other side of the hollow I go, the ground sloping away at a harsh angle. I slide on the pine straw, then roll and hit the bottom with a thud. The fence can't be far.

"Throw it over!" Sarah cries from somewhere to my left.

I sprint toward the sound, my lungs burning, my mind starting to fuzz, and my muscles screaming in protest. I crest the next rise and see Sarah throwing her dress atop the barbed wire. Susannah is already climbing to the top. By the time I get to the fence, she's stuck, the barbs clinging to her dress and digging into her skin. She howls like a wounded animal, but still tries to throw herself across the metal, to make it to the ground.

Chastity drops her skirt, then tosses it on top of Sarah's dress.

"I'm going." Sarah jumps on the fence and climbs. She makes it over the top, then leans forward to try and help Susannah wrest herself free from the barbs.

Chastity begins the climb. "Hurry, we're going to make it!"

Once she's high enough, it's my turn. I'm getting out of here, away from the Prophet. Away from Adam. I can't look back, not even for him.

I take one step toward the fence, then arms wrap around me like iron bars and yank me back into a hard chest. "Where do you think you're going, little lamb?"

Read *The Prophet*, book 2 of The Cloister Series, now.

AFTERWORD

You made it this far, and I hope you keep going. Thank you.

I've written this Afterword because I felt the need to ... not *explain*, exactly ... but to show the underpinnings of this story. I do this knowing full well that this series may offend some people, and that's okay.

The inspiration for this tale came from my love of the dark. I'm certain comparisons will be drawn between it and my Acquisitions Series, which is also a creepy southern gothic of mine. However, the Cloister Series has the added element of religion. As a lifelong resident of Alabama (Roll Tide), I've had quite a bit of religion. There are churches here now that preach some of the same lessons as my entirely fictional Heavenly Ministries. There is also a church in Birmingham that pushed the state senate to allow it to have its own police force. The bill actually passed committee, but died in session. All of these facts were ingredients for this tale.

In addition to influences from my home state, I read extensively about Charles Manson and the FLDS sect. In particular, the books *Member of the Family: My Story of Charles Manson, Life Inside His Cult, and the Darkness That Ended the Sixties* by Dianne Lake and Deborah Herman and *Escape* by Carolyn Jessop and Laura Palmer, informed my crafting of the dark world of The Cloister. I'd like to thank these women for sharing their stories and giving outsiders a view of what it was like inside the funnel of a brainwashing, abusive tornado. Some of the situations in The Cloister Series were actually experienced by women in Manson's cult and the FLDS.

Also, I must thank the brilliantly creative mind of Margaret Atwood. Her *Handmaid's Tale* has lived in my brain since I read it as a teen, and it grows more powerful with each passing year. Along with her, the works of Sheri S. Tepper, especially *The Gate to Women's Country*, is constantly part of my creative stew.

Whenever I write a dark book, I always think of it as a feminist scream. If you just examine the surface, you see abuse, degradation, and horrible situations for women. Dig a little deeper (and read a little further), and you'll find redemption, strength, and above all—vengeance on those who deserve it.

Delilah's story will continue with the next installment, The Prophet.

Brace yourselves.

ACKNOWLEDGMENTS

To my rock, Mr. Aaron. When he read my draft, and I asked him his thoughts, all he could say was, "It's crazy... It's just so crazy." Thanks for the encouragement, honey!

To Viv, who read my draft even though she had her own book to work on. I'm glad you said, "it's not that dark" even after my usual editor quit because of the "emotional and physical toll" of reading such dark content. Eek.

To Kristi, who read it and loved it and didn't judge me. (I mean, if the goodness-and-light K. Webster read it and didn't bat an eyelash, then it's not so dark, right?)

To the ladies of Author Squad, especially Skye, who had my back when I came stressing about how this book will be received. Y'all are some standup writers and humans, and I want to be you when I grow up.

To Becca for taking me on last minute and doing an excellent edit on a book that was a smidge outside your comfort zone.

To Stacey and Trina for always finding my typos.

To Riskay, for singing the song "Smell Yo' Dick" so convincingly and giving me ideas.

To my Rabid Readers who ate this ARC like it was a super tasty treat. Thank you for loving my words almost as much as I love you!

To my Acquisitions for always being there for me. A safe place to post tentacle photos (*shivers*) and such is always a necessity in life, I find.

And to you, dear reader, for joining me on this dark, freaky trip through the looking glass. Sorry-not-sorry about the cliffhanger. You'll get over it in a month when The Prophet releases, promise. Thank you for reading, and for trusting me to deliver a HEA, even in the dark.

xx,

Celia

Dark Romance

Devil's Captive

I'm to be married. It should be a time of joy, but all I feel is dread as I walk down the aisle toward a man who only wants me for my family ties. But my walk is cut short when Mateo Milani enters the cathedral, murders my groom, and takes me for himself.

Mateo is cold, violent, and vicious beyond anything I've ever experienced. The devil with a handsome face and eyes that haunt my dreaming and waking moments.

There's no escaping his grasp, and even if I could run, Mateo would find me and drag me right back to hell. He wants to possess me, stealing pieces of my soul with his cruel words and heated touches.

His motives are sinister, his methods calculated.

I hate him in ways I've never hated anyone in my life. But the part of this nightmare that scares me the most is the way he makes me forget my hatred, the way he commands my pleasure, and the way I crave him when I should want him dead.

The Bad Guy

She was a damsel, one who already had her white knight. But every fairy tale has a villain, someone waiting in the wings to rip it all down. A scoundrel who will set the world on fire if that means he gets what he wants.

That's me.

I'm the bad guy.

The Acquisition Series

Darkness lurks in the heart of the Louisiana elite, and only one will be able to rule them as Sovereign. Sinclair Vinemont will compete for the title, and has acquired Stella Rousseau for that very purpose. Breaking her is part of the game. Loving her is the most dangerous play of all.

Blackwood

I dig. It's what I do. I'll literally use a shovel to answer a question. Some answers, though, have been buried too deep for too long. But I'll find those, too. And I know where to dig—the Blackwood Estate on the edge of the Mississippi Delta. Garrett Blackwood is the only thing standing between me and the truth. A broken man—one with desires that dance in the darkest part of my soul—he's either my savior or my enemy. I'll dig until I find all his secrets. Then I'll run so he never finds mine. The only problem? He likes it when I run.

Dark Protector

From the moment I saw her through the window of her flower shop, something other than darkness took root inside me. Charlie shone like a beacon in a world that had long since lost any light. But she was never meant for me, a man that killed without remorse and collected bounties drenched in blood.

I thought staying away would keep her safe, would shield her from me. I was wrong. Danger followed in my wake like death at a slaughter house. I protected her from the threats that circled like black buzzards, kept her safe with kill after kill.

But everything comes with a price, especially second chances for a man like me.

Killing for her was easy. It was living for her that turned out to be the hard part.

Nate

I rescued Sabrina from a mafia bloodbath when she was

13. As the new head of the Philly syndicate, I sent her to the best schools to keep her as far away from the life--and me--as possible. It worked perfectly. Until she turned 18. Until she came home. Until I realized that the timid girl was gone and in her place lived a smart mouth and a body that demanded my attention. I promised myself I'd resist her, for her own good.

I lied.

Mississippi King

In Azalea, Mississippi, the only thing hotter than the summer days are the men of the King family. When the patriarch Randall King is found dead, Detective Arabella Matthews will race the clock to stop the killer from striking again. Benton, the eldest of the King siblings, has to decide if he wants to cooperate with the feisty detective or conduct his own investigation. The more he finds out about his father--and the closer he gets to Arabella--the more he wants to keep her safe. But the killer has different plans . . .

ABOUT THE AUTHOR

Celia Aaron is a recovering attorney and USA Today bestselling author who loves romance and erotic fiction. Dark to light, angsty to funny, real to fantasy—if it's hot and strikes her fancy, she writes it. Thanks for reading.

Sign up for my newsletter at celiaaaron.com to get information on new releases. (I would never spam you or sell your info, just send you book news and goodies sometimes). ;)

Stalk me:
www.celiaaaron.com

Made in the USA
Las Vegas, NV
30 October 2023

79983041R00203